UNEXPECTED LOVE

A BENNETT AFFAIR BOOK 3

DONNIA MARIE

Duverné
Studios
AND PUBLISHING

To the readers who kept encouraging me to deliver this unexpected love.

CONTENTS

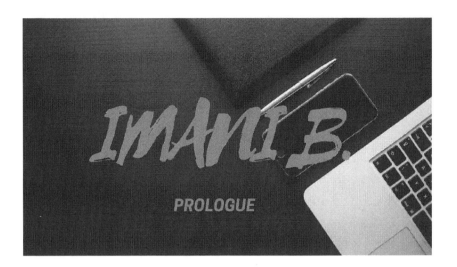

I SKIPPED up four flights of stairs two at a time with my phone, tablet, and notepad which nearly took me out. I mean what better way to add some cardio into my hectic day, than to march upstairs with the devices that keep my life in order in five-inch booties. That wasn't so smart. But I was trying to make it to Shooter in enough time to put an end to a brewing shit storm before it got out of control.

As I made it to the door that was decorated with musical symbols and assorted instruments, I shouted without greeting Riana. "Girl, Where's Shooter? He and I have so much to do because the media is having a field day with this new baby that's supposed to be his." I followed her, and we assembled across from each other.

Riana appeared sluggish, dragging herself from behind the glass booth. "Girl, yeah." Her eyes are low, skin fleshed. "I'm so tired of them throwing my brother's name around like he ain't gon' take care of his kid. He just got the results a few days ago." She paused. "I still can't believe Lexi pinned that baby on Sean the entire time she was pregnant, but yet Shooter is the father. Girl, I can't."

"I spoke to Chelsea, and we came up with a solution for Shooter, but I need him to okay it first. I have been calling him since five this morning to no avail, luckily I remembered him saying he would be here with you today." I'm hungry and annoyed, my stomach reminds me that I haven't eaten all day.

As I lean forward holding my stomach something catches my eye. We weren't alone. All I could think was: damn, damn, damn, in my Martin voice. Who's this handsome latte looking man rising from the couch, moving closer to us? He's so well put together on the outside, sporting a lime green sweater that highlights his muscular build. Solid thighs bulge through his slim yet perfectly distressed jeans. Then he hypnotized me with his deep waves that flowed fluidly behind a clear, crisp, line up.

Riana proceeded to introduce me to the eldest of the Bennett Brothers. I couldn't believe I didn't recognize him at first. He's the guy people run to for legal advice. Plus, he was consistently on some 30 under 30 list all the time.

He shakes my hand, never letting go, "I'm glad to finally meet you in person. You know, put a face to a name that I'm constantly hearing about." Sebastien's deep timbre resonates to the pit of my chest.

Wait. Finally, meet me? What?

He caught the questioning glare and clarified, "Mr. Jones informed me that you're taking Chelsea's place. You're his new Public Relations Agent."

I nodded, retracting my eyes to our locked hands. The spark between us couldn't be missed, and Riana had no problem pointing it out. "I didn't know you two were capable of foaming at the mouth."

Sebastien slipped her a curious glance, simultaneously releasing my hand. I, too, gave her a killer stare, letting her know this wasn't funny.

"Riana?" Sebastien calls her out, sounding like a disciplinary. I do know they have history considering Riana has known his family for years, and she is currently dating his brother Benji.

"Aht Aht," she throws her hand up. "We all grown here, Mr. Bennett. I know I may have jumped the gun, but the signs are evident. I do have one word of advice for you, though." I turned my back to Sebastien to observe Riana, who's walking away from me. "Don't go catching no stroke in that heat between Imani's legs, you hear?"

I didn't know if I should be pissed with my best friend or what. What I did know was how fast I made it to her and pulled her back into the booth.

"Damn Imani, you're kinda feisty, today." Ri smiles as if nothing happened. This would be ok if I knew the man, but this is our very first time meeting. For Christ's sake, I will have to work alongside him since he's Roland Jones, AKA Shooter's, attorney.

"Why are you doing this to me? I barely know him." I pleaded, feeling already defeated.

"Imani, calm the hell down. He's good peoples. Besides, he was salivating over you. Look at him." Riana pointed towards him. Sebastien is back in the chair, smiling to himself, and shaking his head. "He's thinking about what I said, right now." Riana laughed again.

"I hope not. I don't need those problems." I was not in a place to even think about entertaining a man. Seriously or not.

"Didn't I tell you about those damn brothers?" She scolded me like I wasn't just fussing at her. "I knew you would finally meet him, but I should have given you the rules so you won't be as besotted with him." She placed her phone down on the producer's board, sliding her slim thick frame onto a stool. "Number one, don't stare into their eyes. If you do, you will be out of dem draws. *PERIOD*. No questions asked." I can't help the smirk on my face. Too late, we'd already ogled one another for at least fifteen seconds give or take.

"And yeah trick, you already broke that rule. Which is why I made the snarky remark to try to save you. Moving on. Rule number two, do not... I repeat, do not allow them to charm you. Meaning no so-called lunch dates, unless the client is present. Please do not accept any pleasantries because it's a trap. You will not be able to bounce back. Trust me, I know. I'm the queen of finesse and got finessed out of my own damn heart and my birthday suit. Trapped, locked, Benji threw the whole damn key away." Her eyes seemed to roam for a second as if she was thinking about how caught up she really was. "And finally, rule number three. Make sure he keeps his hands to himself. Do not allow him to touch you in any way."

I leaned into her, giggling away, "But he just shook my hand. What now?"

"Pshh!" She falls back as if she's fainting. "It's too late then. You better run for dear life, Mani. That's two out of three you done failed already. You'd been hit with the Bennett Effect. Ain't nothing else you can do. It's only a matter of time."

SEBASTIEN

"STRUTTING around here with no panties will have you splayed out on that desk." I tugged harder, loosening the tie before unbuttoning my shirt. The next thing I see is her dainty fingers flicking her cheekster underwear towards the window that covered the wall. "I'm telling you, be careful, Chelle." Hard chortles filled my office between Michelle Davenport and me. She stopped by to drop off lunch, which was unusual since I never allowed women I was boning to pop up in my workspace. Those who choose to go against the grain were halted by security downstairs before ever stepping foot onto the 42nd-floor into the entrance of Bennett & Associates at Law.

The high-rise building consisted of many different businesses. Still, starting on the fifth floor, no access was allowed unless you were cleared via your access card or security, who went through extra lengths of keeping the building secure. The fifth level held an entire radio station, all the subsequent levels contained companies ranging from PR firms, finance handlers, insurance, and etc. Bennett & Associates at Law was the only law firm in the entire building which spoke volumes about the man who founded the business; my father, Samuel Bennett.

He didn't always have it all together. Truth be told, when I was growing up, my family struggled financially. My mother was eighteen, in college, and my dad didn't stop his schooling either. We lived with my dad's mother and father until both of my parents finished college. I remember one day, my dad argued with my grandfather about being ready to move his family out, but gramps wasn't hearing it. Grandad asserted that it was best not only for my dad to graduate from law school but that he should confirm with my mom that she was mentally prepared for them to be on their own. I could almost imagine his voice as strong as it was years ago, *"Keep saving money for your family, Sam. There's no reason to be running out into the real world, son. I could agree if you and Belinda didn't go and have two more kids after Bastien, but that's where we are. You have six months until graduating from law school. When you do that and pass the bar exam, then you can figure it out. You married folks think life is easy, but this is just the beginning. Marriage and problems are forever, so let me keep giving you guys a head start in the right direction. Your mama and I won't be alive forever, Samuel."*

My grandparents provided the foundation that allowed our family to be stable by the time I hit my preteen ages. I don't remember much about my little brother Sean coming into the world since we're only two years apart. Although, I clearly recall Benji coming along when I was about six years old, and boy was that a transition into the real world.

"Mmm, Sebastien. M. Bennett." Chelle purred, enunciating every syllable in my name. She planted her hands flat on the surface and continued bending over my desk further and further until every inch of her body and kinky curly hair rested comfortably.

No longer did the dress conceal her full bottom but instead rested on her back. Not soon enough, I cupped her ass cheeks, spreading them apart. My slacks had already hit the floor, and I was wholly sheathed, so sliding into a whirlwind of lust courtesy of Chelle was nothing.

Not even four strokes in, Chelle started panting and throwing it back as if her life depended on it. She was no lazy lover by a long shot. She put in work just as much as I did. I pulled the ends of the curly 'fro that she rocked to perfection, watching each loose strand that was out of my reach bounce along the arch of her back, and that curve in her spine blew my mind.

She wasn't a woman I planned to marry. I mean, Chelle was beautiful, could provide for herself, and her career as a journalist surpassed her peers. Several news outlets wanted her, and the offerings to have her weren't slowing down. But Chelle was charting her own path with a journalistic career that allowed her to have a healthy personal and professional balance. How could I be mad at that? Too bad, I couldn't provide her the long-term personal happiness that she was looking for. Chelle has never made it a secret that her end goal was to be a wife and mother, so she completely understood that what we had was on a timer. My workdays did not include a social life. I made it happen occasionally, but I felt no need to change too much since I was happily single. Chelle never made a big deal when I canceled dates, nor did she go on a rant. This was the main reason I kept her around, she understood the dynamics of what we had and didn't expect anything more.

Ragged breaths lingered with perspiration filling the table. Chelle's fingers gripped the edge for support, but then those moans got louder. My office was secluded from the other partnering attorneys, so I assumed no one could hear. But just in case, my palms hovered over her mouth, turning me on furthermore. The low inaudible grunts escaped my airway until I could feel the involuntary muscle contractions from Chelle's cove. I followed almost immediately, and seconds after I went over the edge knocks filled the door.

I pulled out swiftly, maneuvering to the bathroom that was located inside my office. I requested one after we had plumbing issues in the beginning when we first moved into this location. The knock sounded harder and longer this time. "You can clean yourself up, I have washcloths and extra toiletries in the closet near the toilet."

I finished cleaning myself with the soapy cloth and adjusted my pants and shirt while pulling the bathroom door shut. I strolled to answer the persistent knocking but was too late since the intruder barged in anyway. I looked up to the giant who stood four inches taller than me. At 6'3, I wasn't a little dude, but no matter how old or big I got, my dad still seemed to be that man; tall, authoritative, and commanding. Whereas my brother Sean took after him in the looks department, I'd inherited most of his mannerisms... good and bad.

"Smells like sex in this room. Which is odd considering the size of this suite." My dad kept rambling on and observing the area. I leaned against the built-in bookshelf, waiting. "Smeared hand-prints are all over the glass desk. And they're too small to be yours." His buff body settled into the black lounge, "Is she still here?"

He walks in, interrogates me, and finds evidence to support his claim against the crime I so called committed in my own office. In that second, I realized just how irritating I probably came across to my non-lawyer friends and family. Witnessing my dad in action was a clear indicator of how I presented myself to others. You know the whole *apple doesn't fall far from the tree* thing?

Instead of confessing, I sat behind the desk, propping up my elbows. "Mr. Bennett, sir, or if you don't mind me summoning you by your informal moniker, *Dad*. It wasn't too long ago that I came into your office, and your garments were quite disheveled as I happened to stumble over my mother's belongings. Not to mention the Harry Winston earrings that I bought her were on the floor in the corner panel of the window." I reflected for a second considering how far I would carry on with the man who put me on this earth. "Is there anything of real value that you need to discuss with me, sir?"

My dad smiled in a teasing manner, being silly as he always was outside of the courtroom. As a man he's always possessed a ton of personality, as an attorney, he smoothed it out by adding a dose of sarcasm. Many referenced me in the same manner, except I was a bit more serious and people didn't know how to perceive me. *Good.*

"I'm married, Sebastien. I can make love to my woman wherever I please. And to be honest, that wasn't a social call when she arrived at my office. She had done some incriminating things that I had to address. So, I taught her a lesson." He had the nerve to smile after saying those unsavory things about my mother.

I stood quickly from my chair. "Dad, you gotta go. You will not do this to me today. I care about none of your sexual acts with my mother." He followed me to the door and excused himself out, tittering down the hallway. "My firstborn, I love you. Instead of you having meaningless sex in your office with god knows who, you need to be thinking about settling down and bringing your mother and me some grandchildren." He finished his statement and disappeared from my office as quickly as he appeared.

The only thing I could do was hope that Chelle didn't get any ideas of being the one I settled down with. I know she was probably listening to my dad as she was in the bathroom washing away the evidence of our afternoon quickie. Shit, I needed to get a better lock on my office door.

"¿Estás saliendo con Riana oficialmente?" I asked, needing to keep tabs on Benji.

"Y'all so whack. It's all good though, I got y'all." Sean sulked with his profile taking up the left side of my screen while Benji remained on the right. He hated when we spoke Spanish while on FaceTime with him; he felt ignored. It wasn't intentional, but time was scarce, so I allotted what I could for my younger brothers.

I was standing wrapped in a thick Burberry scarf, struggling with the matching gloves, trying to read Benji's expression to the question I asked. Violent winds battered my skin while I scurried inside from the bitterness of the cold. The weather hadn't cooperated at all, leaving the residents of Atlanta to experience below freezing wind chill for weeks.

"Why you always in my business? I'll let you know where our relationship stands when we get there." Benji finally returned, wrapping his hair in a bun.

"Bash, you over there looking like a little bitch with that peacoat on," Sean stated, causing Benji to holler. I pushed the button calling the elevator, before adding, "Your mama."

Sean jerked his head backward, scoring himself a nudge to his posterior from the barber who was already annoyed from the abrupt bursts of movements. Benji curled over in what I presumed to be the bed of his hotel room.

"Hold up, let me hit her line so you could tell her to her face, mama's boy," Sean wouldn't slow down. I couldn't hold it in before exploding into laughter myself in what was now an elevator full of people. I was safe from anyone listening in since the ear pods blocked the entire conversation. My brothers knew I was talking junk since I didn't play about my mom. Out of all of us, Benji and I were equally attached to our mother. But my attachment was more protective than being a true mama's boy. As I got older, I realized I can distance myself and venture out a little more, thanks to my father pushing me into his businesses.

The frozen photo of my brothers indicated my signal weakening. A few seconds later, the pinging sound let me know that the call dropped probably due to me being on the elevator. "Good afternoon Mr. Bennett," the elevator full of ladies cooed. I attempted to respond, but our office's administrative assistant intercepted, "That's a late lunch you're coming from. I hope you haven't been working too hard." She'd been with the company for over five years and still couldn't contain her nerves around my father or me. Her usually colorless skin glowed, mimicking the red decorations on a Christmas tree. The first set of women got off on the seventh floor when I responded to their greeting, "Good afternoon to you all as well, sorry I didn't respond as quickly. Ms. Robbins here didn't give me a chance. But I hope you all enjoy the holidays." They giggled, swaying barely visible hips, but all disappeared when the doors closed.

Bodies filed out as we ascended while Ms. Robbins continued to prattle about plans for her grandchildren and all the family who were due to arrive for the upcoming Christmas Season. Unfortunately, I barely heard her because my mind couldn't get past the workload that continued to grow. For the first time since becoming an attorney and joining my father's firm, I couldn't keep work at bay. This immediately caused regret to settle within me as I started to regret helping a colleague with his caseload. I needed an out, and leaping off this elevator wasn't the way.

Once I arrived on my floor and proceeded to my office, I slowed down as I reached the reception area. I listened as some man went back and forth with the person who was filling in for Ms. Robbins during her lunch break. "Lanette specifically stated that Mr. Bennett would be available for me to speak with. My schedule isn't easily changed, but I made that sacrifice to adhere to his."

The man, who was now damn near yelling at Rochelle, was suited in a white button-down shirt and khakis as he continued fuming. He clearly didn't realize that I had entered the waiting area. He stood pensive after Rochelle insisted that he didn't have an appointment with me. Things didn't get better when she confirmed there wasn't any more she could do since I had no other openings. Silently, I tiptoed to the opposite side where a door would lead me into my quarters of the building. People generally called without notice, hoping to have a chance to meet with me about their legal matters. Not today, though, I would not allow infiltration into the bubble that I created. I needed to get out of the hole, and taking on unscheduled appointments was not the way to get there.

Something was out of place, but not necessarily alarming as I entered my office. It started with a festive concoction of Cinnamon and spices lingering heavily in the warm air and assaulting my senses. I didn't recall the fireplace being left on while I headed out for lunch, but it sparkled and sizzled as I made my way to my desk. A saucer sat in the middle with mini ginger-breads circling a cup of café au lait colored filling. The fragrance from the steam was a dead giveaway that this coffee was specially brewed by my mother. My mama, Belinda Bennett, knew to add carnation milk along with a hint of vanilla and plenty of sugar to my daily addiction. No one except her knew I preferred milk over cream.

The desk phone sounded with my assistant's voice snapping me out of whatever daze I fell into. She was just the person I needed to speak with. "Right on time, Lanette. Who's the man claiming to have an appointment with me? He's trying to convince Rochelle that he's on the books."

"We spoke a few weeks ago. I informed him that you were overbooked with clients and wouldn't accept..." Her voice was unsure and timid.

My agitation threatened to rear its head in a way that would have me lashing out at Lanette. Instead, I tried to ask as calmly as possible, "So how does he have an appointment if I am not accepting clients?"

"Mr. Bennett, sir, I..." She sighed, not knowing in which direction to go. Up to this point, she has been a blessing by knowing my every move and making sure all my clients were taken care of without prompting. This clearly was her flaw. Overstepping and asserting herself when not necessary, making business arrangements that aren't conducive to my sanity.

"Mr. Davidson is a New York Times best-selling author. You know, the science fiction black guy? I've caught you glancing at his books before." Her voice changed from flat to fragile in no time.

"What are you trying to convince me of, Nette?"

"He called distraught, needing legal advice. Of course, I didn't give any since I'm in no position, but Brandi, your paralegal, spoke to him. We figured you could at least point him in the right direction." I spent the past weeks explaining to her that I needed a break and would solely deal with my clients once I canceled out my partner's backlog. Who told her to go against my wishes cause she caught me glancing at a damn book?

"Lanette, send him back. But we will definitely have a conversation after the holiday. For now, consider your holiday break delayed. I'm going to need you to stay and help out with a few things now that I have a New York Times bestselling author to speak with."

"Yes, Mr. Bennett. I'll send him right back, and again, I'm..."

"No offense Ms. Dillard, but I can't do anything with your apology right now. As I stated, we'll discuss your performance after the holiday." Her attempt at an apology didn't faze me one bit, and regardless of how much of an asset she'd been, she could easily be replaced.

One foot tugged at the other, sliding the black Oxfords off my feet as I tried to get as comfortable as possible before this unscheduled meeting. Whoever this unknown man was, he would be coming into my sacred space, and since I personally didn't invite him, I owed him nothing more. But I'd spare him just a moment of my time. If nothing else, I would enjoy this untimely interruption in comfort.

A knock sounded before the man from earlier presented himself. He entered the room with confidence and grace. It was clear that he was used to the best of the best, as he held his composure gearing up to introduce himself. He embraced me with a firm handshake, "Good afternoon Mr. Bennett. I'm Nelson Davidson."

I placed my hand over his, returning the gesture while uprooting myself from my chair. "Nice to meet you, Mr. Davidson. Feel free to get comfortable and have a seat." He sat on the opposing side of the desk, scrutinizing the city backdrop behind me. His globes found the few walls that weren't glass taking in the decor and accomplishments that adorned them. Plaques of recognition filled those areas. Personally, I was damn proud of every award.

"How can I help you this afternoon, Mr. Davidson?"

He unfastened the first two buttons on his shirt, getting comfortable. The bulky clear spectacles on his face reminded me of sunglasses only without tint. Maybe wearing shades without a prescription was the new thing. To each his own.

From his silence, I surmised that he was no doubt at war with a battle going on in his head. Buddy sat there contemplating, but for what? He was now taking up time that I didn't have. He leaned in, forearm hugging the table. "Man..." He started, seemingly trying to decide how to tell me how I could help him. Finally, he said, "My wife and I are at odds. And we've settled on getting a divorce." Well damn. I didn't know what he wanted, but I didn't expect that.

"If the two of you are on the same page, what's the problem?"

"I need my kids. She's made it clear that I can keep the money and all the assets that I've accumulated on my own, but the kids cannot and will not be a part of the deal." I didn't quite understand how his wife could even win a case where he wouldn't be able to be in his kid's life. I asked him tons of questions, gathering all necessary facts to determine where he stood. I was shocked that he had some other legal matters which probably contributed to his wife not wanting him to have access to their kids. But that didn't stop me from feeling bad for this black man who just wanted to be a father. What stirred my soul was the yearning in his eyes, he wanted his kids more than he wanted life. Although it's a strong assessment for a man I didn't know, I was sure of his authenticity because reading people had become a skill I've honed.

"As an entertainment lawyer, I try to stay in the confines of that. You know, drafting, negotiating, managing distribution deals, financing agreements for sponsorships, reviewing contracts and so forth. Sometimes my clients need assistance on personal issues outside of my expertise and depending on the matter, I either opt-in or out." Reluctantly, he nods. I guess trying to determine where I was going with this. I continued, "I love my job, and what makes it better most of the time are my clients. Nevertheless, time constraints and fixed budgets add urgency to my work, which is why I try to fall in line with my job description. Asking me to represent you on a child custody matter with a pending case of DUI adds another load to my already crammed schedule. You deserve an attorney who can supply you with his complete attention, not launching you in an already mounting pile."

I started scribbling notes on the legal pad in front of me signifying the end of this impromptu session. "This paper has the course of action for you to follow that should have you ready to take on your spouse in court. I won't charge you for my time because somewhere in our journey, I feel compelled to be a service to you. However, legally, I cannot represent you or provide you with further counsel."

Shock registered as his eyes narrow, lips curling. He swallowed profusely, trying not to overreact. The confidence that was displayed at the beginning of our conversation starts to dissipate. Still, Mr. Davidson doesn't sit in it too long. It doesn't seem like he is willing to take no for an answer. He clasped his hand over his head, "Mr. Bennett, I need you on my team. Not because of the popularity of your name in the industry, but I know for a fact you can help me win. I've seen what you did for Drayton Brown, Nicole Rodgers, and let's not forget heavyweight champion Marcus 'CrissCross' Armstrong. You don't have to validate this claim, but we both know CrissCross killed that woman, and yet, here he is, living his life."

A slight chuckle escaped as I held a sneer, keeping my mouth together. The death of Mrs. Armstrong was a loaded case, and in this line of work, I knew not to release any confidential information. What the world didn't know was the abuse both parties in that relationship endured. Although it wasn't an excuse or acceptable, CrissCross never laid a hand on his wife. His abuse towards her was of the verbal variety. Now his wife, she was a trip. Very combative and physically forceful. I saw all of this first hand since

I had a connection with Cross outside of me representing him. No matter how bad it got between them, the cops were usually never called. When I got word that police were called because he and Patricia got into an altercation, I knew this was beyond the norm. So not long after I had a conversation advising them both about the dangers of remaining in a toxic relationship, unfortunately, it ended the way I feared. With someone losing their life and the other person getting charged with it.

"I understand you think I'm this efficacious lawyer, but I have fellow colleagues at this firm who are just as good as me, if not better."

Deep octave tones were in full force when he stood, "Sir, I am well versed in all the attorneys in your firm. None of them are you. If I succumb to this case and lose my children, then I am nothing. I live and breathe for my two kids." He roared, slapping his chest aggressively. "My kids are my life. I cannot put that in just anyone's hands. Do you feel me? I need you."

There was no need for me to get as riled up with Mr. Davidson, so I sat there pondering his question. Unfortunately, I had no kids of my own, so I couldn't empathize, but I could sympathize. "I apologize this isn't the outcome you envision, but I'm only one man. Besides, you're an award-winning author of twenty-plus books. You are more than reputable! I know for a fact that other lawyers would be honored to represent you in this heartwarming case." I opened my drawer, pulling out Richard Palaski's card. Not many could top him in this field. He holds a 98% winning rate in the state of Georgia representing his clients in divorce and family law cases. Who wouldn't want that type of representation? Mr. Davidson would thank me later. I stood staring down at him, "Here's someone I trust with my life. He is one of our partners that I can vouch for personally. I can assure you that with him, I can at least follow up on your case."

"I'll pay double your rate."

I strolled off, marching towards the door, practically dismissing him. "Mr. Davidson, my time isn't up for sale." I opened the door waiting for him to retreat from my office.

He snuffed my words, increasing his offer even more. "I'll triple your fee. For my kids, I'll do whatever it takes." He wandered out to the hall as I paused in my doorway.

"I will be out of the office for the next two weeks with the holidays approaching." I waited until his attention was entirely on me before continuing. "I'll have my assistant send you a packet to fill out, and along with it will be all the documents needed for me to get started." I may be busy, but I'm no dummy. Any man willing to pay triple my rate just to keep their kids in their life was someone I wanted to represent.

Mr. Davidson should have been on a Colgate commercial with the first-class smile that had taken over his face. Even his shaved head shined, displaying clear taupe skin, something I didn't notice inside my office. Instead of a stiff handshake, he clutched my shoulder, expressing gratitude. "I'm a grateful man. Thank you so much, and if there's anything I can do to be of help in your life, I swear I got you." I turned my back to him, looking forward to my desk so that I could wrap up for the day, but then he reminded me, "Don't forget that card I handed you." When he first came in, he handed me an envelope that I missed because it was on the floor in front of him.

"Oh yeah, thanks, man. See you soon." I shut the door, ripping the envelope free to read the holiday card enclosed.

I stopped by to see my firstborn, but I missed you. Do you think as a gift to me, you can work on slowing down and finding time for yourself? You've been in and out of town non-stop for months now. Money can always be made but time is more precious, baby. Don't forget to love in between, ok? And before you get wrapped up in work again, take time to indulge in the treats I've left. I know your love for coffee and wanted to be sure to express how thankful I am of you for sending your father and me on that trip. You are too generous.

We love you so much, Bastien.

Enjoy your day. See you tomorrow. You know I only live twenty minutes away, that shouldn't be too much to ask of you.

Love,

MAMA

EVEN THOUGH I was on the West coast, like clockwork, my body was up at 6 am Eastern Standard Time. Since it was only 3 am here, I decided to go back to sleep for a couple more hours. Before turning in, I noticed a message from Riana.

> **RIRI**
> Up for surfing? Hit me back and let me know.

This message wasn't new at all. She sent it yesterday morning, and due to my hectic schedule, I forgot to message her back. In the response box, I had already started typing a few sentences but never finished it. I had to do better.

She wasn't the only one I left hanging, my parents and I spoke only twice since my two weeks stay in California, which is beyond crazy since I usually speak to them several times a day. Let's not mention my nonexistent sex life. There have been no fireworks since I went out with Lennox, who was funny, charming, and sexy as hell. Every time he called or texted, trying to follow up on our next outing, my career always took over. No one had clear access to me, including me. I needed to make myself more accessible so that I could enjoy myself.

I caught some z's as planned before replying to Riana, who in return accepted our meet up for later that afternoon at Topanga

Beach. Before I could head out and meet my homegirl, I only had a few hours to take two mandatory meetings, set my schedule for the week, and indulge in my daily addiction, Jeopardy. Yeah, lame as hell but who cares, Alex Trebek and I were something like homies!

Surprisingly, I wrapped everything up an hour earlier than expected and was dressed in my one-piece wetsuit. I double checked to make sure that I had all my needed equipment for our girls' day out at the beach.

The sun rays blinded me as I squeezed between two sedans, trying my best to park amongst the classic beauties. I squinted, glaring across from me, where Riana was already pulling out her pink and yellow surfboard. It takes no time for me to make my way over to her, "Hey, girl!" I'm stoked, wrapping my arms around her neck. She mumbled her response, "Uh, hey," Riana says sarcastically. The girl can't help her funky behavior, and I love her more for it.

I pushed her away from me gently, "Don't act like you're not happy to see me because..."

"Imani hush, hell yeah, I'm happy to see you. I got so much to talk about." She went on a rant, not even minding the harsh heat beating against our skin. The gentle winds are our saving grace.

"That nigga dick ain't that fucking good where he thinks he can ignore me," Riana said with all her might.

I smirked, waiting for her facial expression to break. Because all she talked about was his dick. I'm assuming Benji's dick?

"Don't laugh at me, hoe!"

"Sorry, I can't help it." I hurled over as tears stained my cheeks. I tried to be serious, but I thought it was ironic that she was complaining about getting dick while I was just musing about my lack of it. "Wait." I gathered the strands of hair hitting my face that threatened to block my visual of Riana. "So, you're telling me that you and Benji haven't talked in a month? No texting, no nothing?"

That question led to her informing me about two other events between them that added to her dismay of one Benjamin Bennett. We strolled towards the shore and prepped for our playtime on the beach. I applied wax to the board to keep me intact when I decided to do my courageous tricks on my blue surfboard but paused when Riana informed me that God has tortured her enough. Those words pissed me off. I'm not the most religious, but I take God's word and promise to us seriously. I wouldn't judge Riana, but I couldn't let her live in the past and feel that her view of failure was His doing. "God doesn't torture, Riana. Don't say stuff like that. Honestly, life is what you make it. We're all battling something, but our outlook and decisions are key in all of it."

The raging waters came toppling over my feet when I decided to leave this conversation that stirred my soul. I couldn't help storming off. Just a bit of fresh air would do to keep me from saying anything I'd regret to one of my dearest friends.

I twisted my neck around, trying to find relief from the pressure I've felt for some days. I couldn't tell if it was stress from work or my body crying for a break. My mood instantly changed with the feel of the grainy sand rubbing against my leg as I strapped the leash that's attached to my board onto my ankle. *This.* This right here seemed to melt all of my stress away. Knowing I'm about to catch a swell in the waters ahead. I lived and breathed for this time at the beach. Not only just the beach itself, but the recreational use it provided me. I enjoyed the flexibility in my career where I can pick up and go with ease and travel, especially when I found myself frequenting California. The only concern I have with living in Georgia is the inability to indulge in one of my favorite hobbies due to the geographical location, and the whole not having a beach thing.

A faint tingle starts to stir within my core. I needed this. The anticipation of dancing on the water has me smiling from ear to ear. Riana silently crept up to join me, and asks, "You ready to hit these waves or what?"

All the BS from earlier is no longer relevant. No matter what, if you place me in my element, I can't stay mad. I smiled at my friend, whom I adored, shaking her wild mane. "Yes, Riana!" I screeched as we positioned ourselves on our boards.

We paddled out in the raging currents that seemed to have picked up in pressure in just a little bit of time. The longboard underneath me staggered uncontrollably as I got acclimated to the turbulence. "Whew, you see that? We gon' catch some amazing waves today. I haven't seen pressure like this in a while," I squealed. I've been waiting for months to do this again. I can almost feel a tear about to slip as I anticipated becoming one with the water.

"Girl, that's what I love about this beach, it boasts some of the best waves and the speeds are incredible." Riana continued, but I have my attention on a beach house ahead that's in line with the swell in the water that's gaining momentum.

We drifted into the water, getting as close as possible to the action. The tension builds, and we can hear the hysterical cries of the sea. It's anger, turned into a force, moving us, viciously. I tightened my grip on the edge as I swung my body upward, landing on my feet.

Next to me, Riana stood with no effort, and I'm super proud of my girl. I introduced her to this happy place of mine, and she's been killing it ever since.

With my body standing tall, I started to elevate. The water carried my weight as if gravity wasn't in charge. I scaled higher, and the gust of wind played musical melodies all around me. It's an exhilarating experience, the momentum, the beat of my own heart tapping away through my eardrums, then the descent through the rocky waters. "I fucking love this!" I yelled at the top of my lungs, but no one can hear me because Riana and I are tossed in separate directions.

The waterfall plunged over my head while Riana rode the top of it on the other end. I pushed my feet forward, manipulating the water to send me into the angle I'm looking for. And just like that, Riana and I came crashing onto the beach, hyped and ready for another round at sea.

This is the most entertainment I've had in a while, and it made me more vigilant in finding a common median to keep me happy. Work and money are cool and necessary but living and spending time with those that matter beats all of it on any day.

It was months ago when Ri and I went surfing. Although I thought it was gonna be the start of me making more time for myself and the things I love, I still hadn't been able to make my way back to the raging waters. Unfortunately, I didn't know when I would make it back, and it wouldn't be today since Roland was in my office with another problem for me to solve.

"Man, I appreciate everything Imani, for real. It's like people are more concerned with where my dick has been than who's paying their bills. You feel me?"

"Yes, as a matter of fact, I do, Mr. Jones." Sitting across from Roland once per week for a mandatory meeting was necessary to make sure he kept the utmost respect in the media. Roland became one of my clients after Chelsea Bennett had been his rep for many years. In the three months of working with him, I've learned more about the judicial system than a law student. His legal name is nothing but a distraction, because his stage name, Shooter, depicts just the guy he truly is.

"Come on, you've been my PR rep for months now, you don't have to be so formal. I need us to vibe and be comfortable with one another." Not one time did he withdraw his eyes from mine. Shooter allowed his thick frizzy hair to grow on his face and head, giving him a rugged look, which his female fans made comments about creaming in their panties over.

I shuffled in the chair, removing the see-through pumps off my feet. Saturdays weren't usually a day in the office, but today I made an exception for him. "I'm still adjusting to you, Roland." His head cocked to the side as if I was addressing someone else. "I'm still trying to feel you out. I got the rundown from Chelsea and Riana about your past - both professionally and personally. Still, it's hard to gauge what angle to take with your career considering you remain closed off." I paused before continuing not sure how he was going to take what I had to say next. "Maybe I should invite Chelsea to all of our meetings since you become this free-spirited man whenever she's around."

He rushed off the cream leather couch and pushed over to my desk. "Imani, I don't trust many. Chelsea is someone I completely trust. At least I'm trying to build that same thing with you. I've done everything you've asked of me."

Imani B. Relations has been stamped as *the* go-to company if you need damage control. In all of my years in business, I've fought hard for that reputation, but Roland and his issues warranted another level of professionalism.

Currently circulating in the press was the reveal of him

fathering one-month-old, Alexandria Cruz. Becoming a dad is supposed to be a blessing, but under the circumstances, Shooter felt pressure and appeared to be running from his daughter's mother, Lexiana Cruz. TMI, PR3SSED, and other bloggers accused him of being a deadbeat, but honestly, he was the opposite. He showered his new baby with more material things than she'll ever need, but seeing him interact with her in person was absolutely beautiful.

I stood up to be level with him, but I still only reached just below his chin, "You want me to unwind and get comfortable?" Blinking and swallowing hard, I grumbled, "No problem. First of all, Shooter, you are on probation. You've apparently violated several of those terms, and now you have a bullseye on your back."

"Nope, Ms. Barasa. That's where you're wrong. I am officially a free man, as of yesterday. That's why I expedited this meeting. I couldn't wait to tell you that you no longer have to send those reports to my P.O."

Wow! I was shocked by this news. This made my entire day. He got involved in a physical altercation a few days prior but somehow managed to not only walk away from the scene, but he got off of probation, too? Damn. Just how salutary is his lawyer? Only a resourceful, charismatic individual could make an impression with the unresponsive judge assigned to Roland's case.

"Yeah, my man Sebastien did all of that. He told me to lay low after the blowup, so I did, and here we are." The smirk that I'd become accustomed to over the last few months crept up gradually, coating his deep cinnamon skin. Who could criticize him after the system held him by the balls for three years? I was just happy to not have a client who was on probation and couldn't seem to stay out of trouble.

Following the rundown of Shooter's upcoming communications plan and schedule, we found ourselves genuinely sharing a few laughs; I was appreciative of this breakthrough with my client. Especially since his sister is one of my best friends. What should have been an hour meeting suddenly turned into three. Once the digital clock on the wall displayed 3 pm, I called it quits.

"What you rushing for, Mani? I'm the one with a flight to catch in a few. I have some bars to lay down with Cole, Ross, and Sean in New York. Then tomorrow evening, I'll be in Jersey for a show."

"I'm not in a rush, but I do have a life," I stated while clearing my desk of all the notes I jotted down during our conversation. Not only did we indulge in the ins and outs of his newfound freedom, but I also got him to view his personal and professional moves in a different light, considering he is a father now.

"You fucking my mans?"

Why would he ask that? Did my reaction to Sebastien show on my face while he was mentioned as Shooter's attorney and the one responsible for getting him off of probation? I halted my steps, shoulders sinking, along with my brows scrunched together. No matter what our work relationship consisted of, I could never concede to Shooter inserting himself into my personal life. A few weeks before, I met Sebastien for the first time and the introductions did not come via Shooter. Although, us being acquainted would have presented itself eventually, but maybe not so early had we both not ended up in the same studio with Riana. Seemingly out of nowhere, I was able to materialize a visual of a naked Sebastien, a name I learned only after Riana not so kindly instructed me to pick my mouth back up before she introduced us. Even though Sebastien's physical traits were a mix of both of his brothers, Sean and Benji, he moved and talked differently. I knew them both and had seen them in action.

Sebastien dominated the room with his presence. Every word expelled through his vocals contained charged atoms that ultimately loaded every fiber of my being with an electrical current.

Sebastien Bennett exudes confidence. He held an edge of arrogance but in a healthy manner. Riana and Chelsea swore by the trio and claimed any women who caught a whiff of them would be cursed and spellbound by the Bennett Effect, and I'll be damned if she wasn't right.

Exasperated, the stout man pleaded, "Mrs. San, you must answer the question thoroughly. I understand you aren't a fan of the current president, but I need the correct name."

The crowd of supporters inside the immigration office snickered at the antics in front of us as we were witnessing history in the making. I glimpsed over to the thin lady whose face was partially covered by a wide-brimmed floppy hat. "Come on, this is the last question Yeay." The older brown gentleman didn't understand what I relayed to my grandmother because I spoke in her native tongue, Khmer. Chhaiyada San, whom I call Yeay, another name for grandmother in our culture, came to the states in the early nineties after her husband passed away. It was a major surprise to my mother that her mother would be joining her in Atlanta as Yeay had always told my mom she would never leave home.

My mom, the former Sophea Chhaiya San, left her family behind in Cambodia to be with my father, who's originally from Kenya. Her family didn't like it one bit. You would think racism only existed in the States but my grandfather wasn't a fan of this black fellow marrying his daughter. Because of the culture, my grandmother stood by his side through it, causing my mom to be an outcast.

"We have no president, sir." Her expression didn't change; in fact, she kept her lips in a hard horizontal line, still resembling a goddess while in her seat. She'd aged over time, and the ridges on her pale copper skin settled, but beauty prevailed. Her button nose was shaded pink from the cool air in the small room we occupied. She cleared her throat, "Sir," her accent thickened. "Trump is the dictator of this country. He's no president. He the demon. The devil."

The man and I chuckled. My grandmother was pissed with having to acknowledge the man who was appointed to govern our land. She had no desire to get her citizenship until the uproar of issues with immigration and deportation. Yeay wasn't willing to risk it. Today she turns seventy-four and what a way to celebrate by becoming a Citizen of the United States of America.

After wrapping up with the gentleman who facilitated the test, we signed documents, took pictures, and completed the process. I couldn't be happier for my Yeay.

The hour drive from the immigration office extended to three because she convinced me to stop at the farmers market, dollar store, and post office. I couldn't take her anywhere without making a pitstop. Approaching the blue and white duplex that I associated with family couldn't come quickly enough. "Yeay," the room erupted. Grandmother shouted in fear, securing her hands over her heart, pretending to be alarmed. I cackled, she got a kick out of making us laugh. My mother pulled Yeay into her thin frame, and the rest of my father's family followed.

Yeah, our unit wasn't traditional, but in examining our past, we've come far as a family unit. My father, Jaali Barasa, purchased homes and flipped them when he immigrated to America from Nairobi, Kenya. Jaali and Sophea met in Cambodia while he was visiting to work on a project with a business partner who also invested in properties. That same year, he set her up with a VISA then moved her to Atlanta in a duplex with his brother and sister. Both of his siblings were married, so it was a full house. I have so many great memories in this blue and white safe haven with my cousins. The first level was originally my Uncle Clifford's spot, which allowed me full access to my older, cooler cousin Nayeli, who'd become one of my best friends over the years. Nayeli wasn't his biological daughter, she came to the states with Yeay. While my grandmother stayed in our unit, Nayeli ended up living with Uncle Cliff, my dad's older brother, and his wife Sheryl because they clicked. Aunt Sheryl stepped in as a mother figure for Nayeli on behalf of her mother, my mom's older sister, who died while giving birth. Again, not the most traditional family, but we loved each other. Imagine what it was like for them, to bond so closely with someone of different faith and culture. The beauty of it all was that they made it work; Nayeli was the daughter they've always prayed for, and she loved Uncle Cliff and Aunty Sheryl unconditionally. On the second level, my mother and father occupied that space, then when I came along, I completed their happy home. The third level belonged to Aunt Zanobia and daughter, my younger cousin Genevieve. The fact that Nayeli, G, and I were all housed in closed living quarters only strengthened our bond as family and friends.

"I can't believe Yeay passed the test!" Genevieve squealed.

"Shoot, she better have. I worked with her for weeks, going over all one hundred questions." I would do it again if I needed to, my Yeay helped me more than I could ever repay her in a lifetime.

"But they only asked her ten?" G wanted to ensure that the

facilitator stuck to the guidelines that we read about, which stated that after a certain age, they could only ask a max of ten questions.

"Yep," I answered coolly, lounging on the couch. Genevieve sat on the other end while familiar Kenyan tunes blasted through the house. Bouncing along to the rhythm was my mom and grandma. Yeay had moves and never stumbled over the beat.

The menu served for the night was a mix of both cultures which only intensified my senses and cravings. Today was a good day and I savored all the love being given at the moment.

THE DAYS FOLLOWING my family's celebration of Yeay's citizenship flew by. Before I knew it, Christmas had come and gone. During the little bit of down time I had over the holidays, I straight-outed out of character and used that time to eat and sleep. Eating horribly led to me being sluggish, so I usually fell right into my comfy bed afterward. I, unfortunately, didn't exercise as I should have, so I knew I would pay for these past two weeks. But for now, I was happy... and full!

Songbirds stirred me out of my slumber. I no longer felt fatigued but refreshed. Ten minutes to six is the time I recalled before staring at the vaulted ceilings in my bedroom. It feels good to be back in my apartment away from the family house.

I coated my lips with Vaseline, a habit I couldn't seem to kick. The shower ran for a second before I hopped in to wash my hair. Hot steamy water beat against my shell, then I reopened my eyes, staring in the mirror underneath the showerhead. Thick coarse hair perched on my shoulders. Taming this beast was no joke. My hairstylist traveled back home for a while, so I was stuck handling it on my own. I parted my strands into eight sections with my fingers, detangling each piece. As I was completing this mindless task, my mind started drifting and the next thing I knew, I was in a full flashback mode thinking about some shit that I shouldn't have been worrying about.

Today's the day. It's time to get real. I removed the impenetrable, black shades that covered the bags underneath my tired eyes. I've somehow become the girl who devoted all her time to loving the wrong person when I should have been focusing on me. I barely recognize the woman reflecting back at me.

Tears clouded my vision as I spoke out loud, "I say I love myself, but do I? It comes a time when you have to learn to be real with yourself, Imani. Progress forward." Damn, I started to feel like I belonged in an institution or sitting in front of Iyanla, begging her to fix my life.

I scribbled on a sheet of paper all that I've accomplished from eighteen to twenty-six years old; seeing the words spoke volumes, but I wasn't convinced it was enough. In those eight years, I've built a business by myself, it was my baby, so it was only fitting that I called it Imani B. Relations, Inc. I ran a thriving Public Relations Company! I busted my ass in my college years by interning at a major PR firm that represented all top names. I understood that in order to take my career to the next level, I needed to work from the bottom up and build relationships with those individuals who were movers and shakers in the industry. I did things most wouldn't care for, like slaving for the top dogs, getting coffee, and running tedious errands, but it paid off.

Amidst all that, I managed to find out what it was like to make six figures, invest in stock, knew the joy of being able to provide for my parents, had been in a relationship with my boyfriend for eight years, and had several great friends, some who have been in my life since grade school. What more did I want?

All of my accomplishments were cool, and I wasn't downplaying any of my successes. Still, more than anything, all I wanted deep down was to travel and live freely without the hassle of living for someone else. Somewhere in the equation, I completely forgot about myself. What I didn't realize was that I was taking care of everyone but me. On top of that, I finally accepted that after eight years of being a girlfriend to a man that I went above and beyond to show that I could be a wife... he never intended to marry me. *My dad always told me, why buy the cow when you can get the milk for free?* He's right, and I knew that.

It's time to step away from the mirror and stop feeling sorry for myself. I made my way to the kitchen with the intention of starting dinner and figuring out how to end my relationship. Unfortunately, Patrick's voice interrupted my planning, for both dinner and his one-way ticket to Breakupville, so now I had to once again listen to his insecurities. "You fucking somebody else, Imani? Keep listening to and following behind ya lil' friends, and you gon' end up just like them, single." Patrick stood up from the black leather couch, marching through the double doors to the kitchen where I stood contemplating on if I should answer his ignorant ass question.

For many years I considered leaving him if he didn't get his insecurities under control, but he never improved. I found myself turning down events and networking gigs because he felt threatened by my colleagues and clients. It took me losing a dope, meaningful opportunity a few days ago for me to say enough was enough. Yeah, it was time to let this go. My mind and heart couldn't take another second of his antics, nor him messing up my coins.

"Why you ain't saying nothing, Mani? I know for a fact you doing you. Just like all the other females. It's cool though, pussy is pussy. You fuck a nigga, wash it out and move on to the next. That's what you do? That's what y'all females do, right?" It took everything out of me to not find the nearest object to strike him. I've never felt more violent towards Patrick than I did at this moment. It was time to go!

A week later, all my clothes were packed and moved out into my new apartment. I never answered Patrick's question before leaving. If he didn't know that I've never cheated on him, or didn't trust me, the sight of my brand new, modern couch let me know that I made the right decision. I left all the furniture behind because I didn't need anything reminding me of my past with Patrick. A clean slate is what I provided for myself. There's no way to have and enjoy love without having it from within.

Now it was time to travel and live freely. First trip on the agenda...
surfing in Phuket.

It's been a minute since I thought about Patrick and that time during my life. Thankfully that was in my past and the only thing I intended to keep doing was traveling. Phuket changed my life, and fed my drive to want to continue to travel.

By the time I finished with my hair, it was nearing eight-thirty and I noticed I missed a call from Riana. "Hey Siri, call Ri."

"Calling, Rye." I need little miss smarty pants to know how to pronounce my bestie's name. For all the cash I spent on the iPhone, the least she can do is talk properly. I keep telling Siri's ass it's *Ree*.

Oil ran through my scalp as I applied it throughout. It didn't seem like Ri would answer, but mere seconds away from clicking end, she hollered, "Big Money Grip!"

I snorted, "I wish."

Riana decided to upgrade our regular phone call with a Face-Time call. I answered the call, then uttered, "You wanna see my face too, Ri?" Red fishnets carved her body, allowing her tawny nipples to crest through the attire. My eyes bugged out.

"Don't even comment." She hesitated. "What you think?" I didn't reply. "Excuse me." Riana waggled her hips. "Answer me."

"I love it, but I wasn't expecting to see ass and titties this early in the AM."

"Oh, hush, it's just me." She readjusted the position of the phone because now her body was fully exposed, head to toe.

"This is what I purchased last night when you pretended as if you couldn't comprehend the description I was giving you." She twirled, bouncing her ass in the camera.

"Stank." I wailed, but truthfully, she was getting it. Riana boasted a big personality, enough for ten people. I loved the girl she was before and admired the women she'd become. Undeniably gorgeous and talented. We met in my early college years when I was an apprentice for a public relations firm. Back in those days, she was a new, young artist signed to a major record label. At first, we conversed only sporadically, but over the years we got to know each other and bonded. I knew I could be standoffish with people, but through trying times in both of our lives, we've been able to help one another, which is how we became best friends. With the addition of Chelsea, nothing significant happens in our lives without the others knowing.

"Whateva. Let me add Chelsea so she can see before she gets too caught up with Sean. You know they're in this honeymoon phase, and they ain't even married yet."

Once Chelsea joined, she and Riana went back and forth as I continued with my daily routine while observing the dynamic between the two. Riana finally draped herself with a robe. My abdomen ached after shouting excessively from the banter between the girls as Sean hovered in the frame clowning Riana. It was nice seeing Sean as lighthearted and comedic. The lyrics in his music were typically hardcore, not showing an ounce of the compassion he shares with those he loves. After the bickering between the crew ended, I added my two cents, and now the gag was on me. Sean couldn't stop cutting up, the size of his 'fro increased as he neared the screen, to get on my case up close and personal. "Oh, don't think you can't get touched too, Imani." The girls cackled. "Know that I know what's really going on."

Riana screamed, "Tell us the scoop, Sean? We wanna know what's going on!"

I gasped, "Know what? There's nothing to tell."

His sneer couldn't be trusted. Those orbs seemed to be filled with information only he was privy to? "I'll disclose all of it if you keep it up, Imani. Just sit back and let me clown BooBoo the Fool over there." He referenced Riana, continuing to roast her until

Benji chimed in, snatching the phone from Ri. I couldn't deal with these fools so early in the morning, I had a meeting to attend.

"Aight, Chelsea, we gon hit y'all up later." Ri offered a goodbye before Chelsea disconnected leaving me and her on the FaceTime call. She filled me in about her current trip in NYC while keeping her conversation rolling with Benji. "Ok, babe, don't forget the syrup. Love you." Benji pecked her on the lips before walking out. "Good hearing from you, Imani. Happy New Year, by the way."

"Same to you, Benji." I shouted, but couldn't see anyone since I stepped away from my phone observing my attire for the day. Black tights, an oversized white shirt, and some Uggs would do.

Riana resumed as if Benji didn't just cut us off. "Whew, this was a long debriefing on my end. What's been new with you? Getting any dick?"

"It's a drought over here, Ri." I gasped, making the sound of a dog feening for water.

"Famine?" She asks, waiting on the tea.

Nodding, "Scarce."

Her whistling caught me off guard. "I know you tend to pray a lot. Why not ask God to provide an abundance then? There's a surplus of dick out there, Mani."

"I do not lack options, it's a matter of who's worth my time."

"So, someone out there getting you wet?" That's when I appeared, and Ri's eyeballs were glued waiting on me. I couldn't entertain this chick.

"You know Imani?" She lingers. "You can tell me all about it. I know exactly who it is too. That boy Ba..." The front door opening could be heard behind her. "You've been holding out on me, and you know I find out everything." She shuffles away, her voice faded with each step. "Hold that thought..."

SEBASTIEN

"THANKS, MRS. GAFFER." *I rushed out of the car, hauling the heavy book bag filled with my football gear. Slamming the door behind me, I made it to the front porch of my grandparent's home and suspended. I couldn't move as a frightening voice stopped me in my tracks.*

"Get off me. Sam's gonna kill you!" My mother cried at the top of her lungs. In my little six-year-old mind, what could I do? I needed to get help from another adult because my mom sounded as if she was in trouble. My dad was at the library studying. Mrs. Gaffer had already pulled off, my grandparents were away on vacation, so I peered over my shoulder, looking out to see that my neighbor wasn't home. The next nearest house was half a mile away. As I was thinking about what to do next, the howling started again and the adrenaline rushed, pushing me to do something. What's going on with mom?

My hands were shaky as I opened the front door, running to get to my mom. Her cries sounded as if they were coming from my parent's bedroom.

"Shut up and relax." This intense shrill grating voice is recognizable as I turn the knob to see who I think it is.

I woke up just in time. Although it was the blaring ringing from my alarm and the fact that I was saturated in sweat, I'm glad to have opened my eyes when I did. The sheets are drenched as if they've been dipped in a tub of water. I hit the snooze button to shut the jarring sound. It's back. The nightmares.

After a few minutes of calming my heart rate and putting the thoughts of the nightmare behind me, I moved through the spacious suite, gathering gym clothes for my morning routine. Today I planned to cycle for a full-body workout since I'd been pushing weights in the earlier part of the week. The plan was to have an intense workout that would eradicate the heavy thoughts on my mind. It didn't help that I wasn't at home in my own bed, but duty calls and I needed to support a friend, so I was in New York City for a few days. The first few days of the holiday season was spent back home in Atlanta with my parents and brothers, so traveling to the Big Apple for my very good friend's celebration party didn't have me missing out on family time. William Goodman has been wreaking havoc in my life since our freshman year of high school, and even after all our years of foolishness, I was happy and not at all surprised that he recently became Mayor of New York.

The commute from my room on the twenty-first floor, to the gym on the fourteenth floor only took a few minutes. In what felt like no time at all, I ran two miles, cycled with a group class, then headed back to my room to prepare for a last minute meet up with my brother, Benji.

Stepping off the elevator and walking through the lobby, I noticed that my Uber driver would be pulling up in about a minute. The air was brisk, and the sun cast brightly high in the sky, but the slight bit of wind felt good against my heated skin. Ten minutes later, I pulled up to the tall building of the Four Seasons Hotel, and people watched on my way to meet Benji at the restaurant for brunch. As I neared the entrance of the restaurant, several individuals in fitted black suits were posted up. This was the standard operating procedure for this hotel since they tended to have lots of celebrities and athletes staying here. I couldn't blame them for wanting to protect their guests and their reputation as one of the best hotels in the city. I was just here to chat and eat, so I had the hostess find a table that was a little secluded but still had a view of the entrance. We didn't have much time because I had a conference, so I was wondering why he wasn't already waiting for me.

As I looked up from my menu, I saw Zino and Benji approaching. Zino was actually Riana's personal security guard, but he'd been looking out for Benji since those two were spending so much time together. I appreciated that he was consistently working with Benji on improving his security team. "What's up, Bas?" Zino reached out to dap me up; I returned the closed fist pound, acknowledging him.

Benji couldn't seem to manage a greeting since he was on the phone. "Nah Maal, I ain't getting in-between shit. Whatever went on with you and Minny, is just that." Benji's deep chortle could be heard as he spoke to his best friend, Jamaal. Within seconds, he ended the call and dapped me up, following Zino's greeting. "Damn, Bastien." He smiled, geeked as ever. "I told you I needed five more minutes. You so impatient."

"Benji, I don't have all day." I returned to view the menu, hoping that we both would make our selections quickly.

"Damn, I forgot my charger, and I'm only on three percent," Benji cried.

"You can't wait until after we eat? You aren't about to waste my time, Benji." Maybe we should've scheduled for another time since I was short on availability.

He looked down at his phone before refuting my suggestion. "Nah, man. Maal going through it, plus I am waiting on a call from my agent. How about we just go back to my room, order in and if I need to take my call, you can just chill until you gotta go. I know you busy, bro."

"Negative."

"Come on, Bash. Plus, Zino won't have to be stressed about Ri and I being separated from each other. It's just easier all around if we order room service. It'll arrive in no time." He begged and I conceded, deciding that for safety purposes and my time constraints, he was right. We rode up to the fifty-second floor in silence. Before we made it to the door, Benji realized he left his jacket in the restaurant, so he and Zino returned to get it. He gave me the key card to enter his room and order the food. I slid the card across the panel watching it turn green before turning the knob to open the door. I stood in the living room of the suite. White and red decorations adorned the floor, walls, and accessories gave the space a glow. Slow jams were playing in the background reminding me that Benji and Riana were now spending a lot of time together doing whatever it is they called themselves doing. Months before, I discouraged the idea of them dating, but seeing Benji and Riana together made me see things from a different perspective. I just pray that this doesn't blow up for them. They both need a win right now.

"Oh, hey, Sebastien!" Her courteous voice came from behind, startling me as I was looking for the phone to call room service. "I thought you were your brother." She stood before me, raising on her toes, offering me a hug.

"Good morning, Ri. This is a dope penthouse." I admired, moving along the ginormous hotel suite.

"Yeah, you like?" She practically sputtered. "Your little bro set this whole thing up. He did a good job if you ask me."

I scoffed, slightly grinning. "Of course, I wouldn't expect anything less from Benjamin. I mean, we are..." I teased.

"Bennett's." Ri pursed her lips, shaking her head, giggling while finishing the chant my brothers and I had been doing for years. We were cool well before she and Benji became an item, and she was something like a little sister to me, so she saw how we got down.

I shrugged before taking in a deep breath. "We decided to eat up here, plus Benji needs his phone charger. Said he's expecting a call."

"Oh, ok. That's probably why he didn't call me to let me know y'all were coming up. It's in the room, you can go in and get it." She aimed a finger toward the master bedroom. "Excuse the mess. I'll be at the piano writing, let me know if you can't find it."

The door silently opened, telling of the upscale quality of the hotel. Their bed was disheveled and sat against a plush headboard, with undergarments disbursed all over, food containers half-open, low sounding music, and before I could find the charger, I heard, "About time, what took you so long? Didn't I tell you I have a call to make in a few?" Step by step I followed the somewhat familiar pitch. It intensified the closer I moved towards the restroom. My dick swelled at the sweet tone. She had no clue of the intruder. She continued talking.

"On a good note, yeah, I might give him all the goods. I don't mind riding his face." Tyrese was in the background talking about making love when I happened to stumble upon the tablet leaning on the mirror.

Bent over, one leg slid into the opening of her tights. My concentration is solely on her dark chocolate, ample bottom. I watch that ass swallow the thin string and immediately I try to refocus. Snapping out of the trance, I murmur, "He must be a lucky man."

Swiftly her spine unfolds. A low grunt spurts out as she spins around to check the screen. Full breasts appear blanketed in an expensive looking lace, black bra. Her washboard abs cave in and out quickly.

I lean back on the counter, taking her in. Eyeing me, she bites the bottom of her lip, then her lashes flutter. Imani's immaculate structure wasn't typical. I'm sure she stood around 5'11, but them thick thighs and supple backside placed her in the Amazonian range. Running and surfing alone couldn't have given her this composition, this had to be some excellent genes showing up and showing out. But I embraced it because her body was here to be worshipped. *Her.*

She hugged herself, shame overflowing, but the eye contact persisted. I broke the ice. "You look amazing, as always." A smile danced on her face. "What a way to present yourself for a meeting."

"The audacity of you to remain so poised as if you didn't invade my privacy." I knew none of this was an issue since amusement lingered in those squinty obsidian eyes.

I played right along. "Considering our current predicament, Ms. Barasa, I'm doing the best that I can. Trust me."

"Trust you, Mr. Bennett? Really? I'm sure you're well aware that some verbiage inflicts different meanings, and I don't think we're quite at the *trust me* phase, just yet."

My eyes twinkled with mirth, as her lips twisted into a gleeful smile. God, she's so beautiful.

We'd never been intimate. How could we? Our relationship surrounded work, with meetings primarily focused on Roland and ways of getting and keeping him out of trouble.

An oversized shirt slides over her shoulders, obstructing the view I found so fascinating.

Fingers took over the screen, "What's the towel for?"

I look down to find myself covering the swelling and pressure I'd battled through our conversation. I smirked, "I had a little mishap before walking in, but all is well."

I changed the subject attempting to ease the oh so good ache in my pants. "The real question is, will you be on time for our virtual meeting?" My phone in my palm had been vibrating for a while, reminding me of our 11:00 am Skype session.

Imani fluidly shifts to the edge of a sleigh bed. "Mr. Bennett, I'm a professional. When have I ever been late for a meeting?"

Riana walks in out of nowhere, announcing, "Oh shit, Mani! I forgot we were on FaceTime. I got sidetracked when Bash came in. What y'all talking about?"

Imani beat me to the punch of answering Riana, "Nothing much, Ri. I was just mentioning to Mr. Attorney at Law over here, how he *came early* to a meeting that we aren't scheduled to have until later." She had the nerve to finish with a sardonic smirk.

"Came early? Hahahaha! Let's hope he isn't like that in real life, sis." Both ladies laughed in unison at my expense, as Benji walked in, fussing about still not being able to find his phone charger.

Riana and Benji left the bedroom on a hunt for the charger. I took the time to turn my attention back on the chocolate beauty who took up the screen of Riana's iPad. "This is no disrespect to you at all. But darling, don't allow Ms. Riana to have you entering into a plea bargain that you aren't ready for. Keep in mind, Riana only bears witness to my *little* brother."

Before she could get a chance to respond, a pinging sound followed by an empty battery icon flashing on the screen, indicating the iPad was dead, therefore, ending our very nonprofessional conversation. It's a good thing we'd be talking later because I wasn't anywhere near finished with her. I was just beginning.

SEBASTIEN

AS I MADE my way into the kitchen, I was elated to discover it was no longer in disarray and that there was a fresh French press waiting on me. Ramona, my housekeeper, was always surprising me by going above and beyond her duties. I knew it was a good idea to keep her around. Aside from the French press, Ramona has my favorite flavors assembled in a new container. I surely didn't purchase it. This thoughtful act from her had to be repaid. I just had to pay her back for what she spent, and figure out a unique way to show my appreciation. She was around my mom's age, so I know she would probably enjoy some flowers and a spa day. All women like that.

Just the thought of knowing that she cared and valued my home as much as I did, meant a lot to me. "Alexa, play my soul playlist." I wasn't the most expressive person, but coming down to a pristine kitchen, and my favorite brew made me want to dance. I started bopping around the trendy bamboo floors, dancing, or at least what I called dancing, and mimicking the Father of Soul, James Brown. Shuffling forward then back I hit the infamous dance, the Mash Potato, killing the footwork. Shimmying left to right, shoulders grooving to *"Get on Up,"* I did my best to recreate the vocals. I glided in front of the mirror, resembling my dad, who was partial to the camel walk. Then suddenly, I stopped.

Focus Bash! I screamed to myself before walking back to my

abandoned laptop. A small sigh escaped at the mere thought of the workload I felt would never let up. A good thing was that I was no longer bound to my colleague's work. A lot of my cases were getting ready to close. The light was shining a little at the end of the tunnel, until this.

"Pete, I'm gon ask you something, and you better not fucking lie to me. Because I swear to God, I will lay yo ass out, exactly where you stand. Were you in that truck when Chelsea got shot?" I barely recognized the aggressor, especially since he was in such rage, simulating heinous acts that I'm not too sure would be approved by most.

The other two men in the room stood back as Pete was being questioned. One was there to ensure that he, too, got answers, and the other clearly wanted to make sure that Pete walked away alive.

"It wasn't me. I don't know who put that shit out there? Man, ask Tim, he was there!" Pete's eyes were beginning to water as he looked towards the man that was there for his benefit. Instead, Pete seemed to be throwing Tim under the bus.

Before Tim could reply, he pulled out a gun and aimed it at the man who wasn't questioning Pete. Next thing, all hell breaks loose as a knife is drawn, and each man is trying to defend himself.

I tapped the space bar on the laptop to pause the nonsense on my screen. My forehead sank to my desk as I felt a headache creeping in. According to my inbox, the email came in a few hours ago at five am. The sender remained anonymous, but I couldn't overlook this damaging video of Sean, Roland, Pete & Tim. I'm not surprised to see Roland in the video as I've always known he had something to do with Pete and Tim being assaulted. But what the hell is my brother Sean doing in the video? Many folks have speculated about Roland being a threat if you crossed him, but I've never seen him in action until now. It's my job to guard him the best way I can legally, but now he was dragging my brother into his rah-rah shit, and I couldn't have that.

It took me a few minutes to begin piecing the video together, but now it made complete sense to see Sean was spazzing about his wife, Chelsea. Months prior, bullets that weren't meant for her found themselves seriously injuring her and leaving her in the hospital. The person behind it was never caught. Except, Sean and I speak several times a week, and he's never mentioned much of the ordeal, only emphasizing being thankful to still have his girl alive and well. It was never mentioned by him or Roland that they had an inkling of who wielded the gun that shot my sister-in-law. I had no time to dwell on all of these new discoveries, instead, I needed to figure out the next steps. If this video leaks, it's going to be detrimental to both Roland and Sean's career.

The treble in the women's voice dislodged me from the thoughts of the video and what could be a damning fallout. "It's jammed packed here in Atlanta today as we get ready for the Super bowl. The Snakes has made their presence known over the past forty-eight hours." Her voice was one that I hadn't heard from for a minute. I hadn't given Michelle any alone time since being with her three months ago. Flipping the monitor down, I stretched my limbs from beneath the table and turned to the flat screen atop the fireplace.

Her co-anchor, Todd, picked up where she left off. "It's crazy for sure. Especially, Magic." I cackled at the nickname they coined for Benji.

"Maybe you can explain this to me, Ms. Davenport, since you're a die-hard football fan. Isn't the extra partying frowned upon before such a huge game?" The russet tinted gentleman pointed to the corner where a video of Benji and a teammate were tossing shot glasses back to back. Jamaal, who is the wide receiver for the Snakes, stood on top of a table in a bar singing. He was definitely drunk. The press had access to all of this because someone felt the need to put it on their Instagram story.

Mahogany ringlets splattered over her forehead as she responded, "Todd, they are young and celebrating. I don't think Bennett or any of his teammates will miss a beat during today's game." Michelle has always taken a liking to my little brother when we talked about sports. She made sure to reiterate my overly protective ways towards him. Being the oldest, I felt a need to protect and nurture both Sean and Benji. Especially when I learned that even the closest family members couldn't be trusted.

I was in and out of the shower in record time, applying the essential grooming products from the Troy C collection to my short hair and body as needed. My dad always emphasized the importance of proper grooming, so that stayed with me through adulthood.

Fiddling through my drawer, I realized I could use some major spring cleaning because there is no reason to have novelty prints on underwear, they are not for men. My mom still felt the need to buy them every Christmas and birthday. Though people can't see what's beneath, there is no need to show personality there. Hell, I had enough packaging below to suffice.

I slid a leg into the pants of the slim tapered jeans. It's my go-to for the day since it works with smart shoes and sneakers due to its design. The garment widens at the thighs narrowing along the way, which I find to be suitable for my muscular physique. The classic fitted shirt was a no brainer, considering a bomber jacket and Chelsea boots would finish the ensemble.

Time didn't seem to be in my favor, so I skipped down the steps two at a time, grabbing my Panerai Radiomir Watch, and floating into the garage and behind the wheel of my car.

With little time remaining before the game starts, I opted out of breakfast, making a note to grab the healthiest snack there.

Once I parked and exited my vehicle, I assembled in an overly congested space of the arena where friends and family of other players were gathered. *Super bowl LII*. I arrived just in time for kickoff and was happy to see that the Snakes had possession of the ball.

Nearing halftime, the game was giving everyone anxiety with the fluctuating scores. One-second, they're tied, then another, one team is up by a touchdown. The game persisted in this manner until the fourth quarter. My heart couldn't rest knowing my brother Benji was playing with a troubled heart. My family had no clue how much I inundated myself with work to keep from elaborating on my feelings of the recently released secrets that forever changed our well-knit family unit.

"You ok, Sebastien?" Dad nudged me away from my thoughts.

"I'm good. Benji keeps fumbling. This isn't good." Anyone watching the game could see that Benji was struggling. "He needs you, dad. I know he's resistant to having a conversation with you, but he needs it if he wants to win. It's as if he's fighting with himself." Benji comes rushing off the field towards us and beckons my father to follow him, leaving my mother and me alone with our thoughts.

My mother moved in closer to me, pushing her lavender fragrance my way. "What, mama?" I smiled, welcoming her hazel orbs.

"Just admiring my charming son, that's all," she giggled. Gripping her shoulders, I kissed her cheeks. "I love you, woman." I shifted and tuned in to the other athletes who were getting water spilled into their mouths, coaches running to and fro, and a buzz of noise filling my eardrums.

I closed my eyes, wanting nothing more than to protect this gem in my arms. When I was much younger, I tried to be her protector and failed. I thought I saved her, but in reality, I was too late because the damage was already done.

My chest heaved up and down once I opened the door to my parent's room. I'm flabbergasted by the sight of my father hovering over my mom, anger roaring through him. I've never witnessed this type of rage from him. Ever. It was scaring me.

Wait, this wasn't my Dad. The resemblance was uncanny, but still, this was not Samuel Bennett. The man who was standing over my mom possessed skin that looked like weak tea stirred with milk. This man was almost identical to the man I called, dad, until I saw the stubble of hair sitting on what's usually a sculpted jaw. My dad had a sharp face and left the house with a clean shaven face.

"Uncle Stan." Sadness crushed me into a million pieces. "My mama," I wept quietly. Tears spilled uncontrollably as I trembled trying to figure out what I just saw and why Uncle Stan was making my mom cry.

Uncle Stan didn't falter in his stance, he just stood there looking at me. And the immense and confusing feelings I felt dissipated when I heard thick sobs escape from my mother. A throbbing pulse banged through my neck before I ran full force towards my uncle. I wanted to hurt him for hurting my mom. I used all my strength, but I missed and landed on my behind. Uncle Stan's steel frame was unparalleled compared to my six-year-old weight and size. I didn't quit though, I jumped on him again, even as he tossed me like a rag doll.

"You have five seconds to leave my son and me alone." My mother finally gained enough strength to push off the bed. When I looked up, I saw her pointing one of the many guns my dad owned at my Uncle Stan. "Five, four..." By the time she got to three, Uncle Stan disappeared from the room, leaving me and my mom in a haze of confusion. What just happened and why was Uncle Stan trying to hurt my mom?

"It's my pleasure to serve you here at Books & Brew Discovery, what can I get you today?" The gleeful teenager took our order with ease bouncing around with her blond ponytail. This isn't a hole in a wall joint, but instead, a bookstore catered to stay at home parents and homeschooled families. When Nelson texted me two days ago to meet here, it made complete sense. I took notice of the abundance of kids sitting in a corner for Storytime and noticed Nelson's two in the mix.

Due to his popularity and frequent visits to the bookstore, he had an official designated work area. It was tucked away from all the commotion of the consumers. No one saw us, but we could see everyone and everything...

"You have no clue how much I appreciate you meeting me on my writing day. I try to stay on track regardless of having the kids with me." Nelson's smile is enigmatic, and I sort of was glad to be a help to him.

Nelson sent all his paperwork and a letter informing me or anyone else who read it, how and why his kids would be emotionally unstable without him. Financial records were attached as well, outlining a blueprint of things he does monthly to provide the best life for his children. Nelson loved his kids! I noticed he paid all their daycare expenses, he furnished a document for the revolving allowance he expends on the kid's clothing and entertainment. The children were barely four years old, but he had it set up so that they wouldn't have to worry about a thing financially.

The prior evening, I stayed up dissecting who this man was and how I could convey to a judge that he can care for kids despite his DUI record. Financially, he could provide immensely, but his wife wanted full physical custody according to the documentation waiting in the office for my response.

We were deep into our menus and decided on what to order when the sound of heavy, small feet seemed to be getting closer and closer.

"Daddy! Summer took my dollars and won't give back."

"No, I don't!" The little girl argued.

The shocker was the clearness in their dialect. They may miss a word or two in their sentences, but the pronunciation was clear. The private daycare was paying off.

Nelson shakes off the dark navy blazer, storing it on the back of his chair. He swoops the little girl with brown curly hair onto his lap and the boy who looked no different than the sister on the other. "I'll give you another dollar, ok, son?" He lands kisses all over the boy's cheeks while swinging his leg excessively, mimicking a ride of sort. Then the trembling leg halts and movement starts in the right leg, giving the girl the same effect, only she gets pecks on the nose, cheeks, and forehead. He buries his mouth into her abdomen. "You leave your brother alone, little girl. Or no more cupcakes for you." She giggles uncontrollably from his face and mouth vibrating on her skin, I imagine she's tickled by the whole ordeal. "I love you, daddy." She announced confidently. The bond is cohesive, and I couldn't imagine a mother being bothered by a love like this. So, I asked him a lot of questions after the kids ate at our table and ran off to a section specifically for their age group.

Nelson has his hands in praying formation against his lips as he stared me down before speaking. "Yeah, man, as I said in the text messages, this is our spot. I strategically chose Books & Brew when we moved two years ago. My wife, Lauren, works a lot of crazy hours, and I couldn't fathom having a full-time nanny for the kids. It's crazy that she's petitioning for full custody when I spend way more time with the kids than she does."

I drew in long deep breaths as the waiter set the coffee on the table. When she sauntered off, I asked again, "Nelson, man, what specifically happened with your wife for her to want nothing to do with you and be willing to take your kids from you?"

"I told you, nothing in particular. We grew apart and I kind of started being standoffish. I no longer participated in the one-sided arguments. Lauren has always been all about herself." He gestures over to the kids who are in a carpeted area, stacking blocks that are mere inches from tipping over. "Savion, don't you dare. What if you hurt yourself?" he scolds. He turns back to me, "I'm the one here with them. Lauren knows that. She also knows that if she tries to take these kids away from me, they'll be surrounded by strangers because she works too much to have to be with them like I am."

I nodded. "Mr. Davidson, my heart is all in. I admire the love between the three of you; however, I'm having a hard time understanding." I glanced down at the paperwork for his wife's name. "Marital problems are one thing, but why is she attempting to carve you completely out of your kid's lives?" I couldn't imagine his wife removing anyone else from Nelson after he's already lost his fifteen-year-old son, Nelson, Jr. According to Nelson this is where his sudden onset drinking derived from. Prior to this incident, he barely even drank alcohol socially claiming he always needed a clear head for his creativity. Especially since writing paid the bills. His son was from a previous relationship, but still, Lauren knew how hard he took it as she was very involved in Nelson, Jr.'s life. If anything, she should allow him some latitude to deal with his loss in a healthier way.

"I told you, we've grown apart since we lost Nelly. And as for the kids, I think she just wants to move on completely from me."

"I'm sorry again for your loss, man. I applaud you for being able to share that with me. Is there anything else I need to know about you? Any dealings you had in your past that makes her feel that you aren't stable for the kids besides the DUI?"

"Well, I can't be too unsafe if I have my kids with me now." I couldn't dispute that. I thought of the same thing when I noticed the kids with him the other day in my office, or when I somehow ran into them at the movie theater and then now, once again, they're spending time with him.

I sipped the hot liquid, savoring the bitter, acidic taste of the coffee before elevating my voice. "You're paying me money to help you, but yet you aren't saying anything. All I hear is a bunch of stuff that doesn't make sense and explain your wife's contempt for you. I need to know the truth and all of it from *you*. I will not show up to court unprepared because you refuse to disclose all the details. I just feel like I'm missing something here, Nelson. Help me out?" It's tedious of me to keep asking him the same question in different ways.

He smirks, "How do you figure I'm withholding information, Mr. Bennett?"

"Did you overlook the fact that I do this for a living? It's my job! And trust me." I lean in close. "I'm *very good* at my job! If you end up embarrassing me because of your own pride and ego, I'll walk away from this case without a thought and with your money."

"Understood, Mr. Bennett. But as I've said before... you know everything you need to know to represent me." This sounded as if Nelson was ending our meeting.

I flicked my wrist, searching for the face of the Rolex for the time I didn't have. A reminder that I had a scheduled phone call in a few minutes gave me a chance to wrap up our meeting.

Nelson wiped the donut residue from his mouth with a napkin before he shook my hand and excused himself. He headed outside on the balcony to grab more coffee while I gathered my belongings, placing them in a briefcase.

Before I could make my escape, a soft voice got closer, "Who are you?" The little girl asks, with icing all over her chin. Then the boy walks up to me, tugging the arm of my flushed flannel sweater. "And why are you wearing pink? Dad says, that's for girls."

Funny, he says that because Nelson complimented me on my attire explaining how the top brought out the cerulean denim and suede loafers. Too bad their dad thought the guy that dresses like a girl is his only hope in keeping his kids.

"Color doesn't define who you are." Both miniature figures looked puzzled. Moving from the stool I was leaning on, I got down in a squat so that I was on the same level as them. "Listen up chief," I pat his shoulder. "You can wear any color and still be whoever you want to be. I like this sweater. I got it from my grandfather, who means the world to me."

"Don't worry, I love your outfit. My mom got some shoes like that too." The girl added more insult to the injury. I groaned. "Yes, both men and women wear loafers. That's what they're called, but these are specifically for men." All three of us chuckled but I could no longer stay at eye level. I stood up cleaning the table. The boy comes and helps, "What's your name?"

"Sebastien."

"My name Savion and dats my sister, Summer."

"I would say it's nice meeting you, but I've met you before, remember?" We cackle.

"I like Chief. It's a cool name." So, buddy likes his nickname.

"Yeah, well, I'll call you that for now on."

Summer jumps haphazardly, "What about me?" She practically screams.

"I'll call you Cupcake because every time I see you, you're eating one."

All giddy, she runs up to her dad who's phone drops to the floor from her abrupt greeting. "I got a new name. He calls me Cupcake."

I'm amazed at how well-articulated these kids are. They haven't even hit kindergarten yet.

"Oh yeah?" He laughs, "Probably because that's all he sees you eat, silly girl." He grabs his phone. "Go clean up, y'all mess, and come back here as soon as you all finish."

Nelson stands in front of me, "Mr. Bennett, I know you think I'm hiding something, but it's all just nervousness. Thanks for being patient with me." Perhaps I would behave in the same manner if I was in his shoes. I'd tough it out and assist him with those kids. He deserved a fair chance, and I would make sure of that.

"Who was that at the door, Rain?" My best friend, Mia, was at home with me as we were working on some ideas for the twins' upcoming birthday. She took her job as BFF and Godmother very seriously.

"A courier with a certified letter." I looked at the letter in confusion before opening it.

"Why are you getting certified legal mail here, shouldn't that be going to your office?" Her thought process was on the same wavelength as mine. I never received important work documents here at my home.

"It's definitely addressed to me, so let me open this first, then we can get back to the party planning." For some reason, I was nervous. Mia stood over my shoulder, and both of us displayed shock as the letterhead came into full view.

"What the hell, Rain? Why are you getting mail from that law firm?" She knew the gravity of this before I even read one word on the page. "You didn't tell me you were going up against them for a case."

"I'm not!" All of a sudden, the paper in my hand started shaking from the tremors rolling through my body. Now the kitchen felt like a chill had come out of nowhere.

Once I started reading, I realized this isn't in regard to what I suspect. The lawyer didn't waste any time on the intent to settle matters in mediation instead of court. Of course, my soon to be ex-husband would choose the cheaper route to get my attention. No one wants to drag a case into court, which wastes time and money, but I wasn't too confident about being able to get rid of him on my terms so quickly. I love my husband, but over the past year, things in our marriage have become intense… in the worst way possible. He no longer gave me the affection I craved, he worked profusely, and if it wasn't for the kids, I doubt he'd even have the strength to pretend like he noticed me. Even with all of this going on, he's still a damn good father.

My plan to leave him was just that, a plan. But then he became enraged, and that made me reconsider any chance of allowing him to be with the kids or me. The level of anger he possessed scared the living shit outta me. Although I've never seen him out of order with the twins, he didn't hold that same control when it came to dealing with me.

"Just calm down. Those thick ass eyebrows look as if they're about to jump off your face." Mia was the joker of the crew for sure, but I wasn't sure if her antics were welcomed or not after opening and reading this letter. "It could have been a letter about something far worse. You act like you're not the one asking for a divorce. He went out and protected himself, fighting for something dear to him. You would have instructed any client of yours to do the same thing." Mia stated, getting under my skin. She sat there with a crisp pixie cut filing her nails. Suddenly, she was *Ms. Composed* and I was still out of sorts. My copper-colored bestie spoke her mind with conviction, but she didn't agree with my decision to end my marriage. She felt as if I was the contributing factor in allowing my marriage to wane. Mia didn't condone the fact that I was busy and dedicated more time than she felt reasonable working as an attorney. Over the past few months, I slowed down trying to work on my relationship but the roles reversed. He was no longer persistent in loving me, but now spent all his time with the kids and at work. All those qualities were great but where does that leave me? And why couldn't he do a better job of controlling his feelings and emotions around me?

Flames of anger shot through me as I finally made it to the signature line. "Are you serious? This day couldn't possibly get any worse." I slammed the document in front of my thick friend. "Mia, read this and pay particular attention to the end."

It took her a few moments to make it through the certified legal document. I noticed her eyes pausing at some areas, and moving swiftly through others. It was clear when she noticed what I needed her to see. "Oh shit! Sebastien Bennett is representing your husband. Damn, Rain, this can't be good."

"Like, we all go way back. How could he even agree to represent my husband? How dare he?"

"Does Nelson know about you and Sebastien's past?" Mia questions.

I shrug, letting my hair down onto my back. I didn't know what to do with myself.

I've seen Sebastien many times over the years in passing, and he's the reason why I finally passed my bar exam. I even interned at Bennett & Associates for a few months before getting an opportunity at my current law firm.

Mia asks, "What's the plan?"

"It's a good thing I know where to find him. Stay here and keep working on the party; I'll be right back!" I didn't give her time to talk me out of it. I knew it was a Saturday, but I also knew there wasn't much in this world Sebastien loved more than his career, so I was willing to bet my marriage that he would be in the office.

Cars were at a complete standstill for half of the ride through the city, only giving me more time to reflect on how this conversation would go with Sebastien. This carried on until seeing my reflection through the shiny complex cylindrical doors as I approached the lobby of the grandiose building that housed Bennett & Associates.

Double doors hitting the wall caused a tumultuous clatter. It wasn't long before I had a face-off with a security guy who questioned me like I was some terrorist. As I was digging in my purse, I heard a familiar voice calling out to me.

"Oh my god! Rain?" Jane Robbins screams, pulling me into a hug that smelled like a carton of cigarettes. I coughed the closer I neared her neck. The lady's skin resembled excess skin on a piece of chicken. No way she'd aged that much since I last saw her.

"Hello, Ms. Robbins." I twirled her around by the hand, "You look fab as always." I couldn't fathom telling her she aged at least twenty years since I've seen her.

"What brings you in today? I've seen the headlines of all your accomplishments. You're busy *busy busy*."

"It's been a while since I've been around these parts as an intern, but now I'm on my own, I could use Sebastien's help on something. Is he in?"

"Oh, dear, you're always welcomed here. Jeff, let her up." Colorful pointy tips accessorize her hand as she drives me towards the bank of elevators that would take me to my destination. "Once you get up there, someone will be at the reception desk to help you out. Good seeing you, sweetie." Ms. Robbins strolled off as I thought of a plan to get inside of Mr. Sebastien Bennett's office.

Getting on and off the elevator took no effort as I approached the reception area, finding it deserted. Since there was no one to help me, I made my way through the immense corridor where Sebastien's office was located and could hear voices from the other occupied offices. Finally, I stumbled upon an eloquently designed nameplate with the man of the hour's name. Without knocking, I turned the golden knob struggling to push the heavy door open before he appeared.

Sebastien seemed to be three inches taller than I remembered, and back then, he already stood at six feet even. Neither he nor his office guest seemed to notice my presence as I watched the two of them har-de-her in what appeared to be the funniest joke ever. His white button-up isn't tucked inside of the dress pants, nor do I see any shoes accompanying his feet. Whoever the wide-hipped girl is, she must be very familiar with him as she appeared to be just as comfortable in his space than he was. I've never seen him so relaxed before. He took his globular arms and wrapped them around her small waist attempting to hug her, as she tried to escape his embrace.

"Imani, don't play. That's mine." His elongated arms reached for a slice of pizza from her extended hand. I noticed she's a tall woman, not much shorter than him at all. Miss Tall didn't have on shoes either, but she too was dressed in professional attire.

"Bastien stop, you gone make me drop it. I won fair and square." She squealed when he intercepted the pizza by stretching her hand towards his mouth. They went back and forth before she conceded and let him have the pizza.

"Fine, you can have it all." She pouted. "I wanted the strawberry creme savers anyway. They all belong to me now."

"What happened to the pack I bought you a few days ago?"

"I ate them all."

Sebastien shifted away from his desk to go and stand behind her while he inspected her body as she looked out of his office window at the amazing views of Downtown Atlanta. Shoot, this woman was a goddess in her own right. I could understand why Sebastien was hooked on perusing her from head to toe. Neatly arched brows hovered over chinky eyes. Her excessive length of hair wasn't a weave. I could tell she was natural, but had it pressed.

Compared to the other women I've seen accompany Sebastien, no one was ever as melanated as she was. Her shimmery mocha skin glowed.

He gripped her seaweed green jeggings, "Wonder where all of them cream savers are going?"

"Pssh, stop it." She turned around to look at him, but her eyes ended up aiming towards the door. She wanted to keep talking, but she saw me standing there.

I wore a smirk and winked in her direction, feeling somewhat like an intruder. I wasn't being funny by winking, but more so, showing her that I come in peace and was offering a genuine welcome. "Good afternoon."

Sebastien hits a ninety-degree curve. Sheesh, he's handsome as all get out. Not that I never noticed. I just knew his handsomeness as he was still growing into it. Now, he resembled a grown man with very pronounced, sharp features. I don't recall a full mustache connecting to a full-length goatee. His hair was kept neat this time, a low fade with a precise line up compared to the days of me working my ass off as an intern when he wore his hair in a higher, kinky curly style.

He once walked around in jeans, sweats, or anything chillaxed. Not anymore. These days, a pair of slacks, chinos, dress shoes, or thong sandals, seemed to be his signature uniform. I only knew about the sandals because I ran into him and his family while they were vacationing at their summer home in Savannah.

Boo nigga; I thought as I chuckled to myself. He must've thought I would go along with the letter and not say anything. I was no dummy to his winning record in the courtroom but I knew my stuff as a divorce lawyer. I hired an attorney from my firm since law 101 dictates that it's not a good look to represent yourself, no matter how good you are.

Sebastien regains his composure, transforming from laid back

Kool Moe Dee to Attorney Bennett. He tucks his shirt in, using his hands to smooth it out. Imani isn't too far behind, propping her palm on the floor to ceiling window, slipping into nude pumps. Sebastien was the first to speak, "It seems as if I need to do some firing around this place. I can't seem to understand how people are getting past security without my knowledge." He shakes his head then walks up to me, hand proffered. "Long time no see, Rain."

A handshake, really? I reciprocated. "It would be longer if you didn't send…"

Imani grabbed her peacoat off the hanger, and Sebastien interrupted my dialogue when he walked off in the middle of my sentence. He gathered the stylish coat from her arms and helped her put it on.

Rude. She's self-sufficient. I mean, she did manage to put her shoes on without his help. He could have at least said *excuse me*, or something.

"I'll leave you to your meeting, Mr. Bennett," the Amazonian stated.

"I don't have any conferences or meetings left for the day." He said to her before turning to look at me for an explanation. "By the way, how did you get in here without clearance or an appointment?"

My nails bumped against each other as I struggled not to resemble a stalker for the second time during this impromptu meeting. Besides, I'm unsure of the relationship between these two. "I told security we had a scheduled meeting."

He stared at me with wide, angry eyes.

"And then I ran into Ms. Robbins." He knew exactly how having an endorsement from Ms. Robbins would gain me entry to this secured floor. "Once I arrived, no one was at the reception desk, so I walked myself back."

Imani was halfway through the suite making her way towards

the door, when Sebastien took a second to have a word with her. "Call me when you get there. And make sure Roland doesn't screw this up. I'll take care of everything else on my end." Then he tried to whisper, "My apologies for this unscheduled interruption. I know we both are short on time, so I appreciate you stopping by and having lunch with me."

"Mr. Bennett," she moves in closer, "I enjoyed my afternoon with you and thanks for replenishing my cream savers stash. I'll call you later with an update." It got quiet, so I couldn't hear the rest of their conversation, but she leaned into his space reaching out for a hug that appeared to be both friendly and sensual. He obliged her by closing his eyes during the hug. Next thing I know, she was gone.

He shuts the door. "Rain, don't come bombarding my space like that. You are more than welcome here, but under no circumstances should you use your previous relationships with my staff to barge in unannounced."

I filled his personal space, smelling what I knew to be *'Avenge'* a fairly new scent from the Troy C product line. "I've always respected you, Sebastien." I gave him steady eye contact, "But I see it's not mutual."

He scoffs like he has no idea of the reasoning for my current state of anger. "Out of all the people you choose to represent, you go for Nelson!" I'm screaming into his face. He barely flinches, letting my hands push into his hard abdomen. I feel my face contorting, but I refuse to cry.

His peanut coated cheek heightens as he clenches his jaw. "What's wrong with me representing Mr. Davidson?" His strides get more prominent as he heads towards the fireplace.

"How can you fight me in court? Why are you coming for me?"

"Wait." His fingers go through a stack of papers. "Lauren R. Davidson." He swallowed, loudly, before focusing on me, then the letter. "I didn't know Nelson was your husband. I know you by your surname, L. Rain Williams. Hell, I didn't even know you were married."

His muscles can be seen flexing beneath his crisp shirt. He runs his palms all over his head before slumping into his seat. "Ok. Off the record, Counselor?" He waves me over to sit down across from him. I decline and sit on the mahogany tables circling the humongous room, but I'm still in front of him. "Why do you want a divorce?"

"Since we're off the record, why?" I would be sure to use this time with Sebastien wisely. "Is he trying to divorce me first?"

"No. But as the letter states, Nelson wants to make sure he sees his kids."

I took a deep breath and held it in because any mention of my kids put me on edge. My best bet was to change the subject. "I'm not happy anymore. I love him, but I can truly say I fell out of love a while ago."

"You guys can't get counseling to fix it? Or find other resources to guide you back to a healthy place in your marriage?"

"No. And I am sure I do not want to repair my marriage. No one knows what it's like to be with an alcoholic until they've been there."

His eyes bulged. Did he have any clue of his alcohol addiction? After I talked more in-depth with Sebastien regarding the seriousness of his drinking, he now understood my fear of allowing him to be unsupervised with the twins.

"Why almost every time I meet him, he has your kids? How is that, if he's a dangerous alcoholic?" I catch the accusatory tone as if I'm fabricating the narrative.

"Nelson is a wise and calculated guy despite his careless moves. When he gets the kids, it's usually during the day. His drinking only occurs at nighttime after he's drafted whatever for his next project. He also doesn't drink when he's expected to have them. The episodes usually occur when it's just us." I take a deep breath to think about how I'm painting this man I call my spouse. He was such a good guy and still had those ways about him, but life had a way of manipulating our thought process.

Sebastien noticed me getting worked up and offered to get me a cup of tea. As soon as he walked out, a weight lifted off my shoulders as I relaxed into the comfy furniture, taking deep breaths until I felt myself calm down. This was the calmest I've felt in ages.

"Wake up, Rain." I cracked my lids, realizing I dozed off when Sebastien stepped out to get tea. He was no longer in his business attire; instead, he had on Nike sweats hanging rather low against his tapered waist. The swiftness of the events made this appear as a lucid dream, but I decided against that when I noticed my reflection in his office windows. I still wore a gray blazer over my fitted red blouse. Denim jeans and black booties enhanced the little hips I carried, making my muscular shaped thighs suffice, adding the necessary curves to my womanly figure.

"I have plans tonight with less than an hour to dip out of here." The lights in the corner of the office shut off. Enough light penetrated the room from the surrounding buildings to keep it from being too dark. "Does it make you uncomfortable that I represent your husband? Do you want me to recuse myself from the case?"

I needed to take a moment to consider the question because the outcome would affect all parties involved. "You don't have to do that, I know you will be fair."

"Even still, you felt uncomfortable enough with me representing your husband that you showed up unannounced to my office. I'll see if I can hand it over to another partner." His hoodie slides onto his frame seamlessly.

I stand to gather my purse to leave behind him. "I appreciate you hearing me out."

I'm out of his office when he turns to me. "If I'm unable to withdraw myself fully, just know I tried. However, I'll see what I can do to make things more amicable for the two of you."

It felt good to express the lingering weary in my soul. Besides God and Mia, I hadn't released all the burdens to anyone. So, having Sebastien as a sounding board for a few minutes was a blessing. Tonight, I would rest up and pray for better days.

THE ATLANTA VULTURES basketball team was having a horrible season. Surprisingly, their luck managed to change just for tonight as they were winning this mid/late-season game. My real obligation, despite the overall team's success, was to Fernando Diaz and Malik Robertson, two of my clients. Many viewed me as a strategic problem-solver, but my client's endless irresponsible encounters and countless losses sometimes deterred me. These two were key players for the Vultures, and I've been repping them for a few years. Unlike other PR Firms who stuck with clients in a specific industry, I had folks all across the board; sports, entertainment, entrepreneurship. I covered it all. It just made me more sought out, for those looking for representation.

The urge to work in different industries started early in my career after my mentor insinuated that I had a special gift that couldn't be taught. The ability to be able to convey messages in a way to move people in a direction that enhanced their careers seemed to live in me. According to her and others, I could talk someone off a ledge.

With my knowledge and natural talent, there was an increase in traffic to my website, and my phone lines were blowing up with all sorts of people clamoring to work with me. More work meant less time to live and enjoy a social life. But I knew and understood the work it took to build and keep this lifestyle. Out of a twenty-four hour period, I'm sure eighteen goes to my business. That's barely a full night's rest. With that in mind, I quickly pulled out my cell phone, asking Siri to remind me to put out a post for an assistant. This may seem like a small task, but it was going to be a start to freedom. I even set a reminder for a month later to work on a full team to give me the ability to go after the dreams I had in mind, starting with a designated time for surfing and traveling. Boy, did I miss that. I knew that things were going to change, and soon. Once I set my mind to something, my heart followed. Fortunately, there was still space in my brain for my clients, and right now, one of my top tier headaches, Mr. Roland Jones was setting up residency in a space where I needed to make room for myself.

Nausea settled inside at the mere thought of Shooter blowing this major halftime performance. He should've been at the arena by now, but Shooter sent me a text confirming he was running late, and that he was on his way. He mentioned the visit with his daughter went longer than expected, and I definitely wouldn't have wanted him to leave her if he wasn't ready, especially since his time with her was limited. I orchestrated this performance for Shooter at this particular game for many reasons. This was the Hometown Heroes game, and having Shooter here would increase the ticket sales and visibility of the team since he was a born and bred Atlanta Entertainer. I wouldn't go as far as calling him a hero, though!

Shooter strolled in with his usual rugged demeanor on display. He and his entourage moved confidently through the vast halls with no cares as if he didn't have an important performance coming up. He slid into the seat next to me, smelling like a pound of weed, but the strong presence of Tom Ford neutralized the fumes. Ranting about his extra-curricular activities to him wouldn't get me anywhere, so I decided to let it go. Shooter was genuinely making a valiant effort to shape his image to fit the goals that he laid out months ago. The more I considered it, the more I got excited to see what his future held.

As I continued to strategize a plan for Shooter in my head, my cell phone lit up with a message from my homegirl Ameka. It was like this message from her was a sign that I needed to make more time for friends and delegate my work to others I trusted. Ameka was one of the few friends that stuck with me through and after college. Similar to my career path, she owns her own business, ARC Marketing & Branding Firm. Not only did we take many of the same classes together, but whatever she learned, she passed along, and I did the same. But, if what I witnessed on her social media was any indication, it seemed like my girl wasn't short on finding fun stuff to get into. We hadn't hung out in forever, but Ameka and I shared some great times in the past. I needed to get with her and see about reigniting our legendary ratchet nights out!

AMEKA CHAMPION
WYA?

ME
In the HORIZON Section.

AMEKA CHAMPION
I'm right behind the players, you coming down?

ME
See you in a sec

A heated glare could be felt emanating from Shooter, but for the most part, we stared at the hyperactive game where men are running up and down the court going back and forth scoring. We were seated two levels above the basketball court, also known as the Horizon section, for those wanting to be nearby but maintain a level of exclusiveness. His head angled, deep glossy brown eyes burned through my orbs, his fingers interlocked. "Imani Barasa?" Shooter definitely posed my name as a question and not a statement. "You don't gotta worry so much about me. A nigga just tryna unwind a bit, so don't go planning ways to fix up my fuck ups, I'm staying out of trouble." He stated that calmly. But that wasn't the end of his dialogue with me. Shooter continued to let me know that the mother of his child, Lexiana is still giving him grief. No matter how hard he tried to keep it cordial, she was always working hard to make him work for his relationship with Alexandria.

On top of that, Shooter seemed deeply concerned about the recent negative press Lexi launched out to the public against him. It was already a shock of epic proportions that Shooter was even tossed in the paternity mix of this beautiful baby girl. No proof existed that the two were involved, so finding out he was secretly smashing one of the hottest entertainers, surprised everyone.

I nodded in regard to his sentiments, but my line of vision faltered to the floor. Figures in blue and black jerseys assembled to and from the seats and into the game. Right before the buzzer rang to indicate the start of a new quarter, my eyes seemed to have a mind of their own as they zoomed in on a tall, well-dressed man sitting on the floor seats very close to the team. I thought it was dope that instead of sitting in the box seats like other owners, he chose to be up close and personal with the team that he part owned. Boss moves. Something I'm sure any woman would find attractive. It's something about his dress outside of those expensive professional suits that shot straight to my lady parts. The tracksuit he was wearing fit his well defined frame as if it was tailored specifically for his measurements. Two neckpieces circled his thick neck. One seemed to be a religious ornament, a cross sitting directly between his breastplate. The other hung closer to his neck.

As I was lowkey eye fucking him, I noticed him having a private conversation with the coach. Sebastien had been accused in the past of being a sideline coach when he should have just been focused on owning the team. Maybe that's what was happening, but either way, I wanted to see what he had on under that jacket. My nasty thoughts were interrupted once again by Shooter, whom, for a moment, I forgot was sitting next to me.

"You might not be screwing him in reality, but mentally he got you fucked up." The Budweiser bottle being slammed onto the countertop startled me as Shooter observed my silence. I didn't intend to tune him out, it just happened every time Mr. Bennett took charge of a room.

I swiveled in my lofty chair, smirking at his remark. "Shouldn't you be warming up for your performance?" I said, putting on my professional, public relations rep hat.

Shooter gasped, then burst into laughter. One foot stepped down before the other. He got up and out of the chair, curling his arms around my neck. "Don't try and change the subject. Tighten up Ms. Barasa, that nigga dick ain't gon walk off, just go get it." Eons ago, this would have been inappropriate and uncomfortable between us, but recently, our dynamic changed. Normally, I would strictly keep things professional. Still, I understood that Shooter was more than a client, and I had no problem letting him get this one off. I allowed myself to smile and embrace the fact that he thought he figured something out between Sebastien and me.

Thankfully, the heat was off of me, as he wandered off, headed to do his half time performance. Before he can fully disappear he looks back at me, over his shoulder. "Just don't take too long to go after what you want. Dem hoes be lurkin'... Trust me, I be know-ing." He had a look on his face that insinuated he was talking to himself as much as he was talking to me.

"Really, Shooter?" His comment made me chuckle but I imagined the hard truth behind it. I've heard women make sly remarks about Sebastien, but none ever phased me since we weren't in a place of intimacy... yet. I could honestly admit, that I wanted him and the surge of attraction for him multiplied as I watched him in action during the game.

I'd descended an elevator in the arena, then walked through endless halls before finally unfolding black double doors, finding myself in the middle of NBA fanfare. The hooting and shaking of the stands were unbelievable. Security guards were all around in black button-ups and slacks. The guards seemed to be occupied, scoping out the scene, and talking through tiny earpieces. The players on the court were enormous, and that says a lot from a woman like me since I was damn near six feet. They were so close, I saw the sweat dripping from many of them.

I kept checking my surroundings as I carefully stepped down the last few steps that would put me on the same level as the court-side seats. A useful review for my shoes was in my future because the last thing I needed was to go tumbling down. My nude-colored above the knee boots were doing an excellent job of holding all 5'10, 190lbs of me up, all without the walk being painful.

"EeeeMonEEEE!" Someone yelled, enunciating every syllable in my name. I kept walking down as this timeless beauty in a cute ass outfit strolled up and wrapped her thin silky hickory arms around my waist. "I've missed you, girl!"

Dark full strands hit the bottom of her chin, her pixie now a full bob. It's been a minute since we hung out. We stayed in touch, communicating through text with random run-ins, but nothing more. She's that type of friend you don't have to see to know she's got your back, a random pop up like this starts and ends as if we've missed no days in one another's lives. That's my girl.

I accepted her embrace, bending a bit at the waist to get down to her level. "Ameeeeeeka." I practically hugged myself in the process since she was so petite. She's warm and comforting, a familiar touch. "I'm glad we have a chance to catch up." My cheeks began to hurt from the prolonged smile I can't seem to rid myself of in her presence.

Not too long after, we're sitting two rows behind black foldable chairs that are occupied by players, assistant coaches, and trainers. Explicit verbiage is thrown left and right between the coaches, fans, and teammates. So much is going on, that you would think this game was a determining factor in progressing to the playoffs. But nope, this game wouldn't change the fact that the Vultures season would be over after their last regular-season game. I loved the support the die-hard fans were showing to the team.

We giggled after accidentally kicking each other as we both tried crossing our legs at the same time. After a giggling fit, Ameka snorted and asked, "Ok, ok, how is Yeay?"

"Girl, she's a US Citizen now."

Her eyes ballooned as she gasped and cuffed her mouth. I nodded my head to reassure her what she heard is true.

"No way! She always talked about returning to her home country, but I see she changed her mind to be closer to family."

"You know she can't play herself with Donald Duck in office." Two teenage girls sitting near us with their parents, grimaced at our obnoxious laughter, something that I can't seem to control in her presence. Ameka took me back to the lighthearted, fun, giggle girl I was in college.

"I'm so proud of her. I need to visit your family soon. Maybe when you all have another get together you can let me know." Ameka leaned into the plush seats, "Because I need all that immaculate cooking from your kinfolk." Her eyes rolled back in exaggeration and her lids fastened shut. "That Lok Lak always hits the spot when your grandma whips it up, or your dad's Ugali when he tops it with his famous fish stew." Slowly her tongue glides between her top and bottom lip. If anyone saw her, you'd swear she was having an orgasm right there. My girl was dramatic as all get out, but Ameka was the sweetest, most giving, and humble human being I knew. She turned all negative situations into positive within seconds, with great reasoning. A skill not very many possess.

She snapped out the trance and stiffened her spine with a smile. "So, what's up with you, Imani?"

I rubbed the back of my neck, unsure what to dish out. "Work! With very little play."

"I know a bit about your work life, I'm referring to this." Her widescreen phone dangled above my eyes, bringing attention to the title, *'On the Up & Up!'* Underneath was a collage of five men, who I noticed were all lawyers. Falling at number two was Mr. Sebastien Bennett, and at number one, I see the one and only, his father, Samuel Bennett. This isn't surprising considering his reputation as the go-to lawyer. I was anxious to see what was discussed and skimmed the online article until I came across the videos of each man being interviewed. My fingers moved fast as hell as I swiped upward on her phone, skimming through to make it to the video where Sebastien is being questioned. Naomi Blasingame, a hazelnut woman, clasped her interlocking fingers over her knees, shooting daggers at a relaxed Sebastien. I couldn't hear the video until Ameka handed me one AirPod, and she placed the other in her ear.

They're both in chairs adjacent from one another. "Mr. Bennett, it's clear you're about your business. Your name has been circulating about not only being a powerful lawyer, but you also co-own the Vultures. Additionally, you invest a lot of money into different causes that are dear to you, and you put in time volunteering. How do you make time for it all, and where are the others like you?"

Sebastien seemed to process the question, placing his calf on his knee. His charming smile showed his charisma. "I can admit that I don't have a lot of leisure time, but we make time for what we deem important. As far as the others like me, Naomi... I'm not sure."

Naomi's bright smile confirmed that she approved his answer. "This leads me to my next topic." The screen splits in half. We can see both Naomi and Bastien on one side and the other, a post from Instagram. "Can you elaborate on the post that PRESSED sent out?" It's clear he hasn't seen the video, and that made me sit up and pay extra attention while I increased the volume to hear the gossip because that's all PRESSED is about.

The beginning starts with an introduction of words, *'Wealthy Bachelor Officially Off the Market?'*

I held my breath as I waited to see the reveal because whoever edited the video had visual effects and sound to go along with the nonsense. A few photos of him by himself were displayed, showing off his sexy attributes, one of him playing basketball with his brothers and friends; and in another, he mingled with other wealthy looking men. A melodramatic sound blasted through the one AirPod I had in, then I saw the caption, *'Sebastien Bennett May Have Been Snatched Away by PR Maven, Ms. Imani Barasa.'* Ameka chuckled at my new found revelation. "Mhmm, you haven't shared this with me yet." She stated.

A few photos of him, Shooter, and myself transition across the screen. The first set of pics weren't incriminating, but the last three said otherwise. One was a hug we shared after dinner, a dinner we shared with Shooter. Another was of him holding my hand while I walked down a flight of steps, he was just being a gentleman. Lastly, the most incriminating one showed my breast, stomach, and groin pressed into him as our faces were mere inches apart, but our broad smiles were the highlight of the photo. We seemed... So happy. His arms rested just above my bubble butt that sits perfectly high, he looked comfortable and at home in this position.

Back to the interview, Sebastien uncrossed his legs and stretched them out. The curve on his face said a lot, and Naomi didn't miss it. She wiggled her brows, then chuckled. She waited for an explanation.

"Ugh..." I couldn't hear the rest, the commotion of the game in front of me is too boisterous and drowning out the sound of the video.

I looked out towards the court and noticed Sebastien's spheres directly on mine. I tried to act unbothered by Sebastien's gaze, so I turned back to Ameka, who was mighty quiet and fully engaged in her iPad taking notes. I went back to the phone and pressed play.

As I was engulfed in the video, awaiting the answer to Naomi's question, I was surprised to hear the next words out of his mouth. "PRESSED barely captured the elegance of the woman in the video if you asked me." My heart galloped at the mention of me. His robust and deep baritone voice was magnified through the small speaker in my ear. It reminded me of getting lost in the ocean after a wave. He continued, "Ms. Barasa and I operate together to produce effective results for our mutual client."

"You address her so professionally, but the photos look very personal." Naomi has a bold personality and doesn't mind prying. That will take her far as a journalist. I watched as she adjusted her thin frames against the bridge of her nose, then she lays it on thick to reel Sebastien in. "As a single, educated black man, the people want to know if you're still on the market or not? Do we... umm, excuse me, do they have a chance, Mr. Bennett?" She snickered, and so did Ameka.

"Does she have a chance?" She gagged, "Thirsty much? She

tried it." Ameka was not happy by Naomi's not so subtle attempt to hit on Sebastien.

I spun in her direction with no words, silently agreeing with her.

Those curly lashes fluttered. "Are you vying for his love, Mani?" Without effort, her body dances in the seat as she glanced at me, waiting for my answer. I just stared at her. I'm sure my smile and blush said it all. We went back to the video.

He pinched his nostrils, finally putting Naomi out of her thirsty ass misery. "Personal or professional, she will and should always be Ms. Imani Barasa to me. I have the utmost respect for her. Most importantly, I enjoy working with her and easily get lost in our conversations. She's a smart woman who knows what she wants. Her work ethic is unparalleled to so many others. I would have to be a blind man to not be drawn to her."

"That's it?" Naomi was a pushy lil' something. The man already answered the questions.

"It's whatever you perceive it to be, Naomi." I noticed that he called her Naomi instead of Ms. Blasingame. It was a turn on and term of endearment when he called me, Ms. Barasa.

"You sure know how to keep people guessing, Mr. Bennett."

"I only speak about what's necessary." He leaned in close, holding eye contact with Naomi. The camera zoomed in as if he's talking directly to the viewer. His orbs are radiating through the screen as if he did the interview knowing I would be on the receiving end. This feels intimate. "I think I've said enough to conclude this interview." He winks, then goes silent as the camera transitions into Naomi, giving her closing remarks.

Damn... that was hot as fuck, and all I could imagine is him calling me Ms. Barasa once we both stripped our clothes off.

"You're missing the bigger picture, Bastien. Look around you." I inspected the arena observing all that's in view. The stands were filled with people who were all here, united as one to push this team one step closer to a championship. "The majority of the players in the league are of color. Can we say the same about the management and ownership? That's kinda stark, don't you think, son?" For years, my dad emphasized the importance of generating several streams of income in different sectors. If the opportunity for a black man to advance and own something lucrative presented itself, you were to jump on it. After lots of convincing, tons of meetings with the majority team owner, Dunlap, and once my dad decided to fund my portion of the co-ownership, I was sold.

The first season of owning a small percentage of the team produced major success allowing me to repay my father the immense amount of money he invested in me. If I'm honest, I was skeptical about my dad putting so much money out because I wasn't 100% sold that this was a substantial investment. I could now admit that I would have been a fool if I'd missed this amazing opportunity. This would feed my family and me far into the future.

The folks sitting next to me courtside probably thought I was going to have an aneurysm. That's how hard the vein was throbbing and showing at my temple. Since I wasn't a coach, but instead part owner, I needed to keep my backseat coaching to myself, and from the looks of things, Coach Oglesbee had it under control. A player on the Vultures team, Malik, was getting elbowed and damn near destroyed by a member of the opposing team. I didn't dream of putting my two cents into how the team was being coached; I just wanted the refs to put a stop to all the blatant fouls. My love for sports wasn't a secret, but when it came to basketball, I went all super fan. Add to that, I partly owned the team, so I was deeply invested in making sure they won fair and square.

"Yee!" I abandoned my chair to parlay with a man I considered a close associate despite his reserved temperament. Emery appeared to be coming from the concession stand so I met him halfway. Our palms smacked against another, "Mr. Coleman, what it do?" I eliminated the corporate talk and adjusted to the person in front of me because what I need to inquire about may hit a nerve. Emery let out a hearty laugh at my affable greeting. His head swung left to right. "Getting it in. All work, no play. It's all goody." Emery ran a nonprofit mentoring program, targeting at-risk youth. His reason for committing to these kids, *'I believe by ten the streets already got a hold of most of our black boys.'* I wholeheartedly agreed with him, we have to intervene early. He's passionate about the boys he mentors and has a strong team of black men who help facilitate the progression of each. Needless to say, it's good to see amazing role models for our youngins.

We proceeded to a more desolate area where it's dark and less frantic. "How's your family back home?" I queried.

"All is well, I'm just getting back actually. What's going on?" His brows lay low, the muscles in his eyes contracted. He always kept a calm composure, never running his mouth; he listened, observed, and moved from there.

"I know you're not a man of many words, nor do I expect you to answer me straight out, but I need you on something."

I explained the video I received through email, giving specifics on the two people who I felt are behind it, Tim and Pete. I never mentioned what I saw my brother Sean and client Roland do. I didn't mention their names at all, but I'm clear in my delivery and my approach to finding out what Tim and Pete really want.

I noticed Em is taking in what I said while he continuously glanced to the left. I followed his sight of vision to the stands where I saw Annabelle, his assistant, along with two boys he mentors. To my surprise, it's the boys' faces from the research I performed a week prior. Montekus and Desmond.

The Ruben Lotus-Cheeks look-alike gave me a cautious stare. "Mr. Bennett, are we talking business, or is this personal?" He quizzically asked.

"Personal," I grunted and switched my stance.

"Tell me what it is you want me to provide, and I'll let you know if I can make it a reality. Yadadamean?" That's it, he was completely letting go of his professionalism and moving in the direction I needed him too. I can differentiate by the way his accent came out blaring, and I too adjusted. I could quickly revert to the Oakland verbiage after spending countless summers with my aunt out there. Those were the good old times.

"I didn't expect to see you pull up tonight but was juiced when I noticed you walking up. Anyway, Tim is Desmond and Montekus' Uncle." I wasn't questioning but was hoping to see him react. Nothing. Just a deadpan expression. Just like I knew Emery to be.

"I don't need anything done underhandedly. I need to know a precise place I can meet him. I have all his information, but I've been advised of so many illegal operations he's running. The last thing I need is to get myself in a situation that jeopardizes my position as a lawyer or the others that I'm protecting."

He swung his head in my direction, brushing his fingertip over his lips. "You want me to put him on blast? My mentees' uncle?" I understood how awful this may have sounded. It's very unlike me, but I'd do anything to protect my brother. Emery was sure to let me know that he wasn't all the way with what I was requesting. "I fucks with you, but it sounds janky, it ain't a good look for me. It's outta pocket if you wanna know the truth. I can't do anything that'll hurt my boys." He released a breath I didn't know he held. He seemed disappointed, truthfully, I am too.

We marched towards the area he kept glancing at earlier, chatting about the dilemma. I couldn't be upset, even I wouldn't jeopardize my trust with a kid or anyone I care about.

Accidentally, I stumbled onto the back of Emery's crisp Jordans. I assumed we were headed towards his assistant until we stopped four rows before it. I stilled, frozen, shocked to see Imani and Ameka. Earlier, they sat in this exact spot, but I didn't think past it after witnessing all the drama on the court.

Emery muttered something into Ameka's ear, the closeness of the two and familiarity makes me think there's more between them. I'm just assuming. I acknowledged Ameka once Emery slid out the way and sat to the right of her.

Moving on, Imani curved her neck, when I descended, and allowed my cheeks to brush in between her collar bone. "It's always good seeing you, Ms. Barasa." Her body elevated as I hoisted her from the seat in a firm embrace. She smelled heavenly.

"Likewise." Her breathing and the vibrations from her giggling tickled the sensitive flesh between my ear and collar. "Excuse me," an older white man motioned, pointing to the suspended chandelier with multiple monitors that broadcasted varying angles of the court and ongoing game. On the four main monitors, Imani and I were in focus. *Not the kiss cam?* I have no problem displaying affection with Imani, but I'm testing the waters trying to gauge if she's down. We'd never kissed in private before, so it was a huge deal that the first time our lips locked, would be in front of thousands of people.

She clenched my shirt with her fist, leaning into me.

I whispered, "We don't have too." She tipped her head; her twinkling focus says she's with it. The invitation to swallow her whole presented when those ample lips parted.

A moan escaped as our lips fused. Rotating in quick succession, our tongues brushed over each other. What I planned to be a slow burn, turned into a full-fledged urgency.

Her energy was a yearning, pulse-quickening, tangent thing. I felt pressure building below. Within seconds, the piercing against her groin from my dick is eminent. She shifts with a grin. Her fingers never faltered, only applied added pressure to my back. We didn't have to communicate any words to concede the level we've entered. "Reach for my jacket and purse. We can exit without anyone noticing your mishap down there."

I can't help the snort that pushed through. Our chuckling had our neighbors taking notice and probably confused at the abrupt stop to our public performance. This has been an ongoing issue since seeing Imani on Riana's iPad, but I wasn't complaining.

I inched away from our position as she spun around with her butt pushed into me. I immediately removed her double-breasted coat from the chair, slipping my free arm over her stomach. She said her goodbyes to Emery and Ameka, then led us out of the stands to our destination. Before we could escape, Emery stopped me.

"Sebastien?" Emery stood to keep his words between us. "I'll do what I can, but under no circumstances am I jeopardizing my boys' trust. So, I'll reach out to the source directly." I appreciated his honesty and his position but mainly felt grateful to hear he'd help out. I nodded walking behind Ms. Barasa with my chin resting on her shoulder. Not caring much of what people thought. I'm single, and as far as I'm concerned, Imani had no one to answer to.

Exiting the congested arena took no time. The anticipated performance from Roland happened almost immediately after leaving the lower level seats. It's the bass that had me and Mani scurrying into a nearby balcony, which permitted us to be captivated by the performance. Roland's energy, musicology, and overall production changed the vibe between us. My guard was down, Imani could have her way with me from now until the bass drop. The lyrics to Roland's *'Want It All'* slipped out. It doesn't matter who believed in or could see your dreams; all it takes is for you to make them a reality. Eat, sleep, breathe it. No excuses. I felt that.

This track served a purpose on those exhausting nights I felt overwhelmed or reminisced on the hours I dedicated to becoming a lawyer to build myself up to my end goal... working at my father's law firm on my *own* merit. People assumed my advancement at Bennett & Associates was due to nepotism. But Samuel Bennett was not that man and would never give anyone anything they didn't deserve, especially one of his sons. This dream of partnering with the firm would be earned.

After standing on our soles for an unaccounted amount of time watching Roland perform, we made it to a private section in the arena sitting in a booth closed off from everyone. Just the two of us enjoying the moment. The game was still in plain sight several feet down. "Good evening, Mr. Bennett, it's a pleasure to serve you and Ms. Barasa tonight. What can I get you two to drink?" The wait staff stood patiently while Imani considered. "Water with a side of lemon, please." I ordered my usual, Coke and Henny.

"I'll have that up momentarily." She glanced over her shoulder, "Mr. Bennett, the pineapple pizza should be out in any second." Imani's brows bunched up as she shakes her head.

The waitress turned fully to speak to Imani, "He also ordered you a Triple Niaburg." Them joints were dope. It's a ginormous burger with three beef patties infused with wine, caramelized onions, herbs, and garlic. Topped with a distinctive spicy mayo sauce. During our previous outings, I noticed that Imani was partial to burgers, usually a much healthier version than the Niaburg, but I knew she would enjoy it. The young lady didn't wait for a response before leaving us to ourselves.

Imani gushed out a breath, leaning over the table to get closer to my face. "Mr. Bennett."

"Sebastien." I corrected her before outlining her mouth with my tongue. Since we got that first kiss out the way, my lips and tongue were drawn to hers. Being courtside with the fellas was nice, but enjoying a private moment with the woman I found myself falling for more each day, is better. A chick rarely holds my attention long enough for me to commit her name to memory. Yet, I yearned to discover the makings of Imani, inside and out. Deep within, I hoped to be the one to satisfy the necessities she felt she needed from a man.

I abandoned my seat, then eased over to the bench with Imani. Lowering my head to her, we melted into one another. Kissing her held so much passion. She spoke so much through nonverbal cues.

We lingered a bit in the same position, lapping at each other's lips, our breathing in sync. "Sebastien," she muttered, keeping her mouth pressed into mine. "You're not worried about our actions in public? You've been so bold tonight."

My head wavered back and forth in response to her question. I had no desire to move from this very spot. With eyes shut, she nodded her understanding. Something inside pushed me to explain my reasoning. I didn't need any misunderstandings about my intentions. We shifted apart before I spoke, "Imani. Do you think I take every one of Roland's staff out to upscale dinners to talk weekly? What we do is the opposite of what I'm used to. Chelsea is a long-time family friend, but even she didn't get this treatment. Don't get me wrong I have a lot of love for her, but running my ideas and plans by my client's PR team is not at all necessary. I'm not compensated for that, nor do I have the time. For you, I make expeditious sacrifices to fill you in because I take pleasure in Imani B."

She blushed hard. "You've been wining and dining me?"

"Courting you, yes." She gasped at that. Surprised. I was happy to know that she didn't recoil at the thought of me courting her.

Toned legs reclined on the seat across from us. Imani's eyes bounced from me then back to that leg that's being caressed by her left hand. The show is stimulating especially how her knee-high boots hit the tip of the denim dress. Simple gestures are exaggerated when performed by Imani. I'm falling hard.

Her nails are trimmed to the perfect length, trailing upward, almost revealing the apex of her sex. I can't help the smirk that's curling over. Anxiety is eliminated, I can tell by the way her back falls against the cushioned seat.

With impatience, her knees swung completely apart while she interlocked her fingers over mine. My palms roved over the junction of her meaty thighs leaving our middle fingers to find their way inside. It's beautiful and slow at first, the pacing is perfect, but her bucking becomes erratic when my thumb brushes her clit. The sound of her wetness brought me to an unfamiliar place. Self-control had never been an issue with me, until now. I've lost it, swiftly pulling my digits out, having her straddle me here, in the private section.

She obliged, rocking on top. Eager to sample those lips again, I dragged my chops from her neck to her mouth. Breathlessly, we moaned, expressing the frustration of not being able to act out our frenzied passion. I couldn't believe we were in here dry humping. Her scent of arousal permeated the air making me thrust upward. She left me imagining how it would feel to be held captive between her. Bunching her dress upwards, my finger glided, playing with the strings of her underwear until I felt the urge to be buried deep inside.

My engorged cock rocked in between us, but unfortunately, my pants acted as a barrier. She freed Mr. Man after unbuckling and shifting my boxers. Then she started fisting him. My balls felt lighter than usual, an electrifying zing continued probing as I rocked into her palms. My shameless fingers were assaulting her pussy from the back. I made a conscious effort to prohibit myself from engaging sexually with her. But I wouldn't deprive myself of a little foreplay.

I kept pumping my digits, rotating against the cushions of her walls. The speed of her jacking me increased, causing both of us to release right there in the confines of the arena. Imani's forehead dropped, the excessive pounding from her neck caused me to pay careful attention. She seemed exhausted but relieved. Her body closed tightly around me when we heard the clacking sound of the waitress approaching.

I planned to place her down as if she was just sitting there, but seeing Imani not shy away from the intimacy we shared, I decided to follow her lead. If she was ok, then I'd hold her in this position for the rest of the night, if that's what she needed from me.

Once again, the room erupted in laughter. The older white man, Judge Crawford, slouched over the podium deliriously. Napkins were used to wipe his tears. Lexiana and Shooter barely breathed throughout their jabs and constant bickering. I tried not to be too judgmental about people I didn't know on a personal level, but this case with these individuals deeply disturbed me. I couldn't figure out if Shooter's baby mother was sincere in her request for extra money for their daughter, Alexandria, or if it was out of spite?

Her Latino Bronx accent thickened, something I didn't think was possible. "Excuse me, your Honor. He can spare fifteen grand a month." She grabbed the iPhone off the table she was standing behind, poking around the screen before raising it, knowing damn well no one could see what she was trying to show as evidence. "Last month, he was out with different *beeches* partying." This time, I cringed along with Riana, who was sitting next to me, supporting her brother. We were both somewhere between astounded and snickering, along with others in the courtroom. Lexiana's lawyer, who kept a straight face the whole time, finally dropped his stance and giggled like a kid. I would label it as unprofessional, but this entire hearing had taken a turn. No one could be at fault.

Lexi appeared to be annoyed that others were giggling at her expense. She continued to try and prove her case. "This is his banking summary. I can prove that there's more than enough to contribute to his first and only born child." She choked up near the end. Then it hit me, she's in love with Shooter. Shooter's extracurricular activities with other women appear to be the main focus of the tantrum she's having. Almost as if this whole thing is to get back at him.

Judge Crawford attempted to get the courtroom to refocus by taking control of the case and turning the floor over to Sebastien. Everyone's attention involuntarily shifted to him because of his tone and the nature of his being. His whole demeanor commanded the attention of the courtroom. People straightened in their seats, awaiting his next words like manna. "My client wants the absolute best for his only child. Mr. Jones is a great father to his five-month-old daughter, on his own accord without involvement from the courts. Ms. Cruz seems to be hinting at something other than his co-parenting abilities." He traveled from his desk to the brown podium, the room follows visually. "She's throwing allegations about his financial status. Who does this concern truly? I've only seen Mr. Jones show her the utmost respect throughout this strenuous process that she continues to draw out. Mr. Jones has been involved financially, physically, and emotionally for the minor child, Alexandria Cruz, since the day he discovered she was his. He was more than willing to work out an agreement with Ms. Cruz before this case ever made it on your docket, Judge Crawford."

Judge Crawford took notice of the many agreeing to his sentiments. At the same time, Sebastien added, "This isn't to make Ms. Cruz appear in a negative light. We're simply making it clear to the court that we've been cooperative."

Shooter interjected, "Judge Crawford, you see this?" He waved aggressively, a black card between his fingers aimed towards Lexiana, who looked stressed to the max. "I gave Ms. Lexiana Cruz an extra bank card from my account to use at her disposal for our daughter."

"Oh, now she's our daughter? Two nights ago, you acted as if you didn't know her."

"No. I said I wasn't there for *you*. And *you* didn't like that."

"Mr. Jones and Ms. Cruz, I will not tolerate the back and forth in my courtroom. I should only be hearing from your attorneys unless I ask you to speak." Judge Crawford was back to business.

After the judge granted the outcome, making the final decision with the bang of his gavel, Shooter locked hands with Sebastien in excitement while Lexiana's eyeballs windmill around. Lexi was hot and ran out of the courtroom without a glance or word to anyone.

Riana and I were standing outside the courtroom, chatting until the Sebastien and Shooter approached. I didn't have time to address Shooter about the hearing due to Sebastien immediately connecting his arms onto mine and hauling me to the other side. He wasn't sweet or tender in the way he was touching me. This aggression isn't normal behavior I'd ever encountered from him, but if he didn't simmer down, we'd both have a case on our hands.

By now, I was used to his touch. Ever since he told me he was actively courting me at the Vultures game, we both worked hard to find time in our busy schedules to go out on a few dates and end it in some heavy petting and fondling. Everything had been going well, so I'm confused as to why he was upset and pulling me away from our friends.

Sebastien stopped near a room, pushing us in a corner away from everyone's attention. I couldn't act as if his abrupt behavior didn't shock me. It did. His face hardened into a scowl, "What was that about? You could have informed me before issuing a statement to the media." He mumbled, forehead practically on top of mine.

With the best sour expression I could muster, I jabbed him in the chest, palms open, and pushed him back, needing space. "Shooter asked me to release a statement, and I agreed. I would appreciate you not running around assuming you know every-thing. I manage his public relations for a reason!" Earlier that morning, Shooter asked me to address a mishap that occurred and was gaining traction due to his butthurt baby mother. I knew not to say too much, nor did I mention the ongoing court case with Lexi to the TMI station. My inside person at the studio made sure to show Shooter on the positive side of the spectrum, something Sebastien should've known was due to my impeccable skills. Our current situation had me reconsidering the connection we've made since our intimate rendezvous at the arena. I thought he knew me better than that to question the decisions I made for my clients.

As if he could read my thoughts, his grip on me loosened, and his touch turned a little more tender as he sealed the gap between us with a tight apologetic hug. "Walk with me for a minute." He interlaced his fingers with mine then proceeded to lead me outside through a side exit.

A burnt, sunset orange two-door vehicle sat secluded from the other cars. I determined that this pretty four-wheel piece of art belonged to Sebastien after viewing his personalized tag, *BASH*. He opened the door and helped me slide into the passenger side. It smelled woodsy with a hint of bergamot and lavender, just like the man that has my emotions on a tilt-a-whirl.

"Imani, I can admit to being wrong for approaching you the way I did. Still, I specifically told Roland not to respond to anything in the media. Before the hearing, I addressed him to confirm he understood." Sebastien explained himself as he closed the driver door enveloping his masculine scent within the confines of the car. "My advice was to him as his attorney, it wasn't my place to do your job."

I bowed in agreement staring out at the overcast skies still trying to decide if I was ready to let it go. It was tough because his scent was driving me crazy, and my body was betraying my mind every second I sat in this beauty of a car.

"You forgive me, Ms. Barasa?" His voice was low, seductively inviting. He extended his index finger to bring us face to face. Our eyes narrowed half-mast while my feminine portal dispenses on its own. Sebastien is gravely handsome, hypnotic, and powerful. Unconsciously, I loosened his ocean blue tie, tugging him near. "Ms. Barasa," he gasped into my mouth. He doesn't have to tell me to climb over the seat and straddle him, I just do.

I launched my mouth back into his. "Imani," he cried. "I'm warning you." I kissed him harder, falling deeper into carnal temptation. The buttons on my blouse are being undone one by one, exposing the tip of my shoulder. Slow passionate kisses trailed the nape of my neck. I lost it. My hips moved relentlessly against his bulging cock.

I'm a loose cannon with this man. I learned this after getting *so* turned on while I watched his nut drip over the back of my hand. I thought about all the fantasies I've had about this moment, especially ever since Sebastien made me cum without the insertion of his dick during the Vultures game. I couldn't turn a blind eye to the fact that I enjoyed how he sucked my tongue when entangled or how he loved finger fucking my pussy from the back. I responded like a fiend who never had dick before.

He spread my ass cheeks while I rubbed against him. I prayed the residue of my reservoir didn't stain his checkered plaid suit. The windows continued to fog, but I'm ready to take it there. Under normal circumstances, I would have required us to be somewhere private, but in the heat of the moment...

I repositioned my dress, as his ring finger quickly moved my soaked piece of string out the way before he inserted his middle finger." Uh," I moaned. I didn't recall him pulling his pants down. The meat in between his legs was completely bare, sliding against my wet slit. Holy cow!

I can't help circling my hands around his masterpiece. I twirled the tip of his dick at my center, allowing him to bury a quarter of his mushroom inside. It's warmed up down there, I am more than ready.

We were connected nose to nose with him inching further into my sex. Our mouths had yet to separate; it was as if we were trying to swallow each other whole. I was ready to take off every piece of clothing that was touching my body. Willing to risk it all... until someone banged against his window, startling us. He didn't move as quickly as I did. My heart raced. I didn't need anyone seeing me in this uncompromising position. Sebastien tightened his grip around my waist, "Chill Imani, I got you." This was becoming a favorite phrase of his. He was always saying, 'I got you' or 'trust me.' Too bad I didn't believe him, especially in this moment. He will have to show me.

"A continuance needs to be in order," He commanded rather than asked. I concurred with a slight chuckle and placed kisses all over his cheeks as we disengaged ourselves from each other. "You should know that term, Barasa."

"Mmm, you want us to resume this later?" I asked, hissing as he removed the last inch from my recently stretched core.

The banging persisted until Sebastien cleared a corner of the fogged window and yelled, "I'll be out in a sec." Darn, that sounds bad. I recognized the figure on the other side. He was one of Sebastien's good friends. Judge Mitchell is the name I recalled from a previous professional encounter.

Sebastien fastened my shirt, paying particular attention to the intricate design of the garment, details that I took for granted. "Baby, let me take care of this, then I'll take care of you." I offered no rebuttal, but still blushed at the idea of us finishing what we started. In his glove compartment, I found napkins and wiped up while he did the same. In what seemed like no time at all, we were dressed and situated before Sebastien got out of the car. He told me to sit still until he came around to open my door.

"Bro, I have a few more minutes before intermission is over." I heard Judge Mitchell announce when Sebastien opened his car door.

Sebastien made it to my side before he responded to the judge, "Can I at least make introductions before you steal all my attention, your honor?" Our almost hot and heavy sex had Sebastien in a much more comical mood than I've ever seen of him. He was actually making a joke. And smiling. He had a beautiful smile.

Brown spurts of liquid splattered out his mouth before he turned to Sebastien, eyes wide open. The coffee cup remained secured as they chortled away.

"Bash, why you cuttin' up?" A big faced Rolex sits on Sebastien's shoulder after the judge's forearm wrapped over his neck. "Introduce me."

Sebastien snaked his arms around my waist, pulling me close to his frame. "Judge Josh Mitchell, this is Ms. Barasa." He paused before continuing. Like me, I'm sure he was wondering the proper way to introduce me. "She's a special friend of mine." I chuckled at that.

Josh offered a hand, breaking the almost-sex trance Sebastien and I seemed to be in. "It's a pleasure meeting you, Ms. Barasa."

"Likewise, Judge Mitchell." I returned his firm handshake as the three of us made our way back to the courthouse. Unfortunately, I was at Sebastien's beck and call because I needed him to take me to my car, which is parked at his office. Ri picked me up from Bennett & Associates, and now that she left, he was my ride.

Instead of going back to his conversation with his friend, Judge

Mitchell examined me from head to toe. Not in a fashion of lust, more so, vetting my intentions with his friend. His questioning glare left me feeling a little exposed, so I pulled my phone out to help divert his attention from me.

I trailed behind them just a tad bit while checking messages on my phone. I had to admit, Buddy had swag regardless of his rank. The thin neckpiece beamed viciously, ready to go to war with anyone. I couldn't neglect the humongous pinky ring on the left hand, he was a whole fashion statement.

As they were walking, Sebastien said something I couldn't hear to Judge Mitchell in a low voice. He nudged Sebastien's shoulder and responded, "Shut that sh—mess up bruh." Mhm, so he seems to have a loose personality with his friend. Much different from what one would expect from a highly decorated judge.

Eventually, the two men fell into a comfortable cadence, laughing and cracking jokes until a dude resembling a slightly darker version of Pitbull walked up. "Good afternoon, Mr. Bennett, Judge Mitchell." Josh didn't reply, only acknowledging with his chin. While Sebastien offered a curt greeting before asking me to give him a moment to handle something.

"Mr. Davidson, you're just the man I needed to see. Though, I gotta admit I'm not surprised that you know Judge Mitchell… since you're no stranger to the courtroom and all." He was only halfway kidding, judging by the tone used to deliver the message.

"You got jokes, Bash. I'm gonna let you handle your business. Don't forget to hit me up, it seems like we have quite a bit of catching up to do." Judge Mitchell embraced Sebastien in one of those bro hugs that showed they were definitely close. He turned to Mr. Davidson, then added, "I hope this is the last extent of us running into each other." With that, he walked off, heading to a set of elevators located in the back of the courthouse.

I finished responding to all the messages I needed to return immediately and shifted my attention to a now tense Sebastien. The seats against the windows were freezing cold, but I sat still and observed the situation in front of me.

Sebastien's unblinking eye contact is hard to ignore. "Nelson, since you haven't returned any of my messages, I may as well go ahead and let you know that I am uncertain about representing you in your case going forward."

"Whhh-what? Why not?" Nelson Davidson was not feeling Sebastien right now. But I was with Mr. Davidson, why did Sebastien no longer want to represent him?

"Mr. Davidson, you asked for help in regard to keeping your children while battling a failing marriage. At the time, you already had a DUI. As a fellow human being, I have compassion, so I took you on as a client despite my already intense roster. That alone speaks volumes. Then I happened to be in court today minding my own business when it was brought to my attention of a DUI arrest involving you the night before. Again. What are you doing, and how is this good for your children?"

Sebastien delivered his message with excessive force. He wanted the man to be a part of his kid's life. What I think Mr. Davidson missed is the fact it takes both of them to win his case, and Sebastien couldn't do that if Mr. Davidson was still racking up charges.

"As I mentioned, I can no longer handle your case and will be referring you to Mr. Polaski. He's the man you want when dealing with custody battles." He declared with finality.

"You represented tons of others in cases like mine!" Nelson announced helplessly.

"This is true," he shrugged. He's so nonchalant. I observed the Sebastien others spoke of. "I don't give a damn who I represented in the past. I'm a *standing my ground on what I think* type of guy. And my decision is final." He was firm. "You don't have to worry about paying me a penny. All payments can be allocated to Polaski. Besides, it's cheaper. I'll be sure to keep tabs on the progress of the case. I know those kids mean the world to you, and I'll do what I can to make sure you get the results you're looking for."

Sebastien walked towards me on the bench and reached out to grab my hand. Decisiveness. Absoluteness. Conclusiveness. Damn, I was turned on again.

"Put me out of my misery and open up those legs for me."

Toes curling with an arched back, I cried for a release. Each flick from his tongue sends waves of pleasure surging inside of me. My arms were suspended above my head, cuffed to the post of the headboard. "Bastien, this feels so freaking good," I wept, driving the heels of my feet into the bed.

"Shhiitt," he growled. I'm shocked to hear any sort of foul language leave his mouth. Nonetheless, I'm riled up. The tongue lashing he's subjecting me to is destructive to my core. Sebastien's eyelids are barely opened, yet I see those lustful eyes gaping at me. Trembling, rocking unsteadily into him, I convulse with an orgasm.

We switched positions, I placed my knees and forearms on the bed, doggy style. He blindfolded me then cuffed my wrist again, this time in front of me. "Don't you move," he roared. Without warning, a wet, extended muscle glided down the crack of my ass. He's nasty *nasty*. Never in a million years did I think I would allow such intrusive behavior, but I was glad I found out it was what Riana made it out to be. It was wet, exhilarating and nasty! Analingus!

I went frantic, shouting incoherent words. "Yeaahh, umm, rigghh... there." Is there a manual for such foreplay? He was precise in his movements, speed, and agility. Unsure if he's making love to me or my ass, I ask, "Which tastes better?"

"I can't decide. Give me another taste."

This has to stop; my pussy can't take any more contact. Already on my third release, I cried out. "I wanna ride you," I hissed, demanding more so than asking. He separated the cuffs and loosened the covering over my eyes. I perused a naked man adjusting himself beneath me just before he allowed our body parts to connect. He fisted his hands, holding his erect dick in place, prodding my entrance nice and easy. The thickness below swirled around until a few inches seeped in.

"Ohhh." I tilted my head back. Regular eye contact was becoming our thing. He made me want to do things that weren't conducive to any of my home training. It's like he spoke things through those thick lashes.

Absorbing the feel of him, I surrendered. I couldn't articulate how happy I was to finally have this moment with him. Uninterrupted. In a real bed. In his slamming ass home. My body went limp as he drove all of him inside. He knocked barriers repeatedly, undoing me emotionally and mentally. No longer caring, his brazen hands kept me in place as he impaled me from beneath. I didn't have to ride him, he took it!

"Damn it, Imani." He shuffled us around looming over me. Sebastien proceeded to do things his way. I screamed in ecstasy, and that alone made him more long and rigid. He slammed into me as my legs dangled over his shoulder. He pumped while I looped my arm around his neck, bringing us closer. I rode him, gyrating slowly, transferring passion that I'd bottled up since we've been kicking it.

"Imani Barasa." He moaned like my name was pain and pleasure in one, sweat falling from his face. Who says a person's full name while fucking? Our lips fused as he propelled harder, bringing me out of my thoughts. His head bent back a bit. "You've undone me in ways you couldn't imagine." His lips were back on mine. Those words, that kiss, all of it was euphoric. "I want you. Not just your body, but all of you, Imani."

Satisfied. Full. My climax came out in drugging waves, and he followed closely behind me. "God damn baby. Slow down." I couldn't. I claimed every inch of his dick, feeling no remorse. I couldn't halt the need to slide my bare yoni over his steel length. I'd been stripped in more ways than one, and I was wide open. My mind was processing all the events for the day. Events of the past few weeks. Events since meeting this man.

I awakened a few hours later to subtle bumps raised over my flesh from the cool air circulating in the room. A damp feeling in between my legs was a reminder of our earlier act. I veered over to Sebastien, who was immersed in his phone, replying to emails, something he does on all our outings. He's a workaholic, always staying busy on and off the clock. This is one of the things we have in common. If I wasn't just in a sex coma, I would have been a slave to my phone as well.

"Can I finally get that tour you promised?" I'm modest in my tone, careful not to interrupt.

"Yep. Give me a second." He kept it short and straightforward without breaking contact with the screen. Lord, please don't let him be the jerk I thought he could be. I wordlessly pray.

"Let's take a shower first." He finished what he was doing and put his phone on the charger, left the bed, then looked over his shoulder, raising his eyebrows in a gesture that seemed to ask if I was going to join him.

The restroom became the sanctuary I needed. A sense of calm descended upon me almost immediately. The frost glossy polish on the counter gave Sebastien's roomy bathroom an ultra-sleek finish. Gold fixtures adorned the place, enhancing the snow-white crown molding circling the establishment. This room had a palatial feel, and the shower area was built for an entourage of people. I could definitely escape into this room alone and never be found.

The water barely grazed my skin before Sebastien joined me in the shower. He pushed me onto the marble wall, kissing me intensely. Another round of pleasure completed in the shower. We were both enjoying ourselves, but I questioned why in the world were we having unprotected sex like we don't know any better? I would talk to him about this before our next go-round.

After we finished, we started the tour and ended up in the kitchen. That's the moment I decided it was my favorite spot in his home. It smelled of coffee: sweet and savory. Pots and pans dangled above our heads on the opposite side of the stove, displaying an organized chef's suite. Nothing is out of place. It made me wonder if it was his doing or if there is a woman that makes frequent visits to his home.

I ended up sitting on his cool marble counter in one of his crisp white t-shirts, while he was at the stove whipping up a meal as he expressed his frustration with several clients. I let him vent, then offered some strategies he could start incorporating to set boundaries with specific clients.

I stared at him as he kept his gaze on me, he wore a slight smirk on his handsome face. I hated to burst his bubble, but it was time to discuss a pressing matter concerning both of us. "So... we definitely need to start using condoms."

He was finished cooking and spooning the meal that smelled divine. Sebastien placed the one bowl with two spoons on the counter, and we both took a tentative sip. I think I moaned loud enough to show my appreciation for his superb culinary skills.

The sound of his spoon hitting the bowl after he consumed a portion of the mussels and clams reminded me that we were in the middle of a serious discussion. He pondered but chuckled before speaking. "I'm glad you brought that up. It was a spur of the moment lapse in my judgment. That should have never happened. I don't usually have unprotected sex, to be honest. It's been years since I raw dogged anyone."

I feel relieved to hear that considering I am on the pill, but STDs are out there. I have to protect myself. "Yeah, I'll make sure to buy and keep some with me, just in case. Seeing as though we had this mishap twice in one day, I won't leave it all up to you to keep us safe."

He chortled, "I have condoms, Mani. I just got carried away." His cell phone chimed, we both read the incoming text that immediately displayed on the screen that was on the counter next to that bowl of sin.

> RAIN
>
> Do you have a moment to talk? Call me when you get a chance.

The message didn't faze him. He swiped up, ignoring it. It wasn't terribly late, but it was well after the 9-5 business time for this to be a client. Plus, if I'm not mistaken, this is the name he called the woman who showed up unannounced at his office weeks ago. Since Sebastien wasn't worried, I decided to let it go and give my attention to my lover and my food.

"It's been about two months since getting tested, I'll provide you the results via email if that makes you feel better. However, I guess I should also worry about you too."

"I don't have unprotected sex with anyone. The last time was two years ago when I was in a long term relationship. I have my results from a few months back as well. I'll send it to you in the morning, Bash."

We moved on from *the talk* to our food and finished our meal quickly as if it was about to disappear. Sebastien cleaned our mess shortly after, reprimanding me every time I tried to help. Instead, he told me, "I got your addiction upstairs on the DVR for your guilty pleasure viewing." He finished cleaning without me trying to help, then cut the lights out as we trekked upstairs back to his comfy bed.

After we were settled, I waited for Jeopardy to return from commercial. I'm stoked that Sebastien thought of me and recorded the episodes. I've missed a whole week of my favorite show and have been a little antsy about catching up. My addiction to the show started when I was younger because my mom would grab Yeay and my cousins, and we'd all sit around watching and guessing. We loved it! What I didn't know is that my mom used this time for us to help Yeay with her English... and it worked. To this day, whenever we were together, we watched it as a family.

It's been too long since I sat down to partake in the high stakes game, so I remained quiet, observing the final bit of the show feeling relaxed and settled.

Bash turned over to his back, flexing his muscles, fully taking my attention off of Alex Trebek and guests. I was overly impressed with the artwork God has created and allowed me to use it for my pleasure. Then an odd blemish on his torso catches my attention. Its deep cocoa, resembling the country of Italy. I can't help tracing it with my tongue, enticing the man I'm fond of.

His goatee rubs against his sternum as those dilated eyes cast down. "Keep that up, and I'll have to take you there to let you get a taste of it for yourself."

"What are you talking about, Mr. Bennett?"

"Italy. I know that's what you make of my birthmark."

Answering his question would have been mundane, so instead I took care of him. After a well-needed massage, I took his girth into my mouth. What I now realized was a marathon of Jeopardy being drowned out by our session. I sucked and fucked his dick until he pleaded my cessation. He made me vulnerable, I had an urge to satisfy his fantasies. This can't get any better. He supplies good dick, five orgasms, and want us to travel abroad. What more can I ask this early on in our situation?

SEBASTIEN

I PUNCHED HRCGIVE into my oversized phone. Harvest Redeemer Church has been a mainstay in me and my family's life for as long as I could remember. The deliberation on whether you should or shouldn't contribute one-tenth of your earnings has always raised questions, but for me, it's the law. Our Pastor, Raymond Shaw, did an excellent job leading his congregation. The end goals were finding God and mastering to swim in the tumultuous sea of distress while living a God first life. If a church managed to properly direct parishioners, it's our responsibility to ensure every entrance to God's Kingdom remains accessible for the next person.

"You ok, sweetheart?" Concern washed over her face.

"I'm good, mom. Making sure I send the right amount," I whispered, never removing my eyes from the total, $1927.00. Sent. Most people would be surprised to know that this is my norm on a Sunday. Anytime I was in town on a Sunday, I was in the sanctuary on the same row with my parents. Just to feel the seats under my legs, to indulge in this spiritually active congregation or the rasp emanating from the depths of my Pastor's soul, speaking wisdom into our lives. Being a part of this church came with ease, which is why I did my part as a member.

We were in our usual seats as my mom looked at me with both pride and love in her eyes. She slipped her forearm underneath mine, squeezing tight. "I'm so proud of the man you've become. At times I feel I don't deserve to be as blessed as I am with you boys."

Severe contractions rattled my chest, making it hard to breathe because it was a hard pill to swallow that my mom was still so troubled. It's a nuisance how she allowed guilt to infiltrate her soul. Especially while we are in church. Here she listens to the word and the lessons by Pastor Shaw, but shouldn't the tears have stopped by now? As a mental health consultant, shouldn't she have healed by now?

She shouldn't feel guilty. She shouldn't be embarrassed, none of it was her fault, and none of it affected her being a great mother. Belinda Bennett served as a vessel between all my kinfolks, not just the immediate family. She's the glue to the circle of friends my parents kept. The Peacemaker. The one that never falls short, smiling through it all. Seeing her distraught and confronting her feelings about the secret that was unleashed at our family dinner last year has been trying for the entire family. Listening to her perspective of the night I walked in on her and my Uncle shook skeletons I thought I buried years ago. Finding out Benji's true paternity added to those long-suppressed skeletons. We all were working our way through it, and Pastor's Shaw message today about dealing with evil was spot on with our current family conflict.

Ephesians 5:11-12 *Have nothing to do with the fruitless deeds of darkness, but rather expose them. It is shameful even to mention what the disobedient do in secret.*

Dad's arms dangled off my mother's shoulder with those long fingers crowding my biceps. Pinning me with his eyes, he questioned, "What's the matter, Bash? You seem out of it."

I was so into the message that I almost missed my father asking me a question. "Nothing sir, got distracted listening to the sermon." I started to think about what else I could do to expose the evil that crept into our family. I knew that my mom wasn't the only one who was dealing with the darkness. I too needed to mention the secret and how it changed me.

My father glared at me, with a low whisper in tow, "Maybe you should stop in and see Pastor Shaw after service is over. Your mom and I have an appointment with him next week."

The service continued as it would normally on any other day, except I didn't leave the chapel. I made my way down a flight of stairs into the area I knew Pastor Shaw would end up after his heartfelt message.

"Sebastien, you've been attending this church since you were three feet tall." I can't help but smile at Pastor Shaw's words. Our family had been coming here for three generations, but you couldn't tell how old it was since undergoing a million-dollar renovation five years ago. Assorted size frames of pictures of senior pastors saturate the wall in his new office. I inspect them hoping he doesn't sense my anxiety or hear the skip of my heart-beat. Although there were many new changes, one old one still stood. Pastor Shaw's open-door policy. I, for one, was thankful he could fit me in today and grateful that my dad suggested it.

Relaxing my jowls felt good. But I tensed thinking about having this conversation with him. "Pastor Shaw, I'm not that little kid anymore. But I'm still dealing with those same demons."

"Just like we tackled it in the past, we can do so again. I was with you during that time and will not leave you this time. I couldn't keep my eyes off you during my sermon. I knew you were troubled. If you hadn't stopped by to see me, I was going to request a meeting with you." He pauses evaluating my expression. "God never promised us peace on Earth, he does promise in HIM you'll find the peace you're looking for. This life is a constant battlefield that humans are trying to conquer but the tools we utilize are what makes it different for each and every one of us. All of our paths have missing pieces to the puzzle, but how do we fix them to align?" A white handkerchief swiftly travels over his bald head, wiping off an immense amount of perspiration. It's cold in this building, so it's confusing to the hot flash he is experiencing.

As an effective communicator who usually exercises firm eye contact, I couldn't give him that today, didn't want him peering any more deeply into my soul. "It is certainly true. Our paths and tools vary from person to person," I replied. "Your message earlier resonated with my emotions this morning. But last week, the scripture, John 16:33, where Jesus says, *'In me, you may have peace, but, in the world, you'll have tribulation. But take heart; I have overcome the world'* stuck with me."

"You remember us going over that scripture when you were a teen? It was as timely then as it is now."

I find myself thinking back to a rainy day, sitting with a black woman alongside my parents. A shrink. They thought I'd be a deranged kid forever since I stayed fighting all through elementary school. Uncle Sam still couldn't come near me without my slick mouth getting out of hand, but I simmered down when I noticed my behavior giving my brother strange vibes. It also helped that my parents found a wonderful therapist for me. She truly connected with me in my feelings as a child. By middle school, I calmed down a lot with maturity and the coping tools given to me, which made me view the day of the assault differently.

I roved my pupils around before it landed on the ceiling as a tear attempted to break through. I wouldn't allow it. I was here to get over this, not dwell on it.

Pastor Shaw's cords shake, "Jesus Wept."

"What?" My voice trembled. It's not a question, but instead, a statement.

"Jesus wept." He restated. "You hated to show weakness back then, and I still sense that now. You won't allow yourself to rid the pain. Even with counseling and other resources you had and still have, you hold your emotions in. All of them. Agony. Pain. Guilt."

He continues after a pause. "Sebastien, Jesus wept. I'm reminding you, even he shed a tear, the one that can do all things took a moment to weep. So why can't you, a broken man, a human that sins, do the same? When Lazarus died, Jesus allowed his emotions to convey amongst the people, over their brokenness of losing a loved one. He stayed by their side through it all, the same way he stands by you through your battles."

"Yeah, but I don't see him raising *'Lazarus from the dead'* in my life." I faced him, removing the barrier I put up between us.

"I disagree. He's risen Lazarus a million and one times in your life. Let's not forget who you are today, how his grace dejected the past to inflict on your future. Unlike many, you had a family that believed in addressing anything that can impair one's mental health. You had an abundance of resources to make sure you stay aligned mentally, physically, and spiritually. The love surrounding you is immeasurable. So even though you have seen the trauma, love supersedes all around you. You can fall all day but you have someone in every corner that will make sure you get up. That's more than a blessing, Sebastien." He takes off his robe and grabs his coat, indicating that our time is up. We walked out through the back doors of the sanctuary towards our cars.

"Sebastien, remember, Jesus wept." Pastor Shaw didn't move until I looked him directly in the eye.

And finally, I get it. The message is clear.

I ZIPPED across town from the office and parked my silver Passat in the assigned parking spot. My younger cousin Genevie sent a text asking me to be there as she packed her things to leave her fiancé after he conceived a third child outside their relationship. Being six years older and watching her walk into some of the traps I've encountered with my ex frustrates me. Nevie devoted so much time to her relationship without experiencing her youth and young adulthood.

In my quest to be supportive, I rushed up the stairs as I heard Nevie at her now ex Nathaniel. "If lies keep spewing from those lips, I'm walking out that door!" Nevie wailed hysterically. Nathaniel isn't bothered by my presence at all. He's parading around as if he's not concerned that she will actually leave him for good this time.

At lightning speed, he walked towards us, sending a gush of fragrant air towards us. I stood my guard, never leaving her side, never letting him talk her out of this move. "Don't act like it's all me, Nevie." I've been in her shoes before. And this, shoulder to shoulder, experiencing Nathaniel and Nevie's rift, is nothing new for me. For years, our family and friends begged her to leave his manipulative ass behind, but finally, it looks like today would be that day.

My day is hectic, and I really don't have the time to be here, but when family or anyone that I love and care about calls, I answer. With that, I performed my best rendition of a statue as Nevie finished packing up all her things, and Nathaniel begged her to stay. I did call one of my homeboys who owns a moving company to take her stuff to storage until she could find a permanent replacement. Thankfully, she would be staying with my Aunt Zenobia until that time.

Although I'm happy that she closed this chapter, I have to find a way to make up the time in my schedule to finish up an important project for a client and get myself ready to be used and used some more by Sebastien for one of our legendary all-nighters. That brought a smile to my face thinking about seeing him and being able to relax, and let go of the weight of this crazy ass day.

As if he was reading my mind, my phone pinged with a text alert as soon as I settled into my comfortable leather seats.

SEBASTIEN

I got off early since you asked me to fit you into my day, hoping to spend some QT with you.

ME

Wish I could meet you earlier, but it's not gonna happen. Something came up, I will have to meet you at your place later. That work?

Before I was able to pull off, Nevie walked up to my car and gestured for me to unlock the passenger door for her. As soon as her ass hit the seats, she cried out. "How did you have the courage to leave Patrick after eight years?" She wrapped her thin, cocoa colored arms around herself in a self-soothing manner.

"Oh, hun?" I reached over the center console, grabbed her hand, and squeezed tight. "You've seen a lot of it. The word lashing he'd hit me with, that made me feel shitty. How he twisted situations around as if I did something wrong when I didn't. Let's not forget how I stopped doing fun things with family and friends due to his insecurities. A man who loves you won't try to control you or pull you away from the things that make you who you are, especially if it's something positive. Patrick never verbally said: *'you can't go out or do this.'* His demeanor spoke more than anything."

I take a deep breath reliving but continuing my flashback. "Do you remember when he would go weeks at a time not saying a word to me in our home? Or he'd come and accuse me of sleeping around with whoever popped up in his imagination? To combat those issues, I attempted to stay in and play wifey without the official and legal title." My eyes rolled at the foolishness I allowed in my life at that time. "And guess what? Nothing changed, it only got worse. I stuck around, hoping he would eventually grow up and live to his potential. All I did was hurt myself."

"What was the first step you took to make your heart stop hurting?" Nevie paused as tears seemed to take over her pretty blemish-free face. "I'm not worried about him moving on to something better, because he clearly didn't deserve me. But my heart and my brain can't get on the same page." I just wanted to get out of my car and walk around to envelop her in my arms and let her know that both her heart and brain were safe with me.

It also made me appreciate what I had and was building with Bash. I didn't feel comfortable bringing that up to her since she just ended her long term relationship. Still, my heart sparkled, thinking about how opposite Sebastien was of Patrick. Insecure, no way. Thoughtful, all the damn time. And he was a man who knew what he wanted from and in a woman. So, I needed to let Nevie know that if she made it clear how she expected to be treated, there was a man out there that would fill that space.

"Let me tell you something, Nevie. Time will make it easier. I promise. If you don't move forward now, one day you'll wake up wondering how and when did you turn twenty-five, thirty-five, fifty-five. And regret is the last thing you want to deal with. This isn't to hurt you in any way. This is me speaking to the old me. When you finally realize who you are, your worth, you will stay gone. That's the moment you become free, the moment you realize you have chosen to put yourself first because you're ready to love you in the best way possible."

"I love you, Imani. Thank you for always sticking by my side even when you didn't agree with my actions."

"Always and forever, Nevie. I will continue to push for the best out of you. I love you."

We stepped out of the car and hugged so tight, it felt as if we were damn near smothering each other. I watched Nevie step away with a more confident gait to the moving truck to give them instructions. And I thought of a way in which I could shorten my workday to get to Sebastien sooner rather than later.

I keyed in the code to the front door and twisted the lock, preparing to let myself in. I cracked the door as the alarm chimed with a lady announcing, *'front door.'* It was barely nine-thirty, and the home was dark, so much so, I needed to hit a light so I wouldn't walk into furniture or a wall. I called and sent a text before showing up, but he never answered, so I could only assume he was asleep.

It hit me like a ton of bricks that I had free reign of his home and all of his security codes. I'm not exactly sure when or how we got here, but I was happy to just be.

I stumbled into the foyer area, removing my flats and taking in the clean, modern scenery. It's quite cozy in this two-story home that only one person occupied. The first time coming here, I questioned Sebastien on the reason for having a six-bedroom home without a family. Of course, he gave me a hundred reasons why he wouldn't allow his money to go to waste on renting any property he could buy now and grow into it when he was ready.

Besides all the massive rooms the home boasted, there were two offices, the one I carefully crept into and one upstairs. Since Sebastien was sleeping, I decided to get settled in here for a few minutes and answer a few emails before calling it a night. I wheeled the lone chair over the hardwood floor gradually, not wanting to make too much noise. A few Red Bull cans occupied a small section of his massive oak desk, a desk lamp was assembled in the corner, and the most surprising piece in his office was the thick red bible that sat almost in the center of his desk. Thumbing through the pages, I can tell Sebastien was either reading or studying it. He's mentioned going to church, but he's never personally invited me. In another corner was a journal, 'The Makings of Bastien' was written on the thick brown leather cover. Inside, I discovered bible verses and how he applied them to his life. I was intrigued by this man, and seeing firsthand how essential his faith was to him, made me think about what forever would be like with this man.

In the midst of me solo planning my future, I realized that I left my laptop bag in the car. If the illuminated sky wasn't enough to stop me, the rain pelting the roof and hitting the window did the trick. Add to that, I'd already set the alarm and didn't want to have to leave the house again, especially since I didn't park in the garage. Sebastien had quite a few laptops, and I was hoping I could use one for my quick tasks. I adjusted the seat to a comfortable setting and was thankful to see his laptop sitting in the center of the desk. I entered the password that was imprinted into my memory, allowing me to log into my email account and check for any urgent requests. As I was opening a new tab to search for an event calendar, I noticed Sebastien had a tab opened that displayed a schedule for an upcoming golf tournament. Then in the lower right-hand corner, I saw an incoming email from the owner of the Vultures. That's when I decided I should have just opted to get my laptop instead of using his. This was starting to feel a little intrusive, like I was invading his privacy. Before I could completely close out all of my tabs, a ding sounded, and an iMessage popped up.

> BROSKI JOSH
>
> Impromptu meet up at the spot tomorrow at 1 pm sharp my G! Don't let pussy have you late!

I quickly shut the top on his laptop, leaving the tabs the way I found them. I was thinking about whether I should tell Bash about the message, then decided there was no use since it would also go to his phone, and he would see it there. Since that was decided, I grabbed the empty cans and tossed them in the recycling can in the kitchen and turned out all the lights before I made my ascent to the place where all the magic happened.

A faint flutter started in my gut, I was elated at the prospect of finally seeing Sebastien. Moving up the staircase swiftly, I discovered a popping sound attached to incoherent words coming from Sebastien's bedroom. The closer I got, the wilder the figures danced against the walls. Then it hit me, the bright orange and red flames of the fireplace welcomed me as I stepped fully into the room. It's no longer cold outside, so the window was open to let in a bit of fresh nighttime air. This adds to the mystique of Sebastien mentioning finding comfort in front of a fire log burning. This seemed to be a tradition he carried even in the off-seasons.

One of Sebastien's legs sunk into white plush carpeting as he lay in the lounge chair, the other rested on the ottoman. I'm bothered by the sounds he's emitting. He's overtaken by fatigue, troubled by the other side of sleep. His skin glistened, lips contorted together. You can even hear the gritting of his teeth. "I can't do it," he pleaded, gripping the armrest. Then an increase in his pitch startled me. "I'm sorry."

This time I collapsed to my knees, holding his face. This isn't an ordinary dream. He's sobbing without tears, unaware of his state. "Ssshhh..." I rocked back and forth with him for what seemed to be an eternity, yet he's still dazed, eyes shut, not yet recognizing my presence.

I understood the body goes into stages of sleep paralysis when the brain activity decreases to a certain level, but this isn't ordinary. I couldn't recall him mentioning any trauma that would indicate nightmares as a side effect.

He stirs around until his mouth lands beneath the cups of my breast, but he's still not awake and aware. A slow leak permeated the sole of my panties but sex only equated to a fragment of the time we spent together.

Usually, Sebastien would be on one end of a room working on his caseload, and I would be working on ways to push a client's brand in a positive direction. It spoke volumes that we were able to do this without either of us compromising the quality of our work. We could grow together.

"Baby?" I cooed into his ear, softly placing kisses along his face. "I'm here, Bash. Wake up."

"What happened?" I knew the answer to that question already. I just posed it to give myself a little time to gather my thoughts and think of how I would explain the situation to Mani. The demons were at it again in the worst possible way. It didn't help that I had an exceptionally long week that started with a phone call from Emery letting me know he set up a meet between Tim and me. At first, Tim was acting as if he was that nigga in the streets, but when I let him know that I was there to squash the beef, he fell into line, and we came to an understanding. I thought I would be able to breathe a little easier, knowing that I got Sean and Shooter out of a situation that could have ruined both of them. Instead, this situation added to the other stressors in my life, both past and present, and now I needed to figure out how to deal. And for now, Imani was the one to help me put the demons and dreams to rest.

The only saving grace is that the nightmares have manifested the one who brings me solace. She's calming me, those vocals, I hear her soothing me, telling me it would be ok, asking me to tell her what is going on.

I breathed out slowly, maneuvering from the chair, shoveling Imani into my arms. Without another word, she drapes her mouth onto mine as I hold her against the wall. Imani is just as worked up as I am, grabbing and holding onto me like I would disappear from her sight. I merely growl. "Let go of my goatee baby."

The dancing fire flames in the room illuminated her skin with shades of red as she moved her hand from my face to my chest, right over my heart. She kept it there until my heart rate slowed down. "Baby, talk to me."

My vision leaves her face to zero in on an empty spot on the wall behind her. "Mani, baby."

"What were you dreaming about?"

Her question bothered me. Even though it shouldn't have, even though she eases the demons. I do trust her. My gut tells me to spill it, but spreading my family's business was something I've never done. Ever. "Revealing layers of my soul will take some time. It's hard for me to elaborate on my inner feelings, and harder for me to talk about past issues that have shaped me into the man I am today. Have you ever heard that everyone has a chapter they don't share with the world?"

"I have," she sounded a little disappointed and even rolled her eyes. "I also know you asked me to be your woman, yet you are holding back. What am I supposed to think after I found you having an obvious nightmare?"

"Some things are hard for me to speak on, Imani. My past wasn't an easy one." I took a moment to release her from my hold and looked squarely in her eyes since both of us had our feet firmly on my heated floor.

Her eyes carried a weird glow. "So, you've suffered from some form of childhood trauma? Is that what you're trying to tell me?"

I made my way to the bed and sat. Imani, situated next to me. "Imani, I'm intentional in my words and think thoroughly before saying things to people. It takes a lot to earn my trust, and you've done that. But don't make me regret it." I paused, preparing to give her the shortened version of my past. "A few months ago, my cousin brought up a situation that happened when I was younger. The incident affected me growing up, but I got past it until he revealed new things that I didn't know about. And unfortunately, the details and consequences have caused nightmares. My dream tonight was no more than a flashback of my stupid past resurfacing its ugly head."

Imani jerked her neck back, "I don't take your trust for granted, and thank you for sharing that with me. I'm still worried about you. Sebastien, you were punching the air, gritting your teeth, and your body was drenched in sweat as if you were standing in the rain showers outside. This thing that's tormenting you is deep, and I don't want you fighting this alone. You don't have to do this alone. I'll be here, holding your hands through the fire."

Something about what she said stirred in my groin and had me getting hard. I wasn't sure if this was the right time, but her unwavering support to me meant the world and let me know that I did the right thing by trusting her with a bit of my past. To show her the effect that she was having on me, I grabbed her at the back of her head and kissed her, stealing her breath away.

Imani moved to my lap, kissing me frantically, rubbing her pussy into me. "Bastien, I've missed you something terrible."

As she slid off of me, I unfastened her pants, peeling them off her skin. "Turn around. Put your hands against the wall and spread them legs, baby." I dropped my shorts and whipped out my steel long dick. Damn a condom, we know each other's status. Plus, she filled me in on her trip to the gynecologist's office, where they inserted an IUD. We were free to raw dawg it as much as we wanted.

"Change of plans." I quickly shift her around setting her on the built-in table in the corner. "I want my face between your legs."

Down on my knees, I spread her cheeks wide apart, darting my tongue into the folds of her treasure. I kissed the opening slowly, seizing her pearl sporadically. "Oohh," she moaned, letting me know she was enjoying what I was offering.

She arched her back, ass rushing into the air. The scent of her arousal stimulated the inner beast that I'd gladly brought out anytime this beauty was in my presence. It's not long before I'm sliding my rod into her, more sensually, then just ramming her. She clawed the wall, standing upward as I thrusted. "Bastien," she cried seductively, banging her hands against the wall. "Right there, please don't stop," Mani squealed. I reached around to rub my finger against her swollen clit. Imani gasped in bliss, turning a little more forceful than usual, throwing her tight, wet pussy back on me. Her hand found its way to the sack of my balls, she milked and massaged with a firm grip, which encouraged me to slam into her harder, faster until we both exploded.

After we were able to catch our breath, I moved us back to the bed. Once I was settled, I peeked over at a sleeping Imani who was out before I could ask if she needed anything. She was softly snoring with the blanket barely covering the body that was like a work of expensive art. I grabbed my phone to check the time and noticed I missed a text from none other than Judge Josh Mitchell.

BROSKI JOSH

> Impromptu meet up at the spot tomorrow at 1 pm sharp my G! Don't let pussy have you late!

My boy didn't know how spot-on he was. Not only did I have to prepare for this last-minute change, but I needed to figure out how I would tell Imani the rest of the horrible truth about my past. She deserved to know, especially since she agreed to be my peace.

IT WAS SUCH A BEAUTIFUL SATURDAY, but unfortunately, I would be spending it building press kits and, in the office... well after my very necessary pit stop. An overage of emails was stored in my draft folder to be sent over for interview dates for fellow clients. While everyone enjoyed their weekend with friends and family, work trolled me. I did plan to add a little family time into my weekend. If there was a party by any member of the Barasa family, you'd be a fool to miss it. Initially, I told my cousin I wouldn't make it to his 30th birthday party due to work duties. But I couldn't miss this milestone birthday, I had to make time by any means necessary. Besides, a few hours wouldn't hurt my bottom line.

My dad moves fluidly to the melodic tunes of Papa Dennis. He can't help the tapping of his left then right foot syncing with the beat. He sings along about falling for a woman, adding my mother's name wherever it fits.

I gushed, masking my face at the giddiness of his affection for my mama. I resembled him a lot, but the ultra-dark coat radiating my skin is a bit off from his. My skin was a bit more radiant, whereas, his ashy bark-like tone was due to the harsh rays he endured growing up from his hometown. Nonetheless, he consumed every God-given feature well, accentuating the clean-cut box fro he's been sporting for as long as I could remember.

Dropping onto his haunches, he rotated his hips. My mother steadied her two-step, moving closer to dad. Her ample backside brushes him. She dips, allowing his crotch to smack her ass as if he's hitting it from the back. I cackled. They're cute, overly affectionate. Her hands rock to the rhythm as she grinds. No one would believe this Cambodian can move like an African Queen. Still, my mother, Sophea, had the Kenyan dance down to a tee, courtesy of my father, Jaali.

"Uko fiti?" He yelled out to me.

"Surely," I replied to his absurd question. I'm more than fine even though he's dry humping my mother at my cousin Aasir's party. Aasir made plans for an after-party with the younger crowd in mind, but while it's still light out, the family, *aka the older people and kids*, kicked it at this local joint. The rhythmic African music and vast amounts of food are taking over the venue. I despised having to break the news that I would be leaving before the sun diminished. But I needed to get to my office by five for a meeting Joshua Mitchell requested via email stating he had a possible opportunity for me. There was also a standing meeting with Shooter after my meeting with Judge Mitchell. To say my day is packed would be an understatement.

Spending quality time with my family was a bonus, so instead of harboring over my parents, I moved on to mingle with others. "Onyx, what are you doing back here?" Aasir gave me this absurd alias when we were kids. He Always emphasized how dark and beautiful his favorite cousin is. *"You remind me of the black jewelry people be wearing. What's it called again?"* He questioned me.

"I don't know, I think it's Onyx."

"Yeah, that's it! We actually talked about that in class. For now, you should make others refer to you as Onyx, Black Beauty, or some shit. Like it's dope how you embrace your skin, you have a glow to you, Mani."

Turning to face him, I replied, "Came out for fresh air before talking to the rest of the party, birthday boy."

"You know, Patr…"

"I already saw his dusty behind." Patrick and Aasir have always been tight, but the thought never crossed my mind that he would be in attendance. It's been almost two years since seeing him. The last conversation was six months after our real breakup, where he begged me to give him another chance. "We didn't speak, I slipped out here before he could say a word." I continued watching the miniature planes graze the cloudless skies around the tall buildings.

"Well, I definitely appreciate you coming out, cuz." Aasir's beautiful smile was on display showing all those teeth that my aunt and uncle had to beg him to brush when we were growing up.

"I got you something."

Aasir cocks his head back at me in disbelief. "Nah, you ain't got me nothing."

"For you, I always go out my way. Don't play." We both had a thing for trying to one-up each other in the gift department. For my last birthday, he got me a new surfboard. A really expensive surfboard.

"So, where's it at?" He's smiling and looking all around the venue as if my gift was gonna jump out at him.

"I couldn't bring it. But check your garage when you get home." Aasir had just purchased a new home in Buckhead with all of that good money he was making as a chemical engineer. So, I thought it was only fitting to restore and pimp out his 88' box Chevy Caprice. He bragged about it being *that car,* the second best thing to happen that year. The first of course was his birth. I got it painted, fitted with new rims and the inside upholstered. It cost a pretty penny, but he was worth it after I found out the price of my new favorite surfboard.

"Word, Onyx? Shit, we bout to shut this party down so I can see what you did." He was dead serious.

"Don't do that, Aasir. You know the family loves to party."

As we were laughing, my dad walked towards us, stepping between us once he arrived. "Uncle Jaali," Aasir hoorays, dapping my father as if it's his first sighting of him.

Their talk spiraled to many levels, and I tuned them out as my thoughts ran wild, thinking about the man that captured my heart. It's been several weeks since I've physically been around Sebastien. We've been limited in our time with each other due to his frequent travel. My increased workload on the West Coast didn't make it any better. Being spoiled underneath his wings wasn't evident until I had to learn to deal with this withdrawal. Not only was I missing his touch, but I also couldn't shake him closing up on me after his nightmare. He never finished the convo with me, but I didn't want to push. Me on the other hand, because we vibed so well, I spilled my guts to this man. I laid out all my insecurities as soon as we confirmed we were taking our relationship to another level. He didn't do the same, and I gotta admit that I don't know how I feel about it.

"Nipe beer baridi," my father ordered Aasir, snapping me back to the group.

"What kind of beer, Uncle Jaali?"

"The normal, Tusker or Guinness."

Aasir disappeared, joining my other family members on the makeshift dance floor. My dad, on the other hand, queried about my whereabouts. My schedule didn't have availability as it did before since Bastien came into the picture.

"Baba, I see you and mama every Sunday. On weekdays I'm busy with clients." I snaked my arms around him, laying my head on his chest, a significant comfort zone for me. No matter the age, I would always be a daddy's girl, through and through. "And guess what, this past week I've been working on boosting your businesses brand visibility." My dad was currently a landlord with about ten properties in the Metro Atlanta area.

He's elated, smiling from ear to ear. "Imani?"

"That's right, I told you I would, and I'm still on it. I created all the pages needed on social media, tweaked your website for optimal performance, making sure your clients will find you. Also, your tenants can now request maintenance through the portal, and online payments are now easier for them and you."

"Thank you, my love. You are always taking care of the family. Your heart is so big with everyone. Whoever you marry will be a lucky guy."

My daddy was a good father, husband, brother, boss, and overall human being. If nothing else, I witnessed firsthand what a good partner looks like. I would be remiss if I didn't bring home someone that my father approved of.

"I can attest to that." Speaking of approval. This one Jaali *did not* approve of. He canceled him the very first time they met. His figure appeared slowly, somewhat unrecognizable, but the gravelly voice is distinct. A whiff of cedar dangles in the air. I know it's him. Patrick's smooth umber tone radiates from the faint light that cast through the rays. "Good evening, Mr. Jaali."

Visually, Patrick was damn near a ten. Still, because of his insecurities, it made his outside just as unappealing as his inside. But something about his demeanor was a little different as he stood in front of me now, he seemed more... *confident.*

"Patrick." My dad shook his hand but didn't reciprocate the gesture of being delighted to see him. Instead, he turned and walked away. "Mtoto wa kike, see you in a bit." Just like that, my dad left us alone.

Maybe he sensed that this moment was a necessity for us both. In all the years since we haven't spoken, I realized that Patrick and

I never really had closure, but I also didn't think I needed it. We were together for eight years. At the time, that was all the closure I needed. Now, I wished him nothing but the best and hoped that he could be happy. As happy as I was with Sebastien, even though he was holding out on me.

"I see you're still daddy's little girl."

"That will never change Patrick. What's up?" I didn't ask him that to enquire about his current place in life, I meant it as a way to ask why he approached me, and why did he feel the need to have a chat with me in private.

He moved underneath the light post where I stood. "I want to apologize for everything that happened between us. I'm not asking you to take me back or anything, but I want to know that we can at least be cool. Or at least cordial. You played a huge role in my life, Imani."

I had no issue with what he asked for, but I wasn't sure it was a good idea. The Patrick from two years ago would ask for an inch, but in the very next breath a whole mile would be taken up. I decided in that moment, there wasn't a need to have him as a friend, I had enough of those. But I could be cordial with him, no hard feelings. "I've forgiven you years ago, Patrick. I couldn't possibly move forward and be happy if the pain and betrayal of our past lingered over to the next man."

"Next, man? Oh? So, you're in a relationship?" His shocking features are hard to not laugh at.

"What did you think I would stay single forever? I'm in love with an amazing man that makes me better. He calls me out when he sees fit, and I appreciate him showing up and supporting me."

His eyelids slid shut, he inhaled deeply. "Understood." He blinked them open, "Are you happy?"

"Extremely." Period. Patrick didn't need to know the inner workings of how Sebastien was everything he wasn't. He just needed to understand just how sure I was of the gentleman who swept me off my feet from the first day we met. Patrick was a good fit for me when I was a young adult, but Sebastien was a man for the woman I grew up to be.

"Well, shit. Ok," Patrick growled, shooting a chuckle to conceal his hurt. I could see on his face that he wanted to be happy for me, but it was hard for him. I wasn't trying to hurt him, I just wanted him to know that I'm good. Actually, I'm better than good.

"Well, I gotta get going, Patrick. Take care." I almost slipped up and said *it was good seeing you*, but I wasn't sure how true that statement was.

"A'ight, I won't hold you up, Imani. Maybe we can work on that friendship thing, huh?"

"I don't think that's a good idea, Patrick." I moved in closer, placing a palm to his chest. "Your time in my life has shaped me in a way that forever changed me, the lesson I hope you took with you is to trust yourself more. Once you do that, you will begin to value your relationship. If you value something, then cherish it, don't wait until the season transpires to try to recover. Maybe next time I run into you, you'll be telling me about the woman who supports and shows up for you."

I was kind of sad that I had to leave Aasir's party earlier than I wanted, but I was thankful to have even had the time to stop in. I spent the drive from the venue to my office, mentally transitioning my headspace from my family and Patrick to upcoming meetings and work duties. I couldn't help but wonder; who knew that closure that I didn't even know I needed would feel so.... *Refreshing.*

The cars spread sporadically throughout the vast parking lot since it was a Saturday afternoon and outside of *normal* business hours for most people. This particular property was located on the outskirts of Atlanta. It was quiet, spacious, and grand enough for my clients to visit without feeling like they were in the hustle and bustle of the city. I've been here three years, and still have seven left on my ten-year lease.

I rummaged through the side door, unlocking it with my key fob, then disarming the alarm to make it to the fourth floor quickly. I didn't have to use my key that opened the door to my suite because my assistant, Hailee, was already in the office running around in her distressed jeans, shouting into the headset, jotting something down on a clipboard. She was handling business. Previously, Hailee was acting as my Junior PR rep, on a very part-time basis. Her role as my executive assistant was a promotion and full-time. It had been just the two of us for a while until I increased my staff by adding a Senior PR rep and a Junior PR rep to Imani B. Relations. We were rocking and rolling, and although it took me a while to build a team that I trusted, I wouldn't change anything about the process.

In a cubicle across the room, my reps were huddled together, eyeing a laptop. "Hey, Imani." Erma, the senior rep, greeted me as she pushed her dreads out of her face. The fact that they showed up to work, without me asking them, on a Saturday, further confirmed I had a strong team.

"Well, good afternoon to you too." I smiled back at Erma before looking over to Corbin, who was typing profusely with aggravation. "You good, Corbin?" Everything he did was in an exaggerated manner, but he knew his shit, and he and Erma worked well together. He was already asking how he could be promoted from a junior to senior rep.

He spun around in his chair, throwing his head back to remove the bangs that draped his forehead. "Ugh, yes, girl. These trolls on the internet will not get the best of me. You know." He stands up, barely to my chest. "Fernando's social media has been poppin' lately."

I nod, enthused with Corbin's work. He handled a few client's social media and supported Erma on direct client relations. "Yeah, I see that. I also see how engaging you are with the fans."

"Right," he rolled his neck. "But I see where he's been back and forth with the guy he got into it on the court with. I'm afraid things may get out of hand next time. I sent screenshots of it for you to review and advise."

I didn't reply. This situation was nothing new. However, I would address Fernando. He's come too far to go backward. "You guys, I can't thank you enough for showing up here today."

"It was Hailee's idea." Corbin points to my personal super-woman, who's still on a call, writing extensively. Once she got off the phone, they informed me of the goals they set forth, and coming in this Saturday is what allowed them to complete it. They didn't involve me because Hailee insisted that I've been in distress and overloaded with work. I could only give her a look of appreciation, never have I been more thankful for her discernment and her ability to put both the company and my personal needs at the forefront. I could almost hear my daddy speaking to me as he advised me to stop trying to do it all. "*Imani, with a reliable and efficient team, all things are possible.*"

Once I was settled at my desk, I looked up to find a very tall man being escorted into my office by Hailee. Leisurely he makes his way to my triangular-shaped desk. His creamy cocoa skin meshed well against the olive suit he was sporting. He isn't fine like my Bastien, but he's pretty darn close.

"Judge Mitchell." I walked up to shake his hand, then asked Hailee to bring us water and coffee before she closed my office door. "It's a pleasure to see you again."

He grasped my hands firmly. "I'm glad you were able to take this meeting on short notice." By the time I made it behind my desk to sit, he's already informing me of his query. "I've heard of you and your company before but was never able to put a face to it until Bash introduced us." He paused to let that settle in then smirked. "So, is what I heard true? Is Imani B. Relations one of the best?"

I nodded as I blushed at his compliment, even though he posed it as a question. "As the first African-American Judge in Cobb County and one of the youngest in the state, you know all about being the best and at the top." His eyes widened. He tried to hold in a laugh. When he shook his head, I noticed the diamonds in his ears and the thin necklace matching the pair.

"You research all your clients before meetings?"

"Yes, sir," I answered truthfully. Speaking with this judge felt no different than talking to one of my homeboys. He's down to earth, charismatic and super smart. Nothing I spoke of went over his head. He's witty as all get out, and I couldn't help thinking who I could pair him with.

"So, you know that I was recently elected as the President of the Black Judges Association and we're known for putting on one of the grandest black-tie galas in Atlanta. The event brings us hundreds of thousands in scholarships, and one of my goals during my tenure as President is to increase that amount to at least a million." The meeting was on track and following the standard process of how I consulted with all possible new clients. He didn't waste time going into details, telling me what he wanted and expected. I couldn't wait to put a proposal together with my team that would take the event to the next level. Especially, knowing it's a group of black judges who are doing great things in the community and for black college students. I can recall how hard it was to get a ticket to the event.

"Why me? Why not go back with RND Relations?" I questioned. I needed to know why, and I needed to gauge if we were going to be a good fit. As pumped as I was, it needed to be right for all parties.

A line sketched between his brows as he pondered. He crossed one leg over the other. "I told you already. I heard you were the best. Plus, I think RND has taken us as far as they could. Time to move on and try something new." He didn't lack confidence, that's for sure. "I know my goals aren't easy and won't fall in my lap. If I really want to fundraise over a million dollars, I need to build a team that speaks to that."

"Ok, that's fair." His reasoning was sound, and I was sure we could give the organization exactly what they needed.

"I may as well admit that I also called Bash this morning inquiring, and he too vouched for you."

The flutters in my stomach had me smiling like I'm in a magazine. I can't help gushing. "I'll be sure to thank Sebastien the next time I speak to him." Damn, the thought of next time makes me sad. Since we've not been able to connect in person, our communication has been through texts, and late-night FaceTime calls. It had me thinking that maybe I could take a day and fly out to Texas, where he's been for almost a week now.

Just when I was ready to bring our meeting to a close, he turned in my direction, gauging his eyes confidently into mine. "You're a good look for Sebastien, Ms. Barasa." Judge Mitchell pushed from underneath the table, revealing a shiny pair of umber spice Derby's. Next, he proceeded to stand, fixing his suit jacket. "I know he's lowkey about certain areas of his life, but be patient with him. He doesn't look like what he's been through. Or even going through." This made me evaluate the fact that I was still sort of having an issue with him not sharing everything with me. Maybe I need to chill out and allow him the time to move at his own pace. Whatever is troubling him would inevitably find its way to me. I just want him to trust me as much as I trust him.

"Excuse me, Imani?" Hailee's sweet voice blared through my desk phone.

"Yes?"

"Your last appointment is here."

"Cool. Send him back in five." I moved folders and tablets around, clearing the space for my meeting with Shooter.

Judge Mitchell wasted no time in giving me a friendly hug, thanking me, expressing his excitement about the opportunity for us to work with each other. I escorted him to the door and went back to my desk to quickly check my phone before Shooter stormed in like he owned the place.

I opened my desk drawer, not surprised to find it full of Creme Savers. Bash may be far, but there's always something in here that reminds me of him. I shut my eyes, placing my head on the desk for a second, reliving our moments, appreciating his culinary skills, especially since I could count on at least one meal to be delivered strictly by him weekly. Or his abrupt visits to my work-place, demanding we go for a run on the track behind the building since he knew the importance of my workout routine. Hell, I can't help but fantasize about the way he had me clawing the walls, or even how his touch seemed to be present in this very moment. It felt so real and made me realize that I just missed the hell outta him.

SEBASTIEN

JOSH DAPPED me up on his way out of the office, surprised to see me, but let me know he would hit me later once he saw the urgency on my face. I needed to make it to Imani. Like right now. I walked into her office. I noticed she was resting with her head on the desk, stroking the back of her neck, face buried between her arms. I just watched her for a second before standing behind her.

If I didn't catch the faint moan coming from her, I would have assumed something was wrong. Except this is familiar. She appeared to be aroused. Instead of calling her out on it, I decided to coax her along.

I applied tension to the spot she was rubbing. She remained in a daze, so I scooted in closer, whispering. "I can take care of the ache you feel if you allow me."

Imani jerked away. Startled. Our eyes met. Without another second, she's out of the chair, hopping into my arms, straddling me. We kiss, kiss, and kiss some more. Her hands moved frantically alongside my head. She caressed my neck, nibbling the lobes of my ear. If I didn't know before today, I knew that Imani missed the hell out of me. Her actions clearly displayed that. I missed her too. Flying to Texas for a convention with my father was one thing, but I didn't expect to be over it. I kindly told my dad that it was time for me to head back. He didn't need to know that it was because of Imani. But it was. Everything I did led to Imani. The absence of sex meant nothing. I just needed her here, under my arms, talking, throwing out stale jokes, reciting something she learned from Alex, or even entertaining her newfound facts she seemed to come up with daily.

Our situation hadn't been right since my nightmare. This made me anxious, causing me to cut my time in Texas short by three days. She's made it clear that my need to leave out important facts in the story didn't sit well with her, but I told her more than enough for the time being. I blamed Sean and Roland for this screw up between Mani and me. Yeah, the nightmares were back, but they are more rampant after feeling bombarded with the assault video I received from Tim.

Additionally, Nelson has been a constant pain in my behind. My nonexistence in his case is killing him, according to his recent text message. Nelson is resilient. He doesn't take no for an answer. Too bad he would learn he's found his match.

"Mmm," She purred into my mouth. "Why are you here? How were you able to come back so early?"

"Simple! I couldn't go another day without your touch." She halted, observing me. I've smeared her lipstick and can only imagine what kind of clown I look like with her springtime pink shade spread across my lips.

"Yeah?" She clutched my neck tighter, desire lingering.

"I love you, Imani."

"I love you to Bash." She circled her nails over my flesh then leapt down frantically. "Oh my God, Shooter is out front. I've got a meeting."

She barely made it to the doorway when I swept her off her feet from the back. "Not anymore." I placed her down to explain. "It's been me all along. I used his name to surprise you. Tonight, I'm taking you out, away from work and all the other madness we have going on."

Her pupils flared, I can see the emotions and happiness show-cased on her beautiful face. I don't give her time to think. Instead, I seized her jean jacket off the coat rack and escorted her out to my car.

Imani, my nonstop machine that spits facts at every second, wasted no time once in motion. As romantic as I tried to be, with the R&B music serenading the background or my attempt to sweet talk, all of it went over her head. "So, you didn't listen to NPR Up First?" Imani scolded.

"No, baby. I've been consumed with my next move with you." I stroked her hand, trying to calm her down.

Imani switched subjects quickly, her questions now geared to where we were going, what we would eat, and oh, back to the news around the world. As quirky, as she may be at times, this is what I loved about her. She isn't hard to please, just as long as you gauge your attention to those dorky facts she liked to rant about.

Imani had a lot to say until we cruised into a warehouse full of people launching axes around. That got her attention.

She mentioned the need to explore Atlanta. I figured in our chaotic lifestyle, this place would be an unexpected stress reliever. With an exuberant smile to match hers, I explained what we were doing here and why.

"Sebastien, you're so lame. Ugh." She attempted to seem annoyed as the instructor trained us, but I knew I knocked it out of the park with this one.

"Remember, it will land according to the direction you send the ax flying. Show me what you got, Mani." Her deep cinnamon fingers clasped the manila coated stem, hands hovering over each other, just like the instructor showed her. I cheered her on while her shoulders sank. She took deep breaths, then repositioned her body in a lunge, hands folded, ax sitting behind her neck. A flick of the wrist, along with her arms shooting forward, sent the sledgehammer rushing toward the wooden board ahead. On the first try, she hit the center black dot, dodging the outer blue and red circles.

"Aaaah," she screamed, circling me like a merry-go-round. "I want you to beat that, Mr. Bennett."

"Oh, yeah. What do I get if I win?" I winked.

Imani doesn't consider anyone in the building when groping me by the balls, allowing her minty breath to graze me. "Whatever you want, Mr. Bennett. Wherever you want it. However, you want it." She's seductive in tone and has the glare to match. My dick stiffened, becoming engorged in her hold. She doesn't act surprised by my current state, further stroking it before squeezing, just enough to affect me, reminding me of her tight pussy. If she kept this up, I'd have to give our reservation up and do some much-needed damage to both our bodies.

I grasped her by the back of her head, bringing her near. I secured her mouth to mine, tonguing her long enough to show my longing. Did I mention how much I missed her?

Eventually, we were able to put our need for each other aside, and I could finally concentrate on slanging another type of wood. We played round after round, though I never hit the bullseye. I recognized this wasn't my best sport. So, I made a mental note to never engage in such activity again. Even though I felt kind of foolish that she beat me, it was worth it since Imani enjoyed herself. So much so that she bragged the whole way home.

Since this whole date was a surprise, I wanted to continue it by surprising her with an overnight stay at a hotel in the heart of the city. It's late by the time we reach our hotel room. Imani is shocked to not only be at this five-star palace but also to see that there's a meticulous layout of food on a beautifully decorated candlelit table.

She danced inside, acting as if this is the first time I've done something sentimental or thoughtful. Our dates usually involved a little creativity, strictly on my end. I've learned to be a free thinker in the gifting department. My dad always said, *"Women don't always know what they want, but they know what they don't want. I can definitely bet, as long as you make her feel secure, tending to her needs, she'll never question your love."* This is vital and important to what I'm trying to build with this woman. This is why I scheduled our dinner away from the crowd, to finally open up about my past so we can both move forward and work on our next chapter.

I've never seen Imani as engaged in my stories as she has been tonight. Over food, we chatted about our moments away from another, the crazy adventures I've had dealing with my dad's silly antics. Listening to her encounters with her family made me confident in allowing our parents to meet soon.

Her spiel about the sudden pop-up and conversation she had with her ex wasn't one of the events I planned on hearing about. I listened. I took in the fact that she wasn't shy to mention that she saw something different in me. I appreciated her expressing herself. This made it easy to invite her into my past.

Controlling the overwhelming emotions trapped inside, my actions led me to the sitting area of the expansive suite. I reclined onto the lounge chair, eyes shut. "What we discuss is to stay between us, Imani." That statement held weight. I only prayed she was as trustworthy as my heart tells me. "For starters," I swallowed hard. My palms started to mist, but the kicker was the unsteady bounce of my knee. I haven't opened my mouth to confront the demon head-on with another human being since I was a child. And the sudden pep talk with myself is playing over and over. If I want things to go farther with us, she should know a bit about my past and my possible triggers.

"At a young age, I walked in on my mother being violated." A beat settled before I could add the part that was the most shatter-ing. "By my uncle."

Sadness clouded her features. "Sebastien." Slowly she massaged my face, pecking my cheeks. "I didn't expect it to be that deep. It's ok, I don't have to hear anymore. I'm so sorry that you and your mother experienced that."

"Babe, let me finish. That's not all." She pried so much into who I was, I'd give it to her, but I wouldn't speak on Benji's paternity. That can come out from the source itself if need be. I respected him too much. Or maybe it's my way of protecting my little brother.

"Seeing my uncle attack her wasn't the icing. It was the result of the attack that damaged the fiber of our family. We all went to see those head doctors."

"Head doctors?" Imani questioned. I wasn't trying to be funny, those were just the titles I used for them growing up.

"Yes, a therapist." No time like the present to just lay it all out there for her.

"Seeing one helped our family as a whole, but the issues for me remained. I couldn't understand why we were still allowing my uncle to be involved in our daily lives as if nothing ever happened? Why did he have this close relationship with Benji or thinks it's ok to kick it with Sean? The only bright side in this was that he knew not to look my way. I made it clear, up until the day he died, he had no place in my life."

Soft breaths of air hit me as she sniffled. "So, you two never made peace?"

"The day before he passed, he requested to see me. My father gave me an ultimatum between him and my job at the firm. You know I was vexed beyond limits. Of course, being young at the moment, I followed through." In this day of age, I would have sepa-rated from my father and did my own thing. I never felt like I needed my father to start a firm, but my respect for my dad superseded. "So, when I showed up, I'm left alone in the hospital room with my uncle, who's my dad's twin, by the way."

She gasped, intrigued by the facts in the story.

"My uncle cried uncontrollably, asking for forgiveness. Usually, I can withstand other's emotions, but that night seemed different. I could tell he meant everything. I also learned of his excessive drug use. I heard about it growing up, but it's a whole different thing hearing him replay the past. It took me a while to admit that his last moments with me were touching, to say the least. He was under the influence of cocaine during the attack but got clean shortly after. He went back and forth with his sobriety, but the family was happy that he attempted to make amends before dying." I stopped for air then reassessed Imani's expression before carrying on.

"Uncle Stan asked my hand in prayer, asking God to open my heart and to allow him to be free because my acceptance of him meant a lot to him. Imani, I believe in God and his word. The church was a staple in my household. I knew God wanted me to let this go and move forward. I had to forgive this man, not just for him, but for me too. But darn, I was so angry. In the middle of his prayer that seemed never-ending, my heart changed with a switch. I embraced him, allowed the uncle who I did adore as a kid, into my life. I wouldn't forget the ordeal, but maybe... Just maybe I can be like my parents and move on. He died the following day. And I attended the funeral and spoke of no harm that he caused. Everything in my life finally seemed peaceful."

Imani just stared, my guess was that she was trying to process it all. "Wow, Sebastien. I had no idea. Just wow!"

"Right, and now the nightmares are back. I think the stress of work and just trying to support Benji and Sean is what is triggering them." I shrugged, releasing a breath.

Today, I decided to view things differently, and for that to happen, I had to change the lens. Ridding myself of all these emotions made me vulnerable in a good sense. It also made me feel another version of peace. I'm glad Imani was the one I decided to share this with. I knew my feelings for her were there and true, so she deserved to know this. Our silence wasn't uncomfortable. I knew she would have answers once she had a chance to let it all sink in, but for now, I just wanted to wrap myself around her body, cut off all of our devices, and think about how we could find a way to do this more often.

FASHIONED REDEFINED, and modern luxury graced the ballroom. The event planners did an excellent job bringing the vision of the BJA to fruition. Because of the expertise of the event management company, it made it easier for my team and me to handle the PR for this year's gala.

Tons of personality crowded the room in upscale formal wear. Tuxedo's that were definitely not rented and ballroom gowns that appeared to be hand-stitched and weaved were in abundance. I was in my element with those in attendance, but having the Mayor, major company CEOs, and the who's who of the judicial world was a huge opportunity for me to market Imani B. Relations. It was a given that Sebastien would accompany me, and he had nothing but praises for me on my execution of getting the word out and having the right people in the room. His praises meant the world to me, especially since I wasn't used to that from a mate.

Weeks before the event, Sebastien strongly suggested that he be the one to purchase my gown. He had a dress made by a young up and coming Kenyan American designer that would match his attire. Sebastien's inquisitive style is uniquely his, so of course, his suggestion was spot on. He doesn't need anyone playing in his closet, and he was very *very* yummy this evening. Sebastien looked astounding in the Multi Floral Jacquard Tuxedo that matches perfectly with the colors in my traditional African Formal Gown. On my end, I wasn't the most comfortable, but the style design Sebastien chose couldn't have fit me better. No one has ever selected clothing for me, let alone hire a designer to make me a one of a kind gown. Tonight, I understood why he took his appearance so seriously. In this crowd, how you looked equated to how you worked.

The theme for this year's gala was *A Seat at the Table: Around the World*. The Black Judges Association was concentrating on getting more Black students to study abroad. Different areas of the room were decorated to mimic some of the most recognizable structures and destinations of the globe. Somehow, they managed to have a structure favoring the Eiffel Tower in one corner, and faux snow-covered Kremlin in another. The event would not have been complete without its own replica of Africa, the scenery of that continent was breathtaking.

"Mademoiselle, you look just as gorgeous as you did the day I met you." Sebastien admired the one-shoulder Ankara asymmetrical dress hugging my curves. This gown was perfect as the original design was vetoed by Sebastien. Surprisingly the Jimmy Choo leather sandals paired with the dress were as comfortable as the wardrobe. I'd been walking in them for over an hour, feeling no different than a pair of sneakers.

"Bastien, quit it. I can't stop gushing."

"That's how I plan to keep you, baby."

I glanced at his shoes. The red bottoms caught my attention. He noticed and answered my question before I could speak. "Santoni Classic Derby. I changed to have something more comfortable, so I can keep up with you. And Josh claimed the red helps bring out the trimming on my tux."

I engulfed the bottom of his lip, releasing just as quickly. I didn't want to linger too long, bringing unnecessary attention to us before formally being introduced as his woman to his family and associates. Plus, I was technically semi-working and needed to keep that mindset. It was just hard to keep my hands and mouth to myself when he was so close to me. "You look so handsome, just the way I found you in the studio that day." I adjusted the red bow tie acting as if my words are just merely that. I meant it though, Sebastien oozed so much confidence in the Dolce & Gabbana ensemble. Did I mention his lips, his jaw structure, the build of his nose, all the elements that reminded me of what a powerful black man he was?

Our evening sped by at an immense speed after the cocktails and introductions. I met most of his partners at the firm or associates he's dealt with in the past. He met my small staff of four but treated them as if I was running a Fortune 100 company. But the best part was being introduced to his parents as his woman.

"Bash baby, she's beautiful," his mom insisted, spinning me around.

And so was she, resembling a slightly older, but no less fabulous Jada Pinkett-Smith. I reciprocated her compliment, praying to be as tight in my body as she was in hers. Mrs. Bennett was a bombshell. Over forty, five years married, three kids, and no baby bump. My future mother-in-law was *#bodygoals*. Even her ass looks tight. The thought had me praying and thinking of ways to increase my workout regimen. I was no small woman, and at almost six feet and two hundred solid pounds, I had to work hard to stay as put together as I was. My father's genes were strong, and he always told me I was built like an East African Amazon Woman.

Samuel Bennett has seen me around before and taken a liking to me from the start, but tonight he knows me as his son's partner. It feels good. "We're waiting on some babies from Sebastien. Can't wait to add more grandbabies to the mix and increase our legacy."

Sebastien's dad had a serious expression as he is throwing the responsibility of grandbabies on me as if he's inviting me to Sunday dinner. He means every word. "Sean's daughter is due in four months, and we have Camden, so that's a plus. Then we have Benji and Riana. Hopefully, a wedding and babies will be in the works soon with them as well. Wait." He smiles. "Riana is your close friend, right?"

"Yes, sir."

"You think she'll leave all that music alone and give Benji some babies soon? We all love her around here."

I chuckled, "I don't see why not. I'd ask Riana if I was you. She feels very comfortable with you and the family." I wonder if she knew she was expected to be having a baby hanging off her titty while she danced and twerked across the stage?

He nodded before turning to his son. "I like her already Bash. I want this same energy when I come to you about y'all having kids, ok?"

We chortled before heading to the tables to sit and talk. Moving closer, I noticed a lady eyeing me. I've seen her around. Then again, all this eye candy holding me close might have been the issue. Too bad, he was taken.

"Ms. Williams? Is that you?" Sebastien's father glowed as he talked to the woman, I found gaping at us. Mrs. Bennett rolls in the same direction, admiring the girl's thick mane running down her back. This chick, Ms. Williams', has her bushy eyebrows spiked up in our direction as if she's confused. It looks as if she's trying to stay away from the spotlight, but it's too late. His parents noticed her.

Sebastien turns to see the commotion. I observed the two of them to see what history they have since his parents seem a little too familiar with her. I try not to let jealousy consume me. I am fully aware of Bastien's position in the media, his job, and around the locals. Plus, he had a past before me. In a town as small as Atlanta, I can't expect *not* to run into an ex or two of his. Except this feels different.

"Mr. Bennett, what a pleasure it is to see you again." Rain is distant with me but open with my parents; after all, they summoned her. She struggled to maintain eye contact, which is unusual. Rain always came off as self-assured, not so much tonight, though. Her straight to the point dialogue made her seem a little short with all of us.

Rain's presence halted us from heading to our assigned table. The hem of Imani's dress brushed my shoe when she subliminally kicked me, asking for an introduction to this blast from my past. But I'd already introduced them when Rain showed up unexpectedly at my office. I went years without seeing this woman, and to now see her twice in a few months was a little weird.

"Rain, this is my lady, Imani. Imani, this is Rain Will... Well I guess you're Rain Davidson now."

Imani didn't seem too friendly with Rain if the firm grip she exchanged with her was any indication. She had no issue giving me a hard glare and an eye roll to finish it off. I've never seen her this pressed. I made enough small talk for the three of us, as the two of them continued to stare and size each other up. Not only was there an attitude from Imani, but she never spoke until Rain was walking away from us in the other direction.

I whispered into her ear, "What was that about?"

"She has been eyeing me since I spotted her. Which tells me she has a problem with me."

"No. We aren't about to do this. You don't have any reason to trip, Imani." I tried to disguise my frustration with a smile; not wanting to cause a scene in front of everyone. Then I kissed her earlobes, soothing her on demand. I've never been the type to take time and settle a woman's feelings. The old Bash would have ended the night by escorting her to her car. Sending her on her way. But Imani was different, and if I had to do a little more to soothe her, then I would.

"Well, it would be nice if this woman stops popping up everywhere. Who is she, Sebastien?" Mani shrieked.

"She's Rain. Someone from my past who I haven't seen in years. That's it."

"But your parents know her, Sebastien." Imani rarely called me by my first name, so the fact that she used it twice in less than two minutes lets me know that she was upset. Although I didn't know why.

As I was getting ready to respond, Josh approached us and pulled Imani away for a work-related inquiry. My dad walked up on me as I was watching her walk away, leaving me in a ball of confusion.

"Son, let me see you for a minute." My dad was the perfect distraction. We walked out of the ballroom and found a quiet corner to have a private conversation. "Is everything ok?"

"Yeah, it's all good, Pops. What's up?"

"I didn't want to say this in front of your mother, but you've been kind of scarce since we returned from Texas, but I need you to make time to come see me. We have something important to discuss. Just not tonight, it's not the time or place."

Now, this was even more stress I didn't need. What did my dad possibly want to talk about? Was it my mom? My brothers? Before I could ask, he continued. "It's not your mom or brothers."

I breathed a sigh of relief. "Ok. I'll make time next week."

"Oh, and Bash. Make sure you keep things under control. You have a lot of eyes on you since you're seeing Ms. Barasa. Some folks aren't wishing you the best and waiting to swoop in. So, if you have anything to deal with, save it for when you're in private."

"I know that, dad." I didn't need my dad tryna school me on event etiquette. This is why I needed to nip this whole Imani/Rain thing in the bud now. I needed to start by finding Imani and getting this night back on track.

I left the hallway and re-entered the ballroom looking for the tall statuesque woman in the form-fitting gown that had me wanting to bite her ass like an apple. Strolling along, I found Imani lingering outside the women's restroom. Instead of heading back to converse with the crowd, I needed one on one time with her. I convinced her to try the hot air balloons that were supposed to be one of the hottest amenities for the night. It was a wise decision to choose this mansion with over ten acres of land because it was the perfect backdrop for the balloons and the estate that was lit up like a sprawling castle. I just hoped that whomever they used as a photographer would be able to catch the extravagance of the event.

Imani was silent as I held onto her arm and escorted her to the balloon that most closely resembled our attire. You know, keeping with the theme of the evening and all. After loading us into the bucket, the pilot, Johanson Nolette, my old-time friend, explained the basics of operating the oversized balloon. Though he's supposed to fly the thing he left us to ourselves. "I appreciate it, bro."

It didn't escape me that Imani trusted me enough to let me take us thousands of feet in the air without the pilot. Johanson waved us off, "It ain't nothing but a chicken wang brotha. I know you can operate this thing in your sleep. Let's not scare your lady here with the shenanigans we used to pull as kids, wreaking havoc in my dad's place of business." His father owned FlyHighAtlanta, one of the top-rated hot air balloon services in Georgia. As children, we went to the several spaces they owned and acted as immature boys going against our parent's wishes of staying out of trouble. My brothers and I can operate the balloons and even knew how to fly a small aircraft. All lessons from Mr. Nolette, Johanson's father, also, one of my father's close confidants.

I shake my head at Jo. "We'll see you in about an hour." We ascend. Imani looks at the scenery as she remains quiet, it's apparent it's not from fear. "Imani, you overreacted inside. Rain was once an intern at my dad's office, and she happens to be Nelson Davidson's wife."

Imani's demeanor changes, chin raised high. "What? I had no idea." She dropped her head unable to face me. "I apologize. I'm working on my trust issues and jumping the gun, Sebastien. In all other aspects of my life, I don't normally overreact. With the business I'm in, I can't. An overreaction could be the difference between a rumor and a life-changing scandal. But in relationships, it's different. Every time I let small things slip with my ex Patrick, it always came back to bite me. I don't want to be naive." I knew all about her ex and the issues they both faced, but the man couldn't stand close to me on my worst day. Then the thought of cheating or manipulating Imani to make myself feel inferior wasn't me. "That's not even including other men that I've dated. I just feel like something in me makes them lie to me, and I don't want that with you."

"I'm not Patrick, and I'm not other men. Let's not dwell on the past and move in a better direction. Plus, we both have a professional responsibility not to show our hind parts in public."

"I'm already a step ahead of you," she purred, hiking her dress up to get on her knees. "You could've said, show our asses, Bash. It's no one around to hear you swearing." My belt loosened, pants were unfastened, then my dick shot out. Imani shoved almost all of me inside her mouth. No prep or anything, just hungry for the cock. She ooh and aah while twirling her tongue over my veiny dick. I wanted to stare into her eyes, but I needed to concentrate on controlling the balloon and make sure that we didn't die while I was getting one of the best blow jobs I'd ever had.

Pop. The sound of her sucking, then releasing the bulb of my dick had me cumming all in her mouth. I peeked down for a sec to notice that she swallowed it, leaving a small amount running down her mouth, eyes half-mast.

I needed to get us back on solid ground ASAP. I pull the string that's attached to a fuel source up the top of the balloon, which will decrease the amount of fire expanding the balloon causing it to descend slowly. It was going to take us at least twenty minutes to land. I spent that time attempting to keep my hands to myself and Imani's mouth off my body parts. We were finally able to act like adults instead of horny teenagers, and the minute we did, our landing zone was in view. Before going up, I warned Johanson to not approach us once we landed without indicating to him why. The balloon hit the ground with a thud signaling it was now safe for me to do what I couldn't wait to do.

The sunset was almost to an end when I bent her slightly, slipping in and out of her drenched pussy. "I've been thinking about being inside of you all day, baby." She responded with a moan frantically throwing her ass back. I massaged her insides, taking my time now that I don't have to worry about us crashing. "I hope you're enjoying this night as much as I'm enjoying this time inside of you."

Imani doesn't respond but convulses around me. Muscles tightening over my shaft. "Sebastien Bennett." Her moans are over the top as I pound releasing behind her. "I love you."

I let out a hearty chuckle. Either Imani meant it or was redirecting me away from the beating I put on her. "I love you too, Ms. Barasa."

"I CAN'T SIT BACK and relax, are you freaking kidding me Mr. Polaski, she's threatening to call the police. I just want to see my kids." Nelson squalled. The glass panel lining the backdoor reveals a helpless man drenched with rainwater. He released the knob, no longer attempting to get in.

Earlier in the day, I notified the young man at the security to block him if he tried to come in. I knew I didn't have legal standing to do so, but he had a crush on me and seemed almost excited about the opportunity to lock Nelson out. Clearly, my plan wasn't thought out to the point of what would happen once they switched shifts since he was now at my door. "I paid for this house, Lauren. This is my home too. Don't make me come after you in court and give you a bigger fish to fry."

"Fuck you, Nelson. You won't ever see these kids if you don't get the hell on. You're drunk. I can't allow you to come in here and show your ass."

"Who wouldn't flip after being stopped from entering his neighborhood? I pay bills here. I came by to tuck *my* kids in. It's been a week, this is killing me, Lauren. Why are you torturing me? If it's another man, you can keep that going. But don't take my kids away from me. I live and breathe for those two."

Assuming the man talking on the other end of the phone is Polaski, he tries calming Nelson down. "Mr. Davidson, I'll see if I can send someone in my place to mediate the situation between you and your wife. In the meantime, go sit in your car and calm down. We don't need to involve the police in this matter."

Nelson backs away from the door and makes his way around to the front of the house. Little footsteps sounded from the stairway into the kitchen. "Mommy, let daddy in, please. It's pouring out there." Summer cried profusely. I'm hurt because she is hurting emotionally. Her alarmed tone crushed me, but a few months ago, Nelson scared me after having a drunken episode. Thankfully the children were fast asleep upstairs while he ransacked the house. Nelson's profanity under the influence is a hard pill to swallow. I couldn't deal with him calling me out my name, then tugging at my wrist when I attempted to push him out. Let's not mention the careless mistakes he made, like urinating in the corner of the living room. It was a horrible evening that I would never ever want to relive.

Crouching down, I caressed the frizzy hair atop her head. "Summer, daddy has to calm down first. I would never do anything to hurt him, ok, baby?"

She nodded, looking around for her plus one. Savion isn't far behind. He skipped down two steps at a time. "Come 'er, Summer. I'm going to read your favorite book." Summer looks to me, then back at her brother. "Only after daddy comes in." She's such a daddy's girl.

Savion watched me without a word. The emotionless twin. He's too serious, but always loving towards his sister. "Ok, we'll sit at the steps, and I'll read it there." He grabbed her hand, leading her to the top of the stairwell.

I opened the front door, lightning illuminated the sky, and cast a glow into the dark entryway. Droplets swish my way from the wind. This reminded me of the beginning of my relationship with Nelson when we started dating officially. The weather was similar to this. It wasn't long after, when I learned I was pregnant and we joked about the sex of the baby. This particular year it rained a lot. Nelson suggested that if it's a girl, we'd name her Summer. Summer Rain. We laughed like crazy. At the time, it was just a corny name. But today, the name held weight. Savion Birk was a surprise baby and was delivered twelve minutes after Summer.

Tears lined my face almost instantly as I thought about my journey with the man I thought would be the love of my life. I still loved him deeply, but his inability to control his drinking has me scared to move forward. I hate where we are today as a family. He went over the top to make me happy in the past, and at times I still saw that in him, but I couldn't keep excusing something that could not only destroy us but our children as well. I wave him over, but he isn't paying attention.

"Nelson!" I called out.

His door opened. A few explicit words slipped out his mouth as he made his way to our sprawling front door.

"You have fifteen minutes to put them down, then you have to go." It hurt me to tell him that. I've never given him limited access to our kids.

"Lauren, all of this," he points everywhere. "I contribute too, just like you. I'll take all the time I need with my kids." He's firm, and I keep my stance as well.

"Fifteen minutes." I don't mean to be this cruel, but as a mother, I never wanted to bring unnecessary pain to my children. Now I was second-guessing even giving him fifteen minutes. I allowed him this much leeway because I understood how hard the last two years have been for him, especially how it affected our family.

"You look at me like you saw a demon. I ain't drunk. I'm tired, I haven't been sleeping. You're keeping the kids from me. I can't sleep. Need I say more? All I want is to see my kids and tuck them in. So, if you don't mind," he walked around me. "I need to get to Summer and Savion."

Polaski called me seven times before I decided to answer. My days in the office were extremely long as of late, and I did my best to stay away from unnecessary disturbances.

"Counselor. You urged me to take on a case that's filled with holes. Due to our relationship, I did it. Now he's having a major crisis, and I'm with my wife. I advise you to make your way over there quickly. If I'm not mistaken, his wife is seconds from calling the police." He didn't even bother with saying hello or even ask if I had the time to handle this issue. "909 Country Club Drive, you got it, Bennett?"

"I'll check in on them, Polaski." The line went dead. I knew he was on edge and needed to be with his wife, but that still didn't mean that I wanted to be the one to have to step in.

I couldn't believe I'm headed over to the Davidsons' home this late in the evening. The drive wasn't too bad, it's the gatekeeper that I found annoying. Every time she buzzed the house, no one answered to let me in. She checked my license and credentials after I told her it's a family emergency, and the couple was expecting me. After I admitted that, she did a double-take and must have noticed who I was, so the inquiries and fanfare began.

I'm no celebrity, by all means, it's the people who make me seem more than I am. And that recent *Most Eligible Bachelor* article and video did nothing to help me stay incognito.

It felt as if the guard held me up forever before I made it to the neo-eclectic home resembling those in California. I rang the bell twice before Rain came to the door. She was wearing a sports bra and matching short set. I kept my eyes trained on her face.

Rain took a split second to take me in before she tensed up. "What are you doing here?"

Letting out a breath, I explained. "Polaski sent me here to check on Nelson. But it seems that everything is ok, so I'll leave."

Nelson appeared at her side, all smiles. He had no clue about how pissed Rain is. Or maybe he did, and he's just used to this side of her. "All is well, Mr. Bennett. I just tucked the kids in. My wife and I had a misunderstanding."

She juts out her hip. "Don't bring an outsider into our home to try to mediate our shit."

"Then, don't go changing the fucking locks on the door, Lauren." That name is the main reason I got thrown off with who his wife truly was. People called her by her middle name, Rain, not her first.

"Get your shit and get the fuck out." She snatched his keys off the hook near the door. Nelson didn't budge for a while before he marched to a set of steps that I assumed would take him upstairs. Rain seized the arm of his jacket, trying to stop him. He shrugged her off and continued on his way.

"Mr. Davidson, we're leaving together." I'm in his face in no time. Hoping to simmer the pot that's boiling.

"Hell no, all of this is her fault. I've been fighting for us for years. All she has been doing is working, building her so-called brand as an attorney, and she's neglected the main people who she claims she does it for." He shifted his body towards her. "You can enjoy the saffron, the kids and I are good on the oodles and noodles. We don't need any fancy shit to make us. Love can't be bought, baby. And time can't be replaced."

Rain launched a sharp jab to the left that landed, but she missed the right, and Nelson caught her fist. I yanked her out of his way, putting an end to whatever this was about to turn into. I'm not familiar with Nelson enough to know how he reacted to this level of violence. I do know Rain is furious and hurt. Nelson hit below the belt, but his words may have been valid. As an outsider looking in, seeing the love and compassion towards him from the kids, he'd done a great job at loving them.

"Mrs. Davidson." I'm careful how I greet her or the level of attention I present. I didn't have time to explain to her husband about our history, but I was sure to make it known at another time when things were less chaotic.

The more I try to soothe her, the angrier she gets. "Fuck you, Sebastien. What me and Nelson have going on is between us. I would appreciate it if you were to let the whole case go and allow us to resolve things outside of the courtroom."

With raised hands, I backed up. "Understood." I wasn't here to solve anything tonight. I just needed to do Polaski this favor and make sure that Nelson left the home without incident.

"Just because you two are working attorneys doesn't give you a right to disrespect him, Lauren. You always use being a lawyer to leverage your way through things." A glass bottle flew straight past my nose, hitting the wall. If Nelson waited two-seconds longer, he'd have glass in his eyes.

I needed to get out of this place, and Nelson needed to walk out with me. Rain doesn't appear stable, and I definitely don't remember her being this aggressive. She's brutal in court, keeping all on their toes, but this, she can catch all types of charges, including child endangerment.

Nelson laughed, further enticing her. "And you say I'm a safety hazard for the kids. You're crazy, girl."

"I'll show your ass crazy." Rain leaped past me grabbing his collar. Swiftly I carved my hand around her belly.

Then an even-toned butterscotch human being latched onto her daddy's leg. "Mommy stop it," she yelled. "Daddy, please go. I don't want you and mommy fighting." Summer gasped for air. Nelson comforted her until she was able to catch her breath. "Daddy is leaving baby." This scene is too much for me.

"Summer come 'er before you get hurt. They are fine." Savion stood there shirtless. There's no reason for kids to have to witness so much violence and foul words. Rain is in shambles with tears. Nelson can barely breathe from all the commotion.

"Lauren, I'm gonna leave, just let me kiss my babies goodnight."

"Hell fucking no, get the fuck out. Haven't you done enough already? Can't you see they're scared, Nelson?" The bickering goes on endlessly. This isn't right, unhealthy. Savion doesn't react much, but he clearly wanted to protect his sister. He hated seeing her so hurt. Rightfully so.

You know what? If these two wanna kill each other, they can go right ahead. I needed to get these kids settled. I took Summer by the hand, letting her lead the way. "Do you and your brother share rooms?"

"No, sir. But I wanna sleep in my brother's bed." She mumbled.

I looked to Savion, he smiled, "Hey Mr. Sebastien. You can come up."

His room has train tracks as the background on the wall. A tv is mounted in the center, and several game systems are neatly placed in the entertainment system. His room was a little boy's dream.

Summer laid on one end of the queen size bed while Savion got on the other. "Are you two, ok?" I questioned, very concerned, but I smiled to make it seem better than what it was.

"They argue all the time, except mommy never hits daddy," Summer clarified.

"They will be ok. You two don't need to worry about that." The kids needed to understand this was adult business, and they were not at all at fault.

I sat in an empty chair near their bed and picked up a book off the nightstand. "Can you read a page or two?" Savion asked.

"Sure thing." I wanted to protect these kids. It hurt me immensely seeing them experience their parents go toe to toe. Seeing Summer's tears almost ruined me completely. I didn't know how I felt about the case after witnessing this, but I knew it was the right decision to remove myself. Polaski needed to get this case solved soon.

I ended up reading a whole chapter, making jokes with the kids and making silly animal sounds that they requested to go along with the book. Initially, it bothered me to make a trip here, but comforting these kids was the highlight of it all.

Summer fell fast asleep when I got out of the chair. I fixed the pillow underneath her head, "Good night, Cupcake."

"You remember her nickname?" Savion was stoked.

"I thought you fell asleep, Chief."

"Wow, you remember mine too?"

"How can I not? I came up with it."

There's a shirt on the dresser, I tossed it to Savion. "Put that on. It's a bit chilly in your room. You don't want to get sick, do you?"

"No, sir."

I still can't digest the intellect of these children. They speak better than most adults, and they were barely kindergarteners.

"Thanks for being our hero tonight." He shrugged. His squeaky voice cracked. "I was kind of scared, but I pray when I feel alone. My dad said there's power in His name. Then you came."

We talked a while longer. I managed to ease his nerves with a teddy bear he found comfort in. Rain asked me to remove myself from their case, and I did that, but what I wouldn't do is neglect the kids. Rain and Nelson had an obligation to put their bickering behind them and put the needs of their children first. If anyone knew about pushing through a tough time and still giving your kids the life they deserved, it was me. Most marriages would not have survived what my parents had gone through, but theirs did, and they taught me that anything is possible if you work for it.

Dɪᴅ I mention the vibes of California can't be duplicated anywhere else? For the past three months, I've been busy working on both east and west coasts, assisting different clients. But the highlight of my time on the west coast was mainly spent training myself for the Woman on Waves competition in Huntington California.

Sebastien visited whenever he could while I was in Cali, making it easier to communicate without feeling a damper in the relationship. "Imani, slow down," my mama yelled as the water shot me into her direction closer to the shoreline. Sebastien and daddy laughed excessively. I've been in the sun in Malibu for a few hours now, trying my best to perfect my stunts.

"Baby, you can't be scaring your mama like that." Sebastien hopped up, tossing me into his frame. He's wearing knee-length swim shorts with a beaded necklace. Bae didn't have to do anything to stand out.

He slipped my blue surfboard underneath his pits. My parents followed behind us to the beach house a few feet away. Sebastien got it for my parents and me. It took a lot of convincing for him to stay along with us even though it had five bedrooms. He says family time is that, no reason to interfere. But daddy liked him, and my parents threatened to leave if he didn't stay the night.

"Khnhom mean avei del trauv niyeay cheamuoy anakher." It's been a minute since my mom spoke in her native tongue.

I looked back at her after she addressed me. I'm the only one who knows Khmer fluently. "Yes, mama?" I answered after she mentioned needing to speak to me.

She departed from dad, leaving him with Bastien. She then proceeds to tug me a few feet away before beginning her rant. "Are you not coming to Pchum Ben Day? Your father tells me after the competition you have obligations to satisfy." The truth is I'm not interested in going to Cambodia for two weeks. Yeay left a week before to attend the country's most prominent holiday, also known as Ancestors' Day. Families from all over the world travel together to pay respects to those who died going back seven generations. Being part of a deeply rooted culture brings out a sense of awareness in you. Kenyans have a lot of beliefs that many would find weird. Still, like Kenyans, Cambodians, or Khmer people, have backgrounds that most wouldn't understand.

"Oh mama," I try soothing the blow, rubbing her arms.

"No!" She didn't want to hear it.

Faint words resonated from the area where my dad and Bash were standing but suddenly it became mute as they listened to my mother chew me out. Dad knew this was on the way. Bash, on the other hand, probably was surprised that my sweet mother had a mean streak.

"Chineye Barasa." It's serious when she calls me by my Kenyan government. Silently, I backed away, not yet ready to deal with her and the answers she didn't want to hear.

"You already missed the Khmer New Year." She pleaded. Having me think back to what exactly had me occupied in mid-April.

"Ok, mama, I'll see what I can do, but I can't guarantee it. Next year though, I'll be there for sure."

"We're not promised tomorrow, Imani." She marched to daddy, cursing underneath her breath. "It feels like you don't take your cultural responsibilities seriously."

I'm embarrassed that she feels that way. I love family time in Cambodia; however, I don't always believe in the traditions, such as feeding monks. Or the thought that in this time for fifteen days our ancestors come back, while their souls wait at a pagoda for food made by their relatives. What I do agree with regarding the holiday is the importance they push on loving and caring for your parents who are considered Gods since they give life, caring for their offspring. As Yeay says, *'Bring happiness to your parents, then you can count on blessings for the moment, and your future with your children will be grand.'*

"I damn near blend in with the cement, no reason for me to be out here sunbathing." My dad tried to make a joke, delivering the corniest lines of them all. Jaali is anti-sunlight. He's never been a fan of the beach, only opting for it because of my love for water.

Bash does his best not to laugh at my dad, though you see his smile in his eyes as my dad continues, "It's ok to laugh, Sebastien. As you can see, my family thinks I'm no funny, but I'm wise. I know better."

"Jaali, I need some reprieve from my daughter and her friend." Mama grabbed Daddy and shooed Bash and me away. "Let dem be. You and I need our alone time." I understood from growing up in a house with extremely affectionate parents, that *'alone time'* was code for sex. She's never been ashamed of her high sex drive. She's made it plain and clear that she frequently overindulges throughout the week and in heated moments, he's who she calls upon.

Her silky mane bumped against her round flat face when my dad groped her. Sebastien took this moment to lift me into his arms, leading us in another direction away from the beach house. He maintained a steady pace for a good mile. His daily four am workout prepared him for this very moment.

We ended up in a secluded area of the beach with the setting sun as the backdrop. Everything about this moment was absolutely perfect, and the conversation with my mom was quickly forgotten. All I could think about was making love under the violet-bluish tint of the sun leaving the sky as Sebastien manipulated my body like I did my surfboard over the waves.

"The thought of me bending you over wouldn't leave my mind, Mani." Once again, he was reading my mind. Sebastien didn't shy away from using dirty verbiage to excite me. It didn't take long for him to push my bikini bottoms to the side and for him to drop his shorts. I didn't notice the towel in his hands, but he placed it on the sand and had me get on my hands and knees as he entered me in one smooth thrust. The more we indulged in the passion, the more he divulged verbally. He fucked me long and hard. Not worrying about who would see us, which had me climaxing within minutes. Grated beads of sand brushed my waist as he used his hands to hold me in place with every plunge. This is thrilling. If Sebastien ever second-guessed our union, hopefully, this would put it all to rest.

It's not until the sun is completely gone that we rest. Exhausted we lay there, bathing suit half-done. "Not one time did you worry about your parents catching us under these circumstances?" Now he asks about someone possibly seeing us.

I gasped, "The way my mom climbed my dad a while ago, no one can tell us anything. Besides, she told me to claim what's mine."

"What?" His cackle sent vibrations up my spine. "Ms. Sophea is a piece of work." He's unable to calm his nerves.

"Seriously, she told me I better suck you dry. For what it's worth, she thinks highly of you. She's no prude. Her confidence is intact."

"Hmm. Explains your high sex drive. Your mom rubbed off on you."

"No more than you've rubbed off on me. You make me want you. Sex isn't boring or just an activity. It's very intimate when dealing with you. Then the long drawn out conversations after every session is special. I feel open."

"That's why you're my girl."

Trickles of wet kisses traced my neck before we shot off into another round.

SEBASTIEN

"IT'S SUCH a disservice for you to cry like that, Senai." I looked into
the camera facing my one-month-old niece trying to get her to
smile while I was in the office finishing up my day. After returning
from Cambodia, Imani and I spent two weeks in Los Angeles with
Sean and Chelsea. Even though Sean and Chelsea could have
hosted us at their estate, we still decided to stay at a hotel to give
the new parents and us privacy.

Time away with Imani was amazing and everything I imagined
it would be. I was also able to finish up some cases and work on
others to the point of just needing to present them in the courtroom, starting first thing tomorrow. Tonight, I was here finishing
up some depositions and playing catch up on anything I missed
while being out.

When Mama Barasa flipped out after hearing Imani wouldn't
partake in their traditional gathering in Cambodia, I couldn't let
that slide. I respected them too much and knew how much family
meant to her, so we flew out the following day after Imani won
first place at the Woman on Waves competition.

I was a well-traveled man who had visited over ten countries,
but nothing compared to the culture of Khmer people. As a
newcomer, they treated me like a king. I ate to the point of feeling

gluttonous, and Yeay, Imani's grandmother, made sure I missed nothing when it came to their culture. The prayer sessions, kneeling in front of statues, or the belief in Buddhism.

Imani admitted to me how her culture on either side didn't align with her current spiritual path since she was a Christian. Although our family values and belief systems are ingrained into us as children, sometimes we grow up and start forging our own path, but never forgetting the teachings that were instilled. During the holiday I witnessed their offering of money, food, and prayer to erase bad karma for their ancestors during their spiritual travels. Imani wouldn't adhere to the practice, but she fellowshipped. Her mother and family thanked me numerous times for the gesture of making sure she attended something so dear to them. The entire experience was something I would never forget. The fact that I was able to do this with Imani was doubly satisfying.

After spending two weeks in Cambodia learning the Khmer culture, I was eager to get back stateside to visit the newest addition to the Bennett clan. My niece Sanai arrived while we were in Cali for Imani's surf tournament, and our connection was instant. She's only been on this earth a month, but she quickly became my favorite. She rarely cried in my presence. Our bond was instant from the start which enticed Imani to poke fun about us possibly having kids sooner than later. I wouldn't mind making that a reality. The only thing giving me pause is the importance for me to partner in the firm and secure my assets first. Speaking of making partner, my dad had been doubling down and getting on me about setting up a meeting, so it needed to happen soon.

"Sebastien." Sean was now in the frame, giggling. "You not used to being around children, and I can tell with those random ass words." He chuckled again, "Disservice. What the fuck?"

I may not be a person who is associated with kids like that, but my heart is pure. My niece stole my heart with her chubby cheeks and set of eyes that looked at you as if she's been here before. "You weren't talking that big boy mess when I stocked Senai's closet with two months worth of diapers assorted in sizes. Or the cans of formula I had delivered, making sure you and Chelsea stay afloat for a while." I knew they could more than afford it, but I wanted to make sure they had enough to get them through without having to send someone out to purchase it, or having to leave themselves to get it. It was more for convenience.

"Hell nah, I ain't trippin. Speaking of which, the bracelet?" Sean went from a smirk to a quizzical look.

I purchased Senai a Cartier love bracelet and a gold necklace she can adjust as she gets older. I'm sure this generous act baffled everyone in the room when I gifted it before leaving for Atlanta.

Sean seemed preoccupied as the office started to dim, reminding me that my time in this building took up a vast portion of my life. While continuing the FaceTime call, I reinserted the papers into the gem clip and placed them in the folder after I scanned all the documents on my laptop. "What about it, Sean?" I was multitasking here, remembering that he asked me about the bracelet.

"You tend to spend money, plenty of it, but there's always a method behind it for you. One thing you don't do is believe in wasting cash, as you claim. So I'm tryna understand the purpose of the jewelry."

Before responding to my brother, I hit send on a text, informing Imani to go ahead and eat dinner. I would be really late making it to her place tonight.

"You're right; however, nothing is a waste when it comes to my niece." She must've agreed, Senai's vibrant eyes exploded at the sound of my voice as if she was searching the room for me. Sean held up her tiny body in front of his screen so that she was covering the entire twenty-six-inch screen of my MacBook.

Witnessing the arrival of Senai made me a believer that I too would one day get to have the experience that Sean had with Chelsea as they welcomed her. Thinking about the whole thing had me anxious, but I would also let Sean know why nothing was a waste when it came to my gift-giving. "Sean, let me school you, youngin." With confidence, my head tilted as he wiped the milk from his daughter's mouth. "Jewelry can be a waste of money, depending on the piece you purchase. In 1970 the Love bracelet from Cartier was created costing $250 a pop which is equivalent to $1600 today. I know this because grandpa had a matching one with our grandmother, but I learned the value a few years back. If you walk into the store today to buy a brand new one, they're over $6,000."

Sean nodded, "I've heard of that before."

"I went into the store to look at pieces for my woman, and I ran across a bracelet for Senai. I made sure she had a bracelet she can grow with, and I love the idea of having a special screwdriver to remove it. She's a child, and we know how careless they are. Either way, she'll always have something of value from me. She'll appreciate her Uncle Bash."

"Chelsea is still raving about not having to leave the house for anything baby-related except for doctor appointments. Thanks, man. You've been a great help and distraction these past few weeks. I love you, Bro."

"Love you too. You know I got you." I looked down at my ringing desk phone wondering who was calling me. "Let me call you right back, Sean. Dad is calling my office phone." I hung up before he could offer additional pleasantries.

"Sebastien?" I answered and heard my dad's voice before the phone could go to voicemail.

"Sir?" I questioned, wondering why he was still in the office at this time of the day.

"I'm on my way out and need a moment of your time." I don't question him, I just simply dropped everything and made my way into his office.

I barely shut the door behind me when he started at me. "Tell me, why do you work so hard? What's your objective at this point in your life?" My dad coming out of the blue with this line of questioning wasn't a good thing. He already knew all the answers to the questions he posed.

I fell into a chair, glaring at him and somehow hoping that he would have just straight up asked me about anything else. "Man, Pops, you know my goal was to be a partner by thirty. Not only did I expect to be a partner, but I expected to expand our entertainment division as well. Now that we're well over a year since I've turned thirty, it's time for me to revamp some of those goals."

"I hear you, son. Do those goals have anything to do with the young lady you've been vacationing with for the past month? Is she distracting you?"

"Pops, she's not. I've been working harder than ever, and if anything, she pushes me. Like me, she wants to know why I haven't made a partner yet?"

"Can you bring in billable clients?"

I couldn't believe my father was sitting here playing me. "What do you mean?" I don't want to cross the line and disrespect him, so I had to watch my tone and demeanor in his presence. "I can't even take on any more clients. I gross more than not only every lawyer in my division but almost every attorney in this firm."

"That part is true. The issue at hand is the clients you represent. Roland Jones. He is a quandary for this firm."

"Come on, dad. Roland is good peoples, just a little rough around the edges. I'm tough on him because he's got too much to lose. Mr. Jones has a reason to get his life together. He has a daughter depending on him. And who am I not to take on someone due to their rap sheet? Isn't that what lawyers do? Turn the tables to paint their client's situation in a way acceptable to society?"

"Is Nelson Davidson favorable too?" I couldn't understand the issue my dad or Josh had with me representing Nelson even though I've already passed his case along to Polaski.

When I was twenty-six, and under my dad's wing, it was cool. He was the best teacher and mentor. Shadowing him allowed me to work crazy hours to satisfy the state requirements. I've had other mentors who pushed me to get out and party, but that was never my scene. I had goals and in order to reach them, I had to do more working and less partying. This lifestyle naturally turned me into a homebody, so much so that Benji once asked me, *'You don't mind being a boring old man in the future?'* I sure don't. I was putting myself in a position to be at the top of my game by a certain age. Meeting Imani and getting to know her made me want to reach my goals quicker. She finally gave me a reason to see that I didn't have to do this alone. Having her beside me also magnified the fact that I wasn't as completely put together as I wanted to be before adding a wife and kids to the mix. The cards haven't aligned in my favor. Yet.

"What more do you all want from me, dad? You know I have more than enough billable clients. So, what is this really about?" According to my last performance review, the partners were happy with my performance. This had to be about something else.

"Sebastien, I'm just worried that you're not focused enough. And some of the other partners agree."

"Wow, I didn't see that coming." I always knew they thought I was some sort of secret playboy since I had a different date at every employee event, and I knew the importance of family to the people who were at the top of this firm. But they were way off base and my dad should have known better than to agree with that notion. "So, when I focus on my career and not a relationship, I'm dinged for that. When I finally start to focus on building something strong with an incredible woman, I'm dinged for that as well. I just can't win."

"No one wants to penalize you for living, Sebastien. But you have to find a way to have balance. And traipsing across the globe for a month is not balance. Continuing to take on high risk clients is not balance. Not pushing harder to meet your career goal and making partner is not balance. Bringing in billable clients is only part of it. But not all of it." He seemed to have been holding this in for a while. "First and foremost, I am your dad, not your boss. And this is me coming to you as your loving, caring dad. Not Attorney Bennett." He took a deep breath before adding, "Just focus, Bash."

I was pissed and didn't totally agree with him, so I needed to get out of his office. I moved closer to the door to walk out, I retracted, feeling the need to add. "As a kid, I wanted to be just like you. Everything seemed so perfect in your world. You painted an impressive blueprint for me and my brothers, but I learned that was only the mere surface. You and mom weren't perfect, but you two worked through any and everything that became stumbling blocks. You don't think I want to be a partner by now? Have a family of my own? I want a wife that can have my back as you have. Imani seems promising and I hope I can be all that she wants. But it's not easy trying to keep it all together."

"I understand. But it's time to stop making excuses and start making things happen." He wasn't gonna feel sorry for me and offer me a lifeline. He was resolute and made his point clear. If I wanted to make partner, I needed to find a way to have it all.

I flew back into my office, almost stewing as I pulled out my phone and FaceTime Sean again. "Do you know dad had the nerve to blow up on me. Like, I don't hold my own in this office." It's not frequent for me to vent to my brothers, especially not immediately after an incident. I normally had time to cool down and reflect. But this pissed me off, and since I told him I would call him back, he would have to hear it.

"You have company coming up, boss." The security officer from downstairs buzzed my phone distracting me from what I planned on saying to my brother.

Sean's questioning glare evaded the screen. "I don't know what to address first. Your beef with Dad or the fact that it's kinda late in Atlanta for you to be getting surprise pop-ups."

Tapping the intercom button, I cleared my voice. "Who's coming?"

"Attorney Davidson, sir."

"She's not on my calendar."

"She's on the list of approved visitors for the firm, sir."

"Thanks." I ended the conversation with the officer. My frustration could be heard in my reply.

"Sean, I'll hit you up later."

He smirked, "That doesn't sound like Imani."

"Nah, it's my client's wife." Technically he was no longer my client, but with my mind on my recent interaction with my dad, my focus wasn't on point... as he clearly pointed out.

"A'ight, well, stay outta trouble and hit me later about ya lil spat with Dad." He hung up in laughter as if any of this was funny.

The knock was heavy, and before long, she strutted in my office like she owned the joint. "How can I help you this late in the evening, Mrs. Davidson?"

Her obsidian dress flared out ascending slowly when she made her way into the chair directly in front of my desk. She crossed her legs, "That's Rain to you. Besides, I just came to apologize."

Instead of being the jerk I could be, I let her ramble about the night I popped up at her house. Since then, according to Polaski, the case is moving forward with mediation taking place in the coming weeks. Other than that, I've been happily blinded to the matter.

"Rain," I wanted to stop her, informing her she didn't have to explain anything to me. "That's between you, your husband, and your attorney. None of it is my business."

She seemed relieved. "Well said. I'll make my way out of here. But I have a question first." Rain stood up and walked towards the sofa near the sitting area observing the few art pieces on the wall.

I pulled the cashmere sweater over my head to stay warm, the room was cooling down. My mind was already shifting to being with my woman after this crazy day. I would give her a few more minutes before kindly asking her to leave after showing up for a second time uninvited to my office.

I stared at her waiting on her question. "What's up?"

"Do you think I'm wrong for trying to keep him from his kids?" Her eyes were full of tears, she's guilt-ridden. Truthfully, I know her intentions aren't to hurt her kids. Given the circumstances and knowing about Nelson's inclination to drink, I can somewhat understand her point.

I vacated my chair, walking around my desk to hold her hand. "Rain, I don't fully know both sides of your marriage. But I know that Nelson is probably not the same man you married after losing his oldest son. That destroyed him, and if he loses the twins, that will kill him. I'm sure as a mother, you'll do anything to protect your kids. But you also have to keep in mind that your husband would do the same. I've seen him in action, and there is no denying that he loves them."

She's shedding tears excessively. There isn't much I can do but let her have it out. "Nelson told you about Nelly? He never wants to talk about him." I couldn't comfort her more than holding her hand since she's not my lady. I won't even allow her to feel comfortable enough to think she can come here looking for answers from me after today, but the least I could do is listen to her. "He wasn't my biological son, but no one knew that. He lived with us and he loved his baby brother and sister, and they loved him. We never recovered from his loss, and Nelson started drinking as a way to cope."

"I'm really sorry for your loss. But I think you all need to work this out. Rain, you're an attorney, you know what court does to families." We both stared at each other. I saw her thinking about my suggestion and the thought that her family would have to deal with a second life-changing blow.

"So, this is what we're doing now?" Imani's physique couldn't be missed, with her belly out in a pullover matching the oversized joggers. The door Rain entered was wide open, which is the reason I didn't hear Imani come in. And the funny part, Rain doesn't give off that she'd been crying just seconds before. She secretly wiped her eyes and put on a nonchalant facade as if the last five minutes never happened. Rain backed away from me as if we were doing something unsavory and had been caught.

Imani was in my face, standing in between Rain and me. "I came to invite you out to dinner at our favorite diner, but it looks like I'm interrupting something. Her again, Sebastien?"

I tried my best not to be an asshole by telling her she was over-reacting and being insecure. I'd address her personally, except not in front of another woman. My mother has always mentioned the importance of being private, never allowing anyone to feel superior to the one you're with.

"Imani," I calmly stated over her obnoxious assumption.

"Sebastien?!"

I looked to Rain, then back at Imani. "Let's not do this. Give me a second to walk Mrs. Davidson out, then we can head to dinner."

"Take all the time you need with her, I'm out!" That's it, Imani lost all her sense.

Rain was already standing, making her way out of my office. I stopped Imani and sat her in the chair Rain just left. "Rain, I am sorry how things are playing out between you and your husband. As you can see, you being in my office is causing an issue in my relationship." I continued to walk her to the elevator. "You can't keep popping up here. Talk to your husband, and if you have any further questions regarding your case, please go directly to Mr. Polaski." I reached inside of my pants pocket to hand her his car.

Rain doesn't evoke any emotion. She's calm when entering the elevator and thanked me for my time. I, on the other hand, can't keep my tremors at bay as I made it back to my office and a fuming girlfriend.

I am sure to shut the door quietly, completely opposite of what I'm sure we were both feeling. There's no one left in the office itself, but I still didn't want to chance someone coming in and hearing us. Imani was no longer sitting down. Instead, she walks around my office with her face in her phone.

After I watched the clock for two minutes, I exploded. "Sit down, Imani!" She stood there unmoved, throwing a dirty look my way. Unbothered. She folded her arms over her breast, hips cocked to the side. Controlling a woman isn't my objective, except she cannot and will not think it's ok to jump to conclusions like that. This could have really been a business meeting, and her behavior would have been embarrassing if that was the case.

I walked to where she was still standing and slipped my arms underneath her ass cheek. Again, she evoked nothing. No fight, no bite. This makes me horny. I'm not sure how we got here when I was just so frustrated with her moments before. I buried my palms onto her pants, snatching them down. One thing for sure is her excitement for sex. Lots of it. In a week, we got it in at least five days with two rounds minimum.

"Bend over." She shook her head no, but did the opposite with her body by opening and spreading her legs apart. Straightening her back. I nibbled on her ear. "It's my pussy any other day," I growled. She moaned.

The bulbous tip of my dick smacks her ass. "Sebastien, I don't want it."

If a woman tells you no and shows disinterest, you stop immediately. No reason to catch a case on what's available in surplus. A saying my Uncle Check drilled in our heads growing up.

Stepping back from the action, I released her. Dick crying for a release. She didn't move but looked over her shoulder. Lust filled her eyes, but pain also appeared. "You said you don't want me. I will not make you feel uncomfortable."

"I'm not about to share you with another person, Sebastien."

I grabbed the back of her neck, "Imani, who do you take me as? I'm a man who knows how to control his dick. I've had my share of women. I know I'm not missing out on anything out there. I don't need Mrs. Davidson or anyone else. I told you we were together. Monogamy is all I've seen between my parents. I want that in my life too." Just like that, my words softened her resolve, and she bent slightly, giving me permission to take what's mine.

"Grrr," I wailed internally, inserting my dick into her throbbing pussy. You can hear me sliding inside the gushing of her salivating sheath. Every inch of my cock is coated, glistening every time I pull out. "You better not ever." I pound harder, knocking into her. "Ever." My pace doubles. "Embarrass me like that again."

She quivered. Screaming, "Sebastien. I'm sorry. I just love you so fucking much."

Her laborious breathing heightened the more she quaked underneath me. Seconds after, I climaxed too, gripping her hips, tightening my hold with every spurt jutting out. "Imani, I love you too. If I didn't, we wouldn't be here now." The high we were both on quickly left our bodies as she asked to talk.

She ran to the bathroom to wash herself up. Coming out, she got right to it; she sought more answers to my past relationships. I explained the best I could. What should have been me working, ended up in a tell-all. We didn't go straight home after our talk. We finally made it to the 24-hour diner and pigged out on breakfast food before we managed to beat the sunrise and hit round two in the comfort of my home.

SEDUCING IS MORE than an act in sexual paradise. The island of Maldives transmitted a sense of peace that's never been experienced by me in any other location. Our villa at this particular resort provided first-class amenities, no different than the commercials we viewed virtually. It was breathtakingly beautiful.

The villas, pools, jacuzzis, restaurants, you name it, all sat on top of the water, glass is the only barrier keeping you afloat. Each villa faces different directions to ensure full privacy. This made it easy to let my guards down, allowing Sebastien to consume my body under the stars, every night we've been here. Last night we barely slept. After a few rounds of lovemaking, we went out exploring, to my surprise it's a boisterous place that many couples from different parts of the world frequent. We had no dull moments and made some associates along the way.

Waking up this morning took no effort. I was excited to be a part of Riana and Benji's special day. It was like a fairytale, but their journey to happiness was more like a dramatic series. In the back of my mind, I always believed the pair would make it in their relationship, but I was lowkey fearful of the outcome of Benji finding out about Santos and vice versa. Seeing how everything fell in place with them, along with Riana's family coming together as a family unit, was a beautiful thing to witness.

"You two seem comfortable, hope you don't mind my husband and I joining you." Riana doesn't wait for Bash and me to answer. She hops onto the oversized chiffon-draped daybed. This, too, is built over water, one we can jump in and out of with no issue.

Sebastien's thumb and index stops flicking my nipple. I adjusted my back into his chest, still pressing into his dick. "Your husband, huh?" I smiled at her, letting her enjoy the idea of having a husband. Riana just walked the sandy beach eight hours earlier and already been constantly yelling out *her husband*. I love this girl to death.

"Uh-huh, that's what I said." Her ring glistened on her finger.

Benji sat on the far end of the bed, motioning Riana over. Not too long after, Sean and Chelsea joined us. As a trio couple, involving brothers, this was cool. It meant the world to me that my closest friends and I were dating brothers.

"Clowns." Sean addressed playfully to Riana and Benji.

"Duck." Benji counteracted, referring to Sean's yellow swimwear.

"Baby." Chelsea snarled with her deep red lipstick. She's glowing, doesn't even look like she was pregnant two months ago. She opts for a classy one-piece bathing suit crossing her legs. "Be nice. Let the Bennett's live out this honeymoon. Did you forget all that Ri has done for us?" He paused to look at the two, zeroing in hard on Riana.

"Yeah, I can't forget. All of our wedding gifts were dope. But what was the dildo for, Riana?" All five of us cackled. Riana and Sean remind me so much of Martin and Pam. You can expect the shits from them all the time. Riana is too overprotective of Chelsea, which was the catalyst to the start of their friendship. Thankfully Ri and Sean have a healthy, fun friendship.

Benji couldn't have known about the dildo. He questioned her, causing a little bit of bickering. I laughed harder at her trying to explain herself. This is insane.

Working to keep the amusement at bay, Ri grabs her bare belly. "Uuh," she acts as if she's puzzled, ashamed. Of course, she's not. "My dearest brother Sean, I love you. Chelsea can attest to that." We go up in cahoots. She's milking this and trying to soften the blow. "It's no offense to you, but you be gone a lot with your career. Therefore, I gave her something to keep her company. That's all B.O.B is for. When she needs a tune-up while you're away."

"Riana," Benji's skin flushed fire brick red as he covered her mouth. "Don't say another word."

She tried to speak in a muffled tone as Benji continued to cover her mouth, "I'm just tryna help a sista out! I'm saving marriages one dildo at a time." Even Benji let go a gut-busting laughter. I can see why she's the life of the party.

Sean smacked Chelsea's ass in agreeance. Chelsea buried her head into his chest, laughing.

"Good looking sis, I appreciate all your hard efforts, Mrs. Bennett." Sean now looked to me and Sebastien. "Big bro, you have allowed your two younger siblings to get married before you. What's up?"

"Let's see." Bastien props an elbow on his knee, brushing his chin. "This month marks a year of meeting Imani, and since then, she's made me reconsider every aspect of my life." I turned to face him. It's hard not to kiss him, but I stared into his eyes, searching for any inkling of where this may go. His gaze was on me, tuning the rest of them out as if this message was solely mine.

"I've fallen in love with a strong-minded woman. She thinks she can boss me around, but soon enough, she'll learn who's the Head Chief in Charge."

"My girl, Mani gottem pussy whipped. Yasss!" Riana hollered, clapping.

Bash and I bumped heads, literally, snorting and parading with jest. It's nice to see this side of him. He isn't uptight. Since entering his life, he's gone from apprehensive to adapting to his surroundings. Allowing circumstances to affect him positively. He evoked a variety of emotions now; he laughs, tells jokes, and allows others to penetrate his world. He's learning to concede to joy, and best of all, he reciprocates to those around him.

He doesn't allow Riana to knock him off course and continues gazing deeply into my eyes. "She's right, you got me going, baby. Going into a direction that only you'll be able to infiltrate. I told myself I had to be in a specific place before marriage and having kids. Today all of that has changed. You will be a Bennett woman, Imani. I'll give you the six kids that you dream of."

"Six kids?" Chelsea and Riana shouted at the same time.

"Man, ain't enough space at our parent's crib for all of that," Sean reminded us jokingly.

"Send that energy this way, Bash." Benji couldn't be any more serious. Riana mentioned the two wanting to start a family soon.

Riana slid off the bed. "Come on, Mr. Bennett. You want babies? We can start practicing now." We shook our heads secretly hoping Benji could keep up with Riana.

"Let's do the same." Chelsea added, jumping off, hauling Sean behind her. "Minus the baby part. Two is more than enough. Besides, Imani is in heat right now."

I straddled Bash, not caring for the eyes on us. Luckily, they got the picture, taking off. "I can't wait until the day you make my dreams come true," I moaned into his mouth.

"Let me give you a preview." He lowered me onto the bed.

"What about others seeing us?"

"You haven't learned to trust me yet? I don't plan to ever mislead you, Ms. Barasa. Trust the process." He untangled the string of the bikini bottom. It's as if I'm floating. Nothing matters but the tongue darting at my clit and his promises of a future being his wife and mother of his six babies.

SEBASTIEN

ANOTHER ITEM CHECKED off my to-do list. Three meetings before ten am, tons of paperwork indexed at the courthouse, and now arriving at Imani's before our twelve pm reservation.

I gently knocked on the door that was slightly ajar. Her favorite go-to year-round candle welcomes me. This only further proves that this random, inexpensive gift that I bought in surplus out of Bath & Body Works was the right choice. She loved it and acted as if it was a priceless product. I'll never forget the tricks she performed to thank me for the thoughtful gift.

"I'm in here, baby," Imani yelled from the bedroom. I moved along the grand living room, passing two ruby wing chairs. The sofa doesn't match at all, yet it fits. The black and white art pieces throughout the home give off a chic, yet modern look. It's like this home is filled with personality. I frequented her place often, but today felt different. Kinda feels like home.

Imani walked out of the bathroom, looking like a mix between an African and Cambodian goddess. She's a good mix between her parents and damn it if they didn't do a good job. For once, she had her waist-length black hair flowing. Usually, it was pulled up or back in a classic, sext bun. I can't help the affection I gave her, she has me all in. After a long-overdue kiss, she sat on the bed, asking me to help her with her shoes.

I felt my pocket vibrating, but I didn't care to answer. I had such a packed morning to free up my afternoon for my much needed Imani time. "Why do you keep teasing me?"

She answered with a spread of her legs, showcasing her red thong underneath her dress. Damn, this girl! I didn't get a chance to respond because now my phone is ringing, loudly. I needed to change the settings where if a person calls back to back, the ringer sounds off.

"Baby, check your phone. You never know if it's an emergency." Imani is big on answering calls, I opted to just let them all go to voicemail.

"Polaski." I said out loud. Imani just shrugged.

I swiped the button to answer, and then he shouted. "Counselor!"

"What now, Polaski?" I replied sternly with the speakerphone on, kneeling in front of Imani, inching up the zipper on her boots. "My lady and I have plans today. I purposely revamped my schedule for two weeks in preparation for this day. I will be on a hiatus for the next forty-eight hours."

I was adamant about not assisting him until I heard the stress in his chords. "It's my wife. Rebecca is in labor, I can't leave her!"

I stood up from the floor, grabbing the phone while continuing the conversation on speakerphone. "Isn't the baby due around Valentine's day?"

"Yes, and life doesn't always go as planned. She's early. Her water broke, and I rushed here, leaving your father with the Davidson's. He's assertive in regard to being there on his own but let's be honest, the man has no clue what he's in for. He's not familiar with the case."

Imani didn't argue at all. But I was a little concerned about her having an issue with me handling the Davidsons' case. "You gonna be ok with me stepping in for Polaski, babe?" It wasn't that I was asking her for permission, I was more or less testing her comfort-ability.

"Bash, this is a unique situation. You heard him. He sounds sick and afraid. And from what he says, this is the end of the case." I was happy to hear her say that. If her response had been anything different, I would have made her stay home while I handled things down at the courthouse.

After we finished putting on her boots, she grabbed her phone and purse, and we headed to my car. The ride to the courthouse where Nelson and Rain were going to hash out their differences in mediation was nothing but positive for us, we laughed the whole way. A small part of me understood that the Davidsons' were more than likely having an entirely different experience.

Once we were out of the vehicle and on our journey over to the assigned courtroom, her struts along my side gave me a sense of completion. This woman had an effect on me. Imani sat in the hallway directly outside of the room where the mediation would take place. I walked smoothly and with confidence, acknowledging Judge Crawford and the reporter. I purposely avoided eye contact with Rain because deep inside I wasn't too sure about being here. It still didn't feel right. But Polaski was correct, I was the only one besides him that knew the case.

To my surprise, Nelson and my father are in a tense conversa-tion, unaware of my presence until I neared. I greeted them both and got the rundown on what's happened in the past three hours of mediation. No resolution seemed to stick as of yet. According to dad, this would more than likely have to be settled in court. My original suggestion was to avoid that route, not due to finances, but more so the time it takes and the toll it takes on an already fracturing family. Coming to terms on a positive note is usually best practice.

According to Nelson, they were on a lunch break, and he was

waiting for me to arrive before he excused himself for a smoke break. "I ain't smoked in years, but someone has to give me a cigarette, this shit too much for me."

The door slammed shut, dad proceeded with his rant, growling into my face. "Why am I now hearing that Lauren Rain is this man's wife? Do you know the hysteria on her face when I strolled in with Polaski? I only accompanied him in case the inevitable of his wife being admitted into the hospital. She's been at the doctor's all morning." He gasped rubbing his forehead. "Rain was like family to us, seeing her so distraught hurt my soul, Son. She's been crying the entire time. She's adamant in obtaining full custody of those children. Joint custody isn't in her vocabulary."

I peeked over to her and noticed that there's no one here representing her. This is somewhat of a surprise. You know what they say about a lawyer who represents themselves… *they have a fool for a client*. She does practice family law, so maybe she decided to forgo one since this is just mediation.

She's shocked to see me in the seat I assume Polaski occupied earlier. My goal is to get this over with and resume my plans with Imani. What Rain and Nelson have going could be resolved in this session if they both just put feelings aside and common sense first. I needed them to see and understand this.

Once lunch was over, and we resumed, Judge Crawford had Rain start. She reiterated the danger of having a drunk man be around the kids. As an attorney, she should understand that during mediation, what she hopes to happen should be discussed, not painting Nelson as an irresponsible drunk.

Her eyes are puffy, and her runny mascara stained her cheeks. "He can see the kids, but I want full physical custody with supervised visitation for Mr. Davidson."

"Are you fucking crazy?" Nelson slammed his palms to the

table. "Out of 365 days, you probably spend a solid one twenty with them. The rest is me. If I don't have them, then who will?"

"I can handle it, Nelson. You can still be with them during approved visitation. I'll abide by all of that."

Nelson is begging at this point jumping out of the chair, at Rain's feet. "Lauren, all I ask is for joint physical custody. We split our time 50/50. I'll pay child support. On split custody, Polaski informed me I am not required to pay child support but I will, 100% of whatever you ask whether I have them or not. Just don't make me go through this. I love the kids. Shoot, I still love you. So, so much." It's like we all stopped breathing. This sentimental moment almost felt private, and the look on Rain's face let me know that she still loved her husband too. He was just a troubled man who needed help and maybe she was tired of waiting for him to get it. As a man who's used to BS and brushing sympathetic words away, it couldn't be dismissed. Is this what kids make you do, fight? Go through the wringer because you love them. I admire him for putting his truth out there.

I tried breaking the ice. "Mrs. Davidson, can you at least consider what he's asking?"

"No, Mr. Bennett, I cannot. If I could, I would. My proposal is all that I'll consider. It's in the best interest of my kids."

My patience went out the window. She was being a total jerk and unnecessarily difficult about everything. I was empathetic to her reasoning in the beginning, but witnessing Nelson trying and laying everything out in the open made me irked with her.

"Allowing this to progress into a courtroom doesn't guarantee a judge will rule in your favor, Counselor. As a whole, this doesn't make sense. I've witnessed cases where a man doesn't even father a child, but due to their diligence in raising and providing for the kid, they are granted some form of custody." I placed the pen I've been fidgeting with down. "Mrs. Davidson, you're notorious in weighing out alternatives in matters you represent, why disregard the concept now?" I'm no longer the attorney coaching Nelson; instead, I wanted to talk to Rain attorney to attorney. How would she advise any other client if she weren't representing herself?

Rain was not happy with what I've just stated. "Sebastien." She pointed a finger in my direction. "I told you to stay out of it. You should not be here representing my husband. You come in here trying to be Mr. Save The Day. But I have something for all of you." She stands, "This mediation is over. I'll see you all in court. Let's see what the judge thinks once he learns how many times Mr. Davidson has been arrested for a DUI."

"This is about the kids, Mrs. Davidson." I get on my feet making one last attempt to talk some sense into her before she leaves. I know that once she leaves, we won't be able to get them back into mediation, and the chances of this being a long drawn out case are incredibly high.

"Well, guess what, Counselor? Since you seem to know your client so well, did he tell you that he's not their biological father?" Rain is now belligerent, gathering her items and trying to leave the room now that she just dropped a bomb. On a typical day, I could read in between the lines, and ninety-five percent of the time know when they are lying. The signs were unclear about the validity of her claim.

Everyone is shocked by her revelation, and the only person who has found their voice is Nelson. "The hell if I ain't their dad. Biologically means nothing." Clearly, this isn't news to him, and now I'm pissed because he never let out this vital piece of information. Especially since I asked him several times if there was anything else I needed to know. He was open enough to let me know about the tragic death of his oldest son.

"Funny, you shall say that Nelson, unfortunately, in our case, you wouldn't stand a chance." She turned to me, I'm on the opposite end. "See the problem with this situation is the parties involved. The father would fry my soon to be ex-husband in court."

"Polaski can and will take care of that. We are well equipped to take on such, but we don't want to have to do that. Mrs. Davidson, you know that per Georgia law, Mr. Davidson established paternity since you were married at the time of the twins birth and he signed the birth certificate. So to have someone else step in to establish paternity would be almost impossible to win at this point." I tried to plead once again with her legal side. She knew how these cases went. It wasn't an automatic win, but it would take some time and legal heavy hitters to have Nelson removed, and another man added. Rain knew this.

A devilish grin made its way to her lips, "We'll see, Counselor."

Something was off. I didn't like the way she was grinning and so sure that he would lose. Before either side could go any further, Judge Crawford stepped in and put an end to the mediation session dismissing us all. It was clear that we weren't going to resolve this case today. Rain was too angry, and Nelson's emotions were too raw. Add to that, the recent news that he wasn't the bio father was another issue Polaski would have to deal with. I decided once I left, no matter what, I was no longer stepping in and working on this case, it felt too close and personal. I needed to stay away for my own sanity.

The room was just about cleared out as Rain, and I stayed behind to gather our documents and folders, and Nelson stood in place, still attempting to silently plead with his wife. I would have a quick word with him about the next steps and be sure to loop Polaski in. Just when I was about to talk to Nelson, Rain interrupted with more shocking news.

"I guess I better save you both the time of finding this out in discovery since we're taking this case to a courtroom." Why did she feel the need to tell me, Polaski was getting this case back? I wanted no parts of it.

"Mrs. Davidson, you can send that information to your husband's attorney."

Rain interrupted me once again. "Mr. Bennett, the twins are yours. So who do you want me to send that information to?" She said that with hardly any emotion.

My heart sank, instantly galloping at tremendous speed. This isn't adding up. Summer and Savion were Bennett's? Not able to put anything together, I glanced at Nelson, his face transformed into one of indescribable hurt, eyes unaware of what to fix his gaze on. I get light-headed, thinking about the news that has both men in this room speechless. Damn it if I couldn't kill her. I could only think of one other time in my life that I'd ever felt so irate. That time, I, too, wanted to kill the person responsible for making me feel that way. I felt the veins throbbing my neck from my increased heart rate, fist trembling, clutching so tightly I can feel evenly clipped nails breaking my skin. The flashbacks of my time with the twins came in waves.

I toiled with the shirt over Savion's head. He's informed me of his love for sleeping shirtless, but this rainy night wouldn't suffice. What makes matters worse is the parents who have yet to see where I went. Or what I was up to with their four-year-old children in their home. Their full-on argument downstairs seems to dissipate, and so do the restless kids in front of me.

Summer is out cold, Savion was complaining about my push of him being fully clothed for bedtime. "Chief, you a special fella, you know that?" He sits up immediately against the headboard smiling. "Why is dat, Sebastien?"

I traced my finger over the smooth asymmetrical spot on his belly. It's dark brown, resembling a boot." You have what they call a cafe-au-lait patch."

"My daddy said it's a birthmark."

"And he's right." I undid my jacket, raised my shirt just enough for *him to see our identical marks in the same spot.*

"Wow! You got one like me too." I nodded at his excitement.

"I can't believe you robbed me of a life with my children? What type of evil woman are you?" I have kids. Not one but two! I've never been so in distressed.

Nelson uttered nothing the entire time as he watched the whole thing play out. Tears were the only way to account for his real emotions. He seemed helpless.

"Why?" I dropped my head, unable to stare into her eyes. "Why would you take away something that's a part of me?"

"WHY?" Sebastien dropped his head, hopeless, unable to stare into my eyes. "Why would you take away something that's a part of me?"

I didn't have an answer for him or at least one that he would like or understand.

He filled the two flutes with sweet but potent red wine before grabbing the thick packet of material I'd been analyzing for months. "How many hours have you studied for this test, this go-round?" He asked after peaking at everything.

I leaned further into the lofty loveseat. Sebastien graduated two years prior to my walk across the stage at Harvard. I ran into him after failing my bar exam, something I was embarrassed about but knew he would be vital in ensuring that I passed the second go-round.

"Maybe two hundred." I wasn't sure why he thought about the number of hours I'd already committed.

"Well, although statistics show an average of four hundred hours is needed to pass the Bar Exam, I think you're ready. I think you were ready the first time, you just let your nerves get the best of you."

I scratched my tingling scalp, wondering, "How many did you do?" I didn't want to focus on me and my test-taking skills at this time.

"Around one hundred and fifty." He's nonchalant with his answer, but I believe him. After all, this law firm office is his father's. Word has been circulating about another establishment they're opening in Downtown

Atlanta in the coming year. He's been preparing for this job since he was in high school, the test was just a formality.

"Come on Bash, do you think I'm truly ready?"

"I said so, didn't I? I have volunteered several hours per day of my time for weeks to help you prep. You're wearing me out, Rain Williams." He finishes with a smile, so I know he's joking and trying to ease my nerves.

Maybe a little something extra from him could help me out as well. I made sure to keep things non-sexual up to this point because I really needed his help, but now that I was ready, I figured one last time couldn't hurt. He attempted to stand, but I hurriedly switched positions and straddled him on the couch. "Do you have a few extra minutes?"

A lazy, yet arrogant grin shapes his face, "You want some dick, Rain?"

"I want you." I purred.

I was sure to make it clear to Sebastien that this was a one last time thing. This wasn't about love or a way for us to restart what we had. He agreed, and we made the best of our situation. The very best. If nothing else, I knew I was ending this with a positive outlook on passing my exam, and countless orgasms.

Sebastien and I decided amicably to dissolve our relationship a week after he graduated. During that time, Sebastien wasn't in a space to devote the time necessary to foster our relationship. His main priority after finishing law school was to pass the bar and make partner by thirty. I knew this because he never forgot to remind me of his goals. Even with that knowledge, I initiated the break up thinking he would fight. Fight for us. We loved each other, he never left me hanging. When my family crumbled into pieces, money got tight, or if I ever felt alone, Sebastien made a way to put me first and made me feel secure. Showed me that a man can love and give unconditionally, so why was it so easy for him to leave me? I didn't see any pain in him at all. And I didn't chase him. I stayed away, focused on school, and worked on securing a place at one of the top law firms. That is until I failed the bar and knew he was a quality resource.

I didn't think I would have to see him again, except in passing as we both became top tier lawyers in the same city. But I was sure to inform him weeks later when I got the results that I finally passed the bar exam. He didn't bring up our encounter, so neither did I. Sebastien did remind me that he was on track for his goals, and he was looking forward to seeing me in the courtroom.

On my end, I had a wonderful man named Nelson Davidson courting me at the time. Unlike Sebastien, who wanted to wait to start his family, I wanted to get started on mine as soon as possible, so when I was more established in my career, my kids would be school-age. Nelson was checking all my boxes, and already had a son from a previous relationship that he adored. He treated me to nice things, respected my hustle, and pushed me further along in my career path. His ambition matched mine. At the time, he was a ghostwriter to some of the biggest names in the entertainment and music industries. He was the reason they were credited for producing NYT bestsellers. Nelson's accomplishments pushed me and was very influential to my success. I was a young twenty-five-year-old woman who was falling for a man ten years older and very well established. He showed me what my future would be like, and I wanted all the parts of it.

Everything was smooth sailing with us until one night we were out for a romantic dinner when Nelson decided to make it official. I paused, eating a meal that I'd had at least a dozen times. This time though, it made me extremely nauseous, and I couldn't finish it. I didn't want Nelson to think that I was sick because he asked me to make it official, I was happy about that. I knew the nauseousness was more about the recent change in my life.

"Nelson, before I give you an answer, you should know that I just found out that I'm pregnant." The silence was deafening.

"Are you in a relationship I am unaware of?" That wasn't the question I expected from him.

"No! It was a fling with an ex, nothing serious at all." I now regret that I allowed Sebastien to play in between my pussy lips, pumping my core a few times before sheathing his cock. Pre-cum is a bitch. "He's not in a position where he's ready for a child. So I'm not sure what to do."

"Well, it's a good thing you decided to be my lady. It looks like we're about to have a baby." The situation became real. "You've already seen me in action as a father, and Nelson, Jr. would love to be a big brother. You're not alone in this Lauren. I'm thirty-five and ready to settle down. I got you and the baby." If I didn't believe he cared, the upcoming weeks revealed it all. A nursery decked in yellow decor became existent in the townhome he rented out for us.

A year later, we were already married and the parents of three. My finances skyrocketed as my career took off, and because we didn't have any financial woes, we purchased a home to accommodate us, Summer, Savion, and Nelly.

Since the moment I found out I was pregnant, I only had one moment of guilt about not informing Sebastien that the kids were his. But it quickly disappeared when Nelson turned out to be exactly who he said he would be.

He was that man up to the unexpected moment when we lost Nelson Davidson, Jr. Our lives have not been the same since. And now, I let my emotions get the best of me by allowing Sebastien and his family the opportunity to come into our lives and take my children. Not only did I have to worry about fighting with Nelson, but now I had to add the powerhouses that were known as Bennett & Associates into the fray. This shit is going to be a disaster and I still couldn't answer Sebastien's questions.

I left the mediation room, leaving Sebastien and Nelson to figure out shit on their own. I needed to get out of here, so I gathered my things and left. I heard Nelson calling after me, but I didn't stop.

Mia rebounded off the bench once the double doors slam shut behind me. I was already talking as I made my way to my best friend and only person in my support system right now. "I can't believe I just revealed the truth about the children's paternity. If only Nelson would have gotten his shit together none of this would have happened. He should have left it alone and accepted my terms. But no, he kept pushing."

"Wait, you told Sebastien the truth, Rain?" She's just as surprised as I am to have let it slip.

"Yes, I told Sebastien Bennett that he is the biological father of Summer and Savion." The second time admitting it out loud was a little easier.

Mia is uneasy, too, a little too unsettled for my liking. My best friend would have a lot of follow up questions, but for now, her eyes focused on something behind me. She looks like she is trying to shut me up with her look.

I turned to find a Dark mocha Pocahontas strolling my way with her face distorted. I didn't know what her reaction would be to this unfolding drama. I'm unaware of how much she knows, but it's not my concern. Before I could think any further on the situation, Sebastien finally exited the room with a sour expression.

"Imani." He looked around until he found her.

She tightened her black peacoat, hugging herself, "What's going on, Sebastien? I just heard that you're a dad? Didn't I ask you several times what the deal was with you and her?"

Sebastien didn't cry in the room, yet the well in his eyes were glossy, puffy. I can feel the love he has for this woman as he rubbed the back of her neck. Sebastien had matured, grown into a man. One who seemed to appreciate what stood in front of him. He's clearly in love. The way he held her hands, caressing them as if she let go, he'd die. He pleaded with compelling hues. "Baby I-I..." He dropped his head, eyes shut. "I messed up." His body straightened. "I should have told you everything about my past with Mrs. Davidson, but I promise you, I just found out about the kids."

Imani craned her neck. "You said to TRUST you. There isn't anything going on with you and her." She glanced at me with the evilest look.

"There isn't. We dated in law school, that's it." He made it seem so casual as if we weren't in love. It stung to hear him make our relationship sound so trivial.

"This doesn't make sense, Sebastien." She started walking away. "I just can't do this..."

He tried to stop her by pulling her into him. "Imani. Please don't leave me. I know you have questions, but I swear I didn't know. I have questions too. The only thing I can piece together is when she kept failing the bar exam and..."

"I only failed once, Sebastien." The nerve of him. "Imani, sweetie. It's not his fault. We had sex one time, years after our breakup and ended up with twins. I kept all of it from him. It's unfortunate and completely ironic that my husband sought his counsel. Nelson also had no idea about any of this. It's just one big mess." My arms shot up.

Nelson sat quietly in the room in a corner, praying. At least that's what it looks like from my angle in the hallway. Imani doesn't allow Sebastien to explain anything. "Fuck you, Sebastien. I trusted you and you played me. Congrats on the kids though, that's a beautiful thing."

Unlike me, he chased her. She couldn't even enter the elevator, he blocked the entryway, telling her she wasn't leaving. Never seeing this side of him, I'm in awe, even a little hurt. What was it about her? Why did he fight for her, and not for us?

"I'm in love with you, Imani. We can fix this."

"No! Goodbye, Mr. Bennett." The elevator door folds in his face.

He moves back into the room to retrieve his suitcase. Next, I notice his odd exit leading to the door for the stairwell instead of the elevator. He looks back to Mia and me, "Do you have any idea the shitstorm your secrets caused? How could you do this, Rain? What about the kids?"

Once again, I had no answers as I watched his back escape to the stairwell, and I crumpled to the floor in tears as Mia consoled me.

SEBASTIEN

AFTER THE BLOWUP with Imani at the courthouse a few days ago, I, unfortunately, had to relive the entire situation over as I explained it to my dad, who left the courtroom and went to pay Josh a visit, then again to my family as I looped them in. Everyone was shocked by Rain's secrecy.

Days later, I'm in my office with the DNA results enclosed in a manila folder. My parents are patiently awaiting the results in my dad's office. They respected the fact that I didn't want to be under everyone and needed to see the results for myself, by myself.

My heart speeds at an abnormal rate as I opened the folder, but a knock sounds off, interrupting me. "Come in." I wasn't ready to see the results anyway.

"Good afternoon." Nelson carefully walks in, making himself comfortable in the chair across from me. I can't lock eyes with him. Somewhere in all of this, I felt guilty. I didn't know about the kids, but I knew I once had a relationship with Rain. As soon as I found out Rain was his wife, I should have done something.

"Hey, Mr. Davidson." I sat back in my executive chair with the DNA results in my lap.

"I'm checking in on you, considering the news. I was in such disarray the other day. I couldn't wrap my head around anything."

"Nelson, you owe me nothing. Things shouldn't have made it this far. As a man, I should have brought it to your attention that I dated Rain the moment I found out she was your wife." I swiveled in my seat, landing my eyes anywhere but on his. "I'm actually in the process of viewing the results. Not sure if you care to know, but you're welcome to sit with me."

Nelson's skin once again tells on him, turning into the shade of Twizzler sticks. His knees began to shake as he fumbled with his hands. "Yeah, let's check em' out."

I decided to not read them out loud but instead placed the two papers in front of us where we both could see the results at the same time. I'm not sure about Nelson's pace when reading, but I saw the 99.9% probability of both kids being mine in less than ten seconds of landing my eyes on the document. My mouth went dry.

"Congratulations, Sebastien." He backed away from my desk. "Christmas is ten days away, let's make the best of things."

As painful as it is for me to know I missed such pivotal moments in my kid's life, I know this puts a dent in Nelson too. Causing intense pain to Nelson and the kids is a fear of mine, yet I still wanted what was fair to me, a relationship with my kids.

"Nelson, I have a question. Not once did you want to know who the biological father was?" I couldn't stop thinking about the fact that he was ok with not knowing that information. "You know what it's like to lose a kid. You never stopped to think that the father would be heartbroken to know he lost not one, but two kids because of someone else's selfishness?" I didn't mean to bring up the loss of his fifteen-year-old son who was struck by a drunk driver while crossing the street, but I wanted to make him think.

He slapped my shoulder, trying to hold on for dear life. "I fell in love with the twin's man. I questioned it but didn't want to make Rain feel guilty where she would go looking for the father. Then I lost Nelly when the kids turned two and coped through alcohol, the same shit that killed him." He sobbed hysterically.

"I'm sorry about all of this, Nelson."

He nodded, "It's all good, life is too short to dwell on things we have no control over." I don't think I could have been as optimistic as he was at the moment. But I wouldn't look a gift horse in the mouth.

Walking out of the room with Nelson at my side, I saw the objects of our discussion sitting in the reception area. Summer and Savion were both engrossed in tablets playing their individual games.

"Daddy, what took you so long?" Summer questioned Nelson making me feel little. He's been their source and example of fatherhood since day one, and it was clear that they adored him.

"Princess. I'm here now." Nelson proclaimed. He's not as enthused as he usually is. Dryly, he moved towards Savion, dapping him up.

"Sebastien." Savion sings, running towards me after his run-in with Nelson.

Naturally, I want to scoop him up and hug him to oblivion, but this would be awkward. However, these are *my* kids. "Hey, Chief. How was your day?" I feel all eyes on me during my first interaction with these two since finding out I am their father.

"Boring. We stayed in the room with 'er," his tiny fingers directed me to Ms. Litman. An older black woman who I learn normally babysits them.

"I'm sure it wasn't that bad, Chief."

Nelson strolled in our direction with Summer in hand, sporting a questioning glare on her face. "If Mr. Bennett here isn't busy today or has free time in the coming weeks, maybe I can let you three hang."

Responding seemed challenging. What was I to say? It's obvious, Summer asked about the trio coming to hang out with me. Deep inside, it's a no brainer, I want the kids this afternoon; however, the whole situation seemed fake. I felt helpless with two children who can possibly never view me as they did Nelson, which bothered the hell out of me.

Before forming an answer, my parents joined us with my mother offering a solution. "They should come to the house. I have my other granddaughter Senai, plus we're cooking a big family dinner tonight." That mother of mine couldn't help herself.

Nelson took me to the side to explain that Rain finally conceded and decided to stop fighting. He also explained that he would have the kids for the next week and that he was willing to allow them the day with my family if he could join as well. Nelson didn't feel comfortable with them spending the day alone without permission from Rain. He even decided to let them ride to the house with me.

By the time we exited out of the building, the kids were secure in the backseat of my Coupe, planning their evening as if they've known me their whole life. The unease of the situation subsided over time. Instead of harping over the past, I would refocus, channel my energy into the present, allow God to order my steps. As for Rain, I couldn't pinpoint how to handle her. All I knew was she would never toil with me as she had with Nelson, and today I'd start planning and executing. For now, I could only thank God again that Nelson was who he was. Because of him, I could start getting to know Savion and Summer.

PILLOW AFTER PILLOW was thrown my way. "Damn, girl, these pillows are soaked." Ri isn't the most sensitive, yet she seems to forget it's a little over a year since we had to play counselor, police, and detective in her crisis with Benji.

"You better stop all that, you ugly as hell when you cry." That made me laugh, this felt like the first time in forever since I've heard that sound come out of my mouth. "Haha, hell, I'm serious. I wouldn't dare let a man see me if I was you." She reclined propping one leg over the other. Making herself comfortable in my beautifully accented chair. It's been a long, challenging week in my luxury apartment. Every room held a theme, mentally stimulating enough to have you in a zone. This was done purposely as a way to entertain others, and give me an escape from reality. Too bad it failed its mission because the reality was dead center in each and every one of my thoughts. I missed being with Mr. Bennett. Let's not talk about the lack of food consumption or how I'm running off of five hours of sleep for the week.

Sebastien called every hour on the hour for the first few days. Now, it's only three times a day. Apologies came in many forms from him; flowers, gift cards, text, voicemails, and a personal masseuse. One night he popped up and sat on the porch for hours in the cold. As pitiful as it was, I found comfort in it. I snuggled on the other side of the door while he poured his heart out, bellowing for forgiveness. At first, I thought he was insane, talking to nobody, until he said, "I'm not crazy, Imani. I know you're sitting on the other side listening. I peeped your silhouette before lying on this frigid porch." I was amazed that he knew that, but wouldn't be a fool to his game. "You know how much I admire and look up to my parents. And I remember you mentioning how you hope one day, you can have what they've been able to build. And how much they remind you of your own parents. Well, those two haven't always seen sunny days. The rain was necessary to water the seeds, Imani. After tonight, I won't overwhelm you, but I'm not backing down either. I love you."

Reminiscing about that night had me doing that ugly cry all over again. Almost immediately, Riana is at my side with a different type of sentiment. "Shhh, it's gonna be ok. I promise. Let me grab something to calm your nerves."

Was she right? Boy did I hope it was true. How could that one day change the course of my future?

Returning from the restroom, I noticed a beautiful, well-dressed, full-figured woman sitting in the seat Sebastien left me in. Paying no attention to her, I returned to my phone as I took another seat nearby. The bickering could be heard on the other side of the entrance before and after Sebastien's dad stormed out. Mr. Bennett comes out unaware of his surroundings, cursing underneath his breath, and more pissed off than I've ever seen his son. He disappeared at the end of the hall, not bothering to return.

Mia is the name the woman gave me, asking how long meditation takes. I admitted to her that I had no idea and was waiting for it to be over myself. We joked about the current gossip from blogs until Mrs. Davidson stormed out with all the confidence in the world in her Fendi pantsuit and life altering information.

"You want me to take him out?" Ri jumped to her toes,

bouncing around as if she's throwing jabs. "He is not the only one with a mean ass left hook."

I sputtered, pausing on drinking the tea in my hand. "Wait, what?" I get where this is going, but I gotta be sure.

"I know of ways we can have his body strategically placed in different parts of the city without fingerprints or dental records. Just give me the word." Riana said that all with a wide grin on her face. Although I knew she was joking, I wouldn't put it past her to have Shooter make someone disappear if she felt that they hurt someone she loved.

She used that same grin to get me out of the house later that evening, for New Year's Eve.

According to the blogs and other social profiles, many were bringing in 2019 at local kickbacks, clubs with stars, or church. I ended up at the hottest club in ATL that occupied a three-story building. Each floor played a different type of genre with too many big names in attendance to name. But I'm still super uneasy. We were given VIP treatment since both Riana and Chelsea were with me. The shots I was throwing back didn't help perk me up and seeing Sebastien several times tonight made it worse. I had no idea he would be here. His attempts to communicate with me failed until Shooter set me up into listening to a dilemma he claimed to have with Lexi. It was all a ruse to allow Bastien to enter our area and stand at his side.

The DJ summoned Shooter to the opposite side of the gigantic club. "I'll leave you two for a sec, be right back." Shooter left the scent of Tom Ford lingering as he left the area in a rush.

I sat on the barstool, needing to give my feet a break from the strappy five-inch heels I was wearing.

"Let me help you, Ms. Barasa." Sebastien's voice is laced with a deep sensual influence. I've never heard anything like it. The magnetic pull is there as he shifts my hair off of my face. We sit there motionless, awkward. He isn't oozing the confidence I'm used to, but I can't blame him.

He's sputtering words quickly, shaking his head. "I've apologized profusely. I don't blame you for being upset. However, certain matters are out of my hands, Mani!" Have you ever heard someone's voice shake before? Tonight, he did just that. The quiver in each word, the shallow breaths in between. He's hurting, but so am I.

"That's exactly my point, Sebastien. You need to take time for you and the kids. Figure out which direction your life is headed in."

"I can do that with you in tow."

I shut it down as he tried speaking, raising both hands. "No, you can't." Tears spillover. Sorrow closed my throat. Sniffling is the most I can muster until regaining my composure. "Finding out about two kids that you fathered is a hard pill to swallow. This is bigger than me, Bash. That stunt she pulled isn't cool. And the thing is, I sensed it from day one that she would be a problem, but I kept pushing my feelings aside, giving you the benefit of the doubt."

"If you know that this is all because of her, why are you torturing me? Allow me the opportunity to at least talk to you about everything."

I slammed the shot glass I just tossed back down. By now, I've taken three to the head. "You had a nerve sprouting off how I should *trust you* and believe how different you were, yet you didn't have the decency to tell me the true nature of your relationship with her. Even after I asked you numerous times."

He choked on his words, pleading. "It's not the way it seems." I appreciate Shooter for leading us towards this secluded spot. This area is reserved for privacy. "It's been so many years since being with her that it felt unnecessary. She's the past, no baggage."

"Except there is plenty of baggage, Bash."

His shoulders collapsed. "Right." Shortly after, his head follows. I go on to explain that it's not the kids, but more so the inability to be straight forward about having sex with a woman I clearly felt uncomfortable around. He asks me to trust him until he gives me a reason not to, you see where that led us.

"I love you, but our time has come to an end, Sebastien." Detaching myself from my barstool, I observed the subtle movement when he stopped breathing. He glared into my eyes as I continued. "I can't stick around with a man I can't trust."

"Trust? Don't you think you're being a little unfair, Imani?" The tension begins to boil, his brows knit collectively, eyes squinting as he inspected me.

"Yes, trust. No matter how you slice it and dice it, you lied to me, even if it was by omission. Best of luck to you, I hope everything works out with your kids. I'm sure you'll soon find out what an awesome father you are, Bash."

He's on his feet, following close on my heels, "Imani. Just hear me out. I have a plan." I kept walking and he kept yelling after me. "Imani!"

In a knick of time, Shooter arrived with Sean, Chelsea, and Riana.

Chelsea pulled me into her, walking me a few feet away to keep me from breaking down in front of the clan. It's too late, that ugly cry is out. Ri whispers, "No! Not like this. I said to never do this in front of a guy." I can't find the humor this time. This is too painful.

They took me home, and I swear I felt like dying. This heartbreak hurt a million times more than it did when I left Patrick. But just like that time, I would be ok.

DROWNING IN GRIEF. Those are the three words I would use to describe my days following the New Years' Eve Party. Work is almost nonexistent. It's been two weeks since attempting to work from home. My dad decided to have all my cases reassigned after realizing getting me out of this funk would be harder than he perceived.

Summer and Savion have been making their way to my parent's home weekly since the reveal. Nelson and I communicate when it comes to the children. Yet, I haven't had the strength to have a conversation with their mom. I didn't want to put myself in a situation where things turned sour. Hate is a harsh word, but at times that's what I felt in regard to Lauren Rain Davidson. I prayed twice a day for healing and discernment. So far, nothing has changed.

I was sprawled out on the bed, staring at the crown molding ceiling for the umpteenth time. How did I lose a woman my soul connected with, yet I gained two irreplaceable beings? It's hard to weigh these factors. But I was happy to have my kids. Too bad, I had to lose my lady in the process. I promised Imani a family, the big one she dreamed of. Just the thought of not being the man to father her children has me already planning the death of the man who will get that opportunity. I also have to think about how she feels, knowing that she wouldn't be the first woman to bear my seeds. The whole situation was messed up.

This morning, I realized I had several new voice messages, but decided to listen to Chelsea's since hers was the latest. "Hey, stranger! Senai hasn't been the same, not hearing her favorite Uncle's voice in a while. Senai and I have had several sleepless nights. I would appreciate you giving her a call." This makes me laugh and reminded me there will be brighter days.

All of a sudden, she becomes muffled, sounding as if she's hiding something. "Who are you over there telling lies to, Chelsea?" It's *her*, Imani. I replayed the last five seconds over and over just to get a taste of the woman I'm missing so very much.

"But, yeah, she has teeth now and won't stop biting people. Give her a call at your earliest convenience. Don't wait until she starts walking." The voicemail is still going, but there's another pause before Chelsea continues. "Girl, mind your business and hurry up. Riana is waiting on us, Mani. And I wasn't talking to anybody." Then it ended, and I no longer heard Imani's voice. I only had those few seconds of her sultry voice etched into my brain.

Time heals all wounds. That saying rang through my mind before I called my family to come over. If anything, I learned through the demonic forces that tried to kill me in the past was the importance of reaching out when you no longer can hold on. Allowing someone else's guidance, ones you trust to help you come through whatever struggle you're facing.

I don't know when it happened, but it couldn't have been shortly after I called my family to come over and visit when I fell asleep. Despite having my eyes shut, I sensed it all. Pizza, wings, and something fruity was being served or already eaten from the crowd of people in my home. The background is filled with static from footsteps, music blaring from the flat screen opposite of me, and someone changing channels on the small TV in the kitchen. Sean and Benji seemed to be unable to keep my name out of their mouths. "He's gon' bounce back," Benji insisted.

"Bro, we got here at two, six hours later with all this chaotic noise his body hasn't even stirred a bit. Bash hasn't gotten any sleep. It's obvious. We need to make rounds and check-in daily while we are still in Atlanta." Sean was running his plan past Benji. It's crazy seeing my younger siblings plot on ways to see about me. Typically, it's the other way around, me caring for them, seeing about mom and dad, checking to make sure that everyone has all necessities mentally, physically, and financially. Just because we're all in good places in our lives doesn't mean we don't have struggles. I'm a clear product of this.

Slowly my eyes readjust to the confines of the living room. My neck is stiff, painfully so. Our father is the culprit behind the remote, struggling to find something to watch.

"Y'alls gots mo drama den da Maury Povich show." Uncle Check hollered into the living room. He's almost all gray now, frizzy braids seeming as if they're about to fall off his scalp.

"Come on, Unc, go eat your food so we can get out of here. Troy leaves the shop in an hour. He's doing us a favor by staying later. And don't forget Stacy will be at your place in the morning to braid you up. I know that's backward, but we get in where we fit in." Benji tries to get Unc off-topic, realizing I am up and aware of the chatter.

"Shiddd, with all these new DNA reveals, we need to be focused on monetizing all dis good shit. I could use some monies in dese pockets here." Everything Uncle Check says makes me laugh, except today, his tongue is lethal, poisonous to my veins. He makes light of a lot, including his downfalls, but I couldn't roll with it now.

Me awakening switched gears in everything. All of a sudden,

everyone seems to be more cheerful, as if they weren't just diagnosing me. Mom gave me a rundown on the kids; how Rain allowed her to take them out to the movies, and for ice cream. She gravitated to those kids once everything was proven. You couldn't tell of her absence at the beginning of their lives.

Pops took it the hardest, not showing much emotion until I explained everything I could recall from that one intimate encounter. He's happy about the twins and finds Savion to have similar characteristics as himself. "Summer is a split image of Senai and as feisty as her too." He mentioned during our chat one day.

Like old times I'm surrounded by my immediate family, no extra people. This gave me a sense of peace, knowing I can be vulnerable and more readily open to receiving constructive criticism as they love to throw my way.

Sean and I left the older gang to indulge in a friendly competition of truth or dare, as childish as this seems this was our thing. Having to gulp down shots if we chose neither. Luckily for me, I refrained from the drinks and finally had a sufficient amount of food intake.

Josh pops in, out of nowhere through my back door, he's the only one with the spare while my relatives had direct access through the code entry. He interrupted our game with his announcement. "All I'm saying is a nigga thought you were dead in this bitch. You haven't returned any of my calls or texts." We exchanged hands, embracing in a tight brotherly hug. In the workplace, you see a well put together African American man. Well-articulated, diverse, can carry any conversation regardless of the subject; Joshua Mitchell is an overall well-rounded man. But when you put him with his boys, he's Josh, that dude from the slums of Chicago, born and raised. We met in undergrad and have been boys ever since.

"Nothing keeps me down too long," I said convincingly.

The fanny pack running across his chest catches my eye, where he slips a miniature card out, handing it over.

Upon opening, I notice a $100 gift card to Starbucks, attached there's a note: *'I won't act as if this matter isn't a load to carry, but I know the man you are. You are more reliable than most, you have a vision, and you have the ability to turn all the negative into positive. Remember, there's not just you in this, but you got me. You got your brothers. You got your parents. Nothing can withstand this force we're coming with. Don't go through this alone. Let us be there for you as you've been for us.'*

There was a small quote at the bottom. I remember the day I recited it to him, encouraging him to never forget it as he made his way to the bench. *"Adversity toughens manhood, and the characteristic of the good or the great man is not that he has been exempt from the evils of life, but that he has surmounted them."* –Patrick Henry

He earned another brotherly hug. And Benji wasn't too far behind. "Y'all in love or something?"

"Shut up, Benji." I locked him into a headlock, pressing my chin on top of his silky hair.

Benji waits for Josh to leave when he decides to play the role of parenting. "Maybe this blow is what you needed to get you the healing you deserve from your childhood, Bash. Dealing with all of that, then adding two kids is fucking crazy. Don't neglect your mental health, bro."

A standing ovation is all I surmised from his talk. It's uncomfortable hearing your little brother preach truth into a situation you didn't ask his advice on.

"Ok! I'll make that a priority. Hopefully, I can start in the early part of next week."

The corner of his mouth quirked up. "That's all I ask of you, bro."

Heading inside from the back porch, I noticed everything was put away. It's clean and free of noise. My parents left a note stating they were leaving and to give them a call if I needed anything else. Uncle Check was the only lively voice coming from the front of the house inside of Benji's car. He's chatting away with the driver, talking nonsense.

Peace has settled over me by the grace of God. He sent angels to help me regroup and move forward. Settling in front of my fireplace, I see my life as shopping for a new pair of shoes. This only makes sense. I no longer fit my favorite pair that I walked through these past few years. Instead of forcing it, I'll learn to grow and love my new ones.

Lisa Stewart came highly recommended by a handful of associates I trusted, except I never thought I'd be personally using her services. This is our third meeting in the past two months, and each time feels painful. Pulling out pieces that I stored away doesn't come easily, especially in regard to the situation with my mother and uncle.

She's as observant as me. Hazels burning my orbs until an answer is formulated. "You're correct, I've always been aware of my Uncle's mishandling of my mother. But the day Tavious divulged Benji's paternity is also the day I learned and understood that Uncle Stan had more than just assaulted my mother. He raped her."

Mrs. Stewart's thin eyebrows spiked up. She sipped out of a

steaming white mug. "You're saying what you initially forgave your Uncle for hurts all over again since learning it was more serious than you knew."

"Yes, this is all new to me. I'm thankful for Benji and how things turned out, but hearing what I witnessed was deeper than what the visual eye perceived tore something in me. I wanted to kill my Uncle all over again." Pushing myself off the lounge chair, I walked towards her window, breaking eye contact. "The dreams came back that very night, reminding me of how I failed her. I could have possibly prevented it, but I had our neighbor stop at the local donut shop, something she allowed me to do on Fridays."

"Then, Benji would not be here. Your parent's revealed to you all about the trouble in the marriage before this moment. How Benji came into play saved them in a sense."

I nodded while turning into her direction. "As a grown man, my views are different, and it still baffles me sometimes on how they swept it under the rug as if nothing happened. Like it's all ok. Its not until my current situation with Imani did I realize that we all have our path and ways of handling situations. I try not to judge and allow everyone to walk through their relationship as they feel they should. It's not my business how they did it, but I'm grateful they worked through it. Benji did have a healthy, loving relation-ship with Uncle Stan." I chuckled at the thought. "Now I'm in a weird place dealing with two kids, and I'm still trying to get a grip on how to adjust and be sure the kids are as happy as they were before I arrived into their life."

She's behind her desk, pointing for me to have a seat. "You have grown since our last session. You need to acknowledge that everyone is set on their own path, and though yours may have changed some or is not what you had in mind, it's still yours. You can't control the world, that's not your place. This is great, Mr.

Bennett." She clasped her fingers. "How's the adjustment coming along with Summer and Savion?"

"When Rain isn't cutting up, things are fine. It bothers her for me to reach out to Nelson instead of her for our kids. I only do this to keep the utmost respect for her. I don't trust a thing she says. She threatens me all the time, but she doesn't want problems, so her threats are empty."

She crossed her arms, "You don't think you will have to work on that sooner rather than later?"

"Of course. I plan on speaking to Rain to establish a median where we're both happy in co-parenting." What should have been a quiet sigh came out rough. "I feel slighted by this whole situation. She took my rights away before they could breath. How are those kids supposed to accept me? What if that never comes?" The kids are almost five. I'm well aware this period of adjusting wouldn't hurt them as bad as I make it seem, but I see the love they have for Nelson and what he reciprocates. He doesn't deserve this pain either. I'm assessing everything.

"Alright." She moved towards the door. "Is it ok for us to let Lauren inside now?" I shrugged, accepting the fact I agreed to let her come for the last thirty minutes of the session. Dr. Stewart suggested this set up for us to move on and further a positive relationship.

Rain walks in, greeting both of us. She gets a simple *sup* out of me. She's parallel on the other couch, answering a few opening questions. Even volunteers to express how we ended up here. "Be thankful I allowed you to run free and live without baggage. You had nothing to slow you up, Bastien!" She hits her chest.

"Fuck you mean baggage?" She took me over the edge. I hadn't cursed this much in years. "They aren't materialistic things, they're my kids. A piece of me, Rain!" She lost her tongue.

"You weren't even gonna tell me. It took having your back against the wall when you realized shit wasn't going your way."

"I was."

"When Rain?" I moved in closer. "You confronted me about representing David. You didn't inform me of the simple fact that this man I am talking to frequently has fallen for two kids that are mine! You gave a complete stranger my fucking rights. I've never been so humiliated in my entire life. I don't know what they were like as babies when they first walked, talked, ate. Nothing. You took that from me." The rant continued. I could go on forever on how much I missed over the last five years. Rain tried cutting in, but I shut her down. She had no words before, and I could care less to hear it now. "No need to worry about me taking care of mine because I've felt enough pain for a lifetime. Which is why I guarantee you those kids will be fine. I won't allow another second to pass by without being the best I can be and loving them. For that, I will continue my counseling sessions, but for you, I have nothing else to say. I will continue my communication through Nelson." Rain's frown deepened, tears trickling slowly. Mrs. Stewart seemed affected as well, but I didn't care. This is our reality.

We were approaching our thirty minute mark, so I tried dismissing myself, pulling my sweater off the rack. Involuntarily I found myself ranting in the process. "You had this man drinking and being reckless around my fucking kids. You two were fighting in front of my children. I would have never allowed my kids to see me so deranged. Truthfully, you weren't such a great example yourself, Rain."

She can't take it anymore. Her bedazzled wrist swings into me. She tried hugging me, apologizing. "We can fix this. I am so sorry, Sebastien, I swear I can change. This wasn't supposed to end in this way."

I looked down into her eyes. "It's just the beginning, Mrs.

Davidson. You know what did end, though? Imani and I. Taking on this case has ruined one of the best things that has ever happened to me. You're untimely bullshit fucked all of this up. Guess who has to fix it? *ME!*" I punched my chest.

She snatched my arm when I tried to leave out the door. "You are more worried about a bitch than ways to keep your kids happy."

"Bitch?" I tilted my head back. "No one has shown more animalistic characteristics than you, Rain." She strikes my cheek lazily, attempting a soft blow. It's apparent she's forgotten the intense training I have in defense, which is how I blocked the right hand she threw to my abdomen.

"Mrs. Davidson, you have to leave. Violence isn't the way to solve any of your problems. This is toxic." Mrs. Stewart straightens her pencil skirt.

"Mrs. Stewart, I'll call tomorrow to schedule my next appointment." I shook her hand before looking over to Rain, who was picking up her purse to depart. I tried to exit quickly to prevent myself from catching a case, except I have a few more words. "The fight you put up with Nelson won't work over here. I *will* find a way to be a part of my children's lives legally."

SEBASTIEN

8 Months Later

"SEBASTIEN." A voice whispered. I glanced in the back of the truck at the little person who appeared bulkier in his full body armor.

"What's up, Chief?"

Savion had a size-able coniferous tree in between his feet, attempting to secure it for the ride home. We were starting a tradition in picking out and decorating a tree for my home.

"I'm thirsty." He whined.

It's been almost a full year since I've gotten the DNA results and have been working closely with Nelson on the arrangement. Adapting to the kids wasn't the easiest. I quickly learned they only liked the word *yes*. A *no* earned them tears and *maybe's* eventually turned into a yes. By our third week into this new arrangement, I nipped it in the bud. Never did I want to seem like the mean one, but structure is essential. More than anything, the fact that I established a healthy, respectful relationship with them since the beginning has made the transition easier for us all. We were still learning and growing together.

I placed Summer's limp body into the back seat, securing the seatbelt over her lap. Never did I appreciate the leather seats and amenities of this 1500 Denali Truck until having children. So far, drinks have been wasted, fingerprints smeared onto the tv, and window screen and wrappers of all sorts scatter the flooring of the vehicle. Every week there's evidence left in the back seat of my kids, who have clearly taken over and now run things. From the moment I purchased this truck eight months ago, I was at the car wash at least once a week trying to get it cleaned in preparation for picking them up or getting it cleaned after dropping them off.

"Chief, we'll get you something to drink when we get to the house. In the meantime, come catch you some Zzz's like your sister. We'll need plenty of energy to put the Christmas tree up and decorate it tonight." What I learned over time is that Summer didn't fight sleep, and Savion had FOMO. Fear of missing out. He only went to sleep when he was dead tired and nearly delirious.

Nelson and Rain had the kids for Thanksgiving Day & Black Friday, and I picked them up this morning. I would keep them until I dropped them off at school a week from now after their break. What made it more exciting is knowing they would be with me on Christmas; My *very* first Christmas with *my* kids at *my* house with *my* entire family. And the tree was the start of our traditions.

This year hasn't been easy, but Nelson and I had become like brothers keeping the system working without me even needing to communicate with Rain. He decided to get help, and I was proud of him for that, although I was a little confused as to why he took that troublemaker back. But our choices have collectively made our arrangement work, and the kids seemed to be dealing with everything healthily.

An hour later, I realized I needed to stop by the office for some paperwork, so we hit a quick detour. I didn't plan on doing a lot of work since the kids would be with me, but there was one important document I needed to get notarized by Monday morning, so I needed to pick it up tonight. We pulled up to a spot right in front of the building, and I had security keep an eye on my vehicle since

I was just running up and coming right back. *At least that was the plan.*

I toted sleeping beauty on one hip while Savion walked next to me, holding my hand and asking tons of questions. This required some serious manpower. We took the elevator to my floor. The dinging sound announcing the arrival to our destination woke Summer up. Meanwhile, Savion dashed to my office, hoping to get to the TV and tablet I had set up for them in the corner. Once I got them settled, I made my way to my desk and decided to order food and answer a few emails since they both looked comfortable and not in a rush to leave.

At the desk, I was typing a quick email, with every few minutes glancing at the two kids who are making my office into their own. Savion occupied the mounted tv over the fireplace, which has box-like figures running all over the screen. I learned all about this game, Roblox, after it repeatedly appeared on my bank statement. He obviously was making purchases in the game when using my devices.

Summer used my dad's lounge chair for her personal comfort as she looked to be dozing off again. Months ago, I noticed her wheeling it from his office into mine, but I didn't stop her. The relationship between my dad and Summer was special to watch. Summer and Savion had other grandmother's, but not a grandfather. Summer had my dad wrapped around her cute little pecan colored finger, and whatever the little girl wanted from him, she got it. Hence the reason that thousand dollar chair has not been moved from my office.

"Cupcake put your socks back on. It's a bit chilly in here." I scolded the girl with the gigantic ponytail on top of her head before she could fall asleep. I could now see that she's the spitting image of me, more so than her twin brother. Funny how you turn a blind eye to something clearly in your face.

"But, Poppa." She definitely knew how to finesse me. She's been more receptive to the significant change that's been imposed on their lives.

One of the most memorable nights with them was back in May when they requested a meeting with me. What in the world could they know about running a meeting? It took a measly second to find out. I was intrigued by the entire thing. We found our small party of three seated at my table in the formal dining room. The table that was only in use when I hosted the family at my home. I was giggling as they truly prepared and used the time to pretend like it was a real meeting. But what I ended up learning changed me forever.

"Dad had a long talk with us. He says you are our dad too. He says we have to listen and be good to you like we are with him." Summer was very matter of fact. I'm stunned at her straightforward and candid way. I listened intently, observing the body language from these two little human beings. The hard work I put into law school seemed to be just for this very moment. My plans to thoroughly discuss this matter would come after I conjured something, but Nelson beat me to the punch. I sorta appreciated this.

I nodded, smiling from ear to ear. "Nelson said all of that?" I quizzically laugh.

"Yes. Dad said God loved us so much that he gave us two daddies." Savion piggybacked off of his sister, sounding so confident in Nelson's word. I now remember his fears and how important it is to not see his parents fighting. I reassure them nothing will change as far as the love between those two, and I'm just another human being that they have to count on. Or how I, too, am glad to play an integral part in their lives. Summer asked if it was ok for her to call me Poppa, and Savion still called me Sebastien. I didn't want to push him into calling me something different, but I would be lying if I said my heart didn't flutter each time I heard Summer say, Poppa. And the fact that I knew she was referring to me and not Nelson.

"Only a few more minutes, and we're outta here, Cupcake." I watched her finally concede and put her socks on before making her way to my lap while I worked.

"Ok, Poppa. What's a Puppet-ish-ion of a name change?" She's an inquisitive one.

"If you can't pronounce the word, then there's no reason to inquire about it, Cupcake?" I sang while rocking her on my lap and printing out paperwork. After dealing with the two, I became the multitasking king in this firm.

"Awww, Poppa." She props her elbows on the desk, holding her chin. "I can read. I am five years old. But I don't know what sound the last letters make." The average joe would think I was being a dick to my kids, but it's the total opposite. I challenged them, making games out of anything regarding reading and spelling. Since Nelson did a great job starting them on their love of words, I would build upon it. Except this time, I exited out of the screen I was in and into something a little more kid-friendly, preparing to shut down soon so we could head out.

"T-I-O-N is SHUN. Peti-SHUN." I could at least help her out with the one word she was struggling with.

"What's a petition?"

"Why do you ask so many questions?" I stared her down, not folding. She gets pretty intimidated when I give her a stern look, but this doesn't seem to faze this cocky lil' girl."

"Con-Contempt for court." She struggled to get one of the legal words I taught them right.

"It's contempt OF court."

Her contagious smile lights up the room. "Yeah, that word. You say it means to not follow orders." She's ten toes down off my lap and prancing around. "You are in contempt of ME. We promised to talk about anything and any questions I have, I can ask you." Yeah, she's a brain whiz. I learned early on she doesn't forget anything, and her confidence level is through the roof. A straight shooter.

"You're right, but in the line of work I'm in, it doesn't permit me to give too many answers or tell you everything. At least, not right now."

"You taught me that permit means to allow. Your job won't allow you to tell me things? That's not nice." With folded arms, she stormed back over to her lounge chair, pushing Savion off.

"Get outta my chair, Savion."

"Summer! Move." Savion pushed her back off, and they started to tussle.

"Both of you sit down now!" The fear in their eyes said it all. They didn't like it when I had to raise my voice, and neither did I. My expression softened. "You don't go stomping your feet and pushing your brother when you can't get your way, Summer."

I glanced over at a shirtless Savion. This boy hated being fully clothed. "First of all, you need to get your top back on. Second, I better not see you shove any girl in that manner again, let alone your sister. Got it?"

"Yes, sir."

It took another hour to finish all my assignments. To my surprise, once it was time to leave, my office was spotless. The kids cleaned up after themselves and made it look brand spanking new. I led them into the break room, where I placed the apple juice, a box of pizza, cinnamon rolls, and wings that were delivered.

They hadn't spoken a peep since their crazy behavior, which slightly bothered me. Since I was still fairly new to parenthood, I still had this feeling of wanting to always make the kids happy and not have them upset with me. Daily I strived to see them smile, even if it's through a simple FaceTime call. In such a short period of time, my love for them grew to a level that I can't even begin to describe. No matter how tough I thought I would be, every day, a barrier inside broke in me, making me softer, allowing these kids to steal another piece of my heart.

The same week we found out they were mine, my dad took me to the side and had one of the most unforgettable conversations ever with me. *"Being a dad, one who wants to really be involved with their kids brings on a different kind of sentiment, Bash. There's a break-down of your inner emotions, vulnerability, and realizing the world doesn't revolve around you is what kids do. They even make you feel young again, pushing you to thrive in the moment. God blessed you, son. The circumstances aren't right, but he placed them in your life when he saw fit. Keep the counseling sessions going, pursue God as you've been in church and prayer. Allow yourself to grow mentally and spiritually, and you will automatically grow as a father. Summer and Savion need you. No matter what you think they have, they are yours. God gave them to you, he trusted you out of all people with these precious lives. Don't let them down."*

Spinning out of control fluidly as if gravity no longer existed is the best explanation to describe his movements. Levitating, in a manner that seemed surreal, his shoulder hit the wooden floor, back rounding out smoothly, letting his body transform into a robotic figure. Then the funky beat picks up having every able person in an uproar. My dad was the leader of the fan club and was hyping Jamaal up to continue his breakdance. It's no wonder he's the life of the party. Known as one of the top wide receivers in the league, who plays alongside his best friend, Benji. One who many would never know of his popping and locking skills. Luckily for myself, I witnessed him growing up with my little brother and finding in my heart to look out for him when possible.

Regardless of the festivities taking place for Benji's birthday at my parent's home, matters in my life hadn't eased up. "What kind of concoction you got going on here?" Nelson's silver wedding band couldn't be missed, reminding me of the tension still between Rain and me.

Shuffling away from the obnoxious crowd, we make it to the heart of the home where there are endless assortments of pillows scattered across the loveseat and sofa. Nelson preoccupies one with a slight snare.

"Oh, this?" I question taking a small sip of the brown mixture. "The Bash House Special. It's my typical Henny, coke, and a few other ingredients I won't dare disclose." Communication between the two of us increased dramatically, considering I didn't communicate with Rain. Never would I let the kids in on the discourse I felt for their mother, but Rain felt it, and I kind of didn't care. Every day there's a text message of apologies. She went as far as delivering coffee to my office twice a week through a service provided at a local coffee shop across from my job. Nelson had no clue of these gestures.

Meanwhile, the pain of missing out on the kid's life simmered day after day. The bond between the kids and I strengthened daily. They took to the idea of calling Benji and Sean Uncle. To this day, I'm unsure how this came about, but they hung around my parents a lot, which is the only way I saw this to be possible.

"You're doing great with the kids, you know?" Nelson nodded, waiting for me to acknowledge his statement.

"Yeah, you think?" I can't help giving him a once-over as I notice the holiday button-up sweater that's paired with green suede loafers. I chuckled. "Savion mentioned your lack of taste in the fashion department."

He quickly resembles an apple, darkening in color with every chuckle. "What?" He guffaws. "Nah, I still got it. I've always been a bad dresser."

"Bad in a good or bad way?" I laughed some more before adding, "I like the ensemble you are rocking, but let the kids tell it, loafers are for women, and the color pink makes a man less than what he stands for." I teased, bringing up exactly the joke Savion once criticized me on.

"Aw man," he shot up from the couch. "Our kids are a tough crowd."

"Who are you telling, man?" I loved that he's always said *our* kids from the moment those test results came back. Nelson was really a blessing, and our situation could have been very different if he was a different man.

"Daddy!" We both turned to Summer. This could have been awkward if I didn't know that she was talking to Nelson. She gives him a hug, then comes over to sit in my lap. "Poppa, Cam, and Savion keep hitting me." She's dramatic, barely able to catch her breath.

Cam barely makes it around the corner before falling at the foot of the stairwell. Sean blurted, "Camden, we hit on girls now?" Sean being a disciplinary, is a joke, but not to the kids. Cam is shaken, barely able to look up at his stepfather. "Get up, Cam. Not only are you going to apologize, but you won't be seeing the game systems for the week." Sean was extremely helpful to me during this transition as he also has a co-parenting situation going on with Cam's biological father, Randall. They had a rough start when Sean and Chelsea got married, but now they let bygones be bygones, and Cam knew he had two dads who didn't play.

"But Sean. I'm sorry." He pointed aggressively at Summer. "She threw hot chocolate all over me. Look." The stain is visible, splattered on his red shirt. I see Savion hiding behind the door, I don't call him out. I'll deal with him later.

"Apologize, Cam."

"Are you gonna tell mom?"

"Should I?"

"No, sir." He pushed off the floor, walked into the living room pulling Summer off my lap giving her a hug and apologized. He's different from other kids, most would have provided a snarky apology from afar, but he was sincere. Chelsea raised this boy with the utmost respect, and it showed. I even admired Sean being firm, not allowing something as little as this go by. I could take notes.

"Sorry, Summer."

"It's ok. Can we play hide and seek now?" She doesn't wait for a reply. They scattered, leaving no trace of their existence.

"Y'all in here planning to get married or somethin'?" Sean sits with me and Nelson. "I mean y'all raising kids and shit, I ain't heard a word on Rain." It's been a long while since we've bumped heads. If Nelson hadn't brushed the situation off as smooth as he did, Sean and I probably would have been fighting.

"If that's what it takes to keep the kids happy." Nelson said that with a serious face.

Sean and I glanced at another before locating Nelson, who laughed his comment off. "Bruh, it's a joke. But I'm serious about getting along." We join in on the laughter, and start to explain how it can be tricky co-parenting, but if everyone acts like adults, it's a beautiful thing.

Nelson fumbles into a knapsack lying in the corner. He retrieves a folder where I later learn contained papers that would help me be able to move forward legally with the kids. "I appreciate that, Mr. Davidson."

"Rain already knows you're taking the kids to school on

Monday and she'll pick them up after. Hit me if you need anything." With that, Nelson is kissing the kids goodbye and out the door.

Sean and I decided to join the crowd of bodies, chatting away in the family room. A very pregnant Riana vacuums her plate while laying her head on Chelsea's lap. They made themselves at home on the loveseat since both of their bodies consumed it. Chelsea looks to be laughing at her cellphone, apparently she's on a video chat. "Tell her to come get her man and stop playing." Riana can be heard a mile away, screaming at the receiver.

"Stop, Ri." Chelsea smacks her hand away from the phone.

"Oh my God, is that his daughter?" I can't help but be nosy, realizing Imani is the one on the other end. I shouldn't have been able to hear them, but I did.

"Umm yeah," Chelsea tried for a whisper, noticing she's caught by me.

"She's so beautiful. Looks just like her father."

"Yeah, and that father has been a sick puppy ever since you left. Give him a chance to explain where he's at in his life now." I appreciated the plug from Riana, but I never stood around to hear the rest of the conversation. I still thought about Imani, but after so many months of no communication, I was beginning to accept that there was a strong possibility that a future between us was not likely.

Her body leaned into mine, grabbing Summer. The twins were sleeping, which is the only reason I was coming inside while Nelson was away on a book tour. I carried Savion to his bedroom, putting him down since they already had on their pajamas.

"Sebastien, you mind giving me a second?" I smell the Bailey's on her breath, wondering if her asking to speak to me was liquid courage.

"No." I stood in the doorway, refusing to step foot in the trap she's set up. She clutches the sash around her robe, feverishly rubbing her foot over the other.

"You have to understand my position at the time, Sebastien." She calls to my back as I continued to the front door. "You made your intentions clear. A family was not in your plans, and you didn't fight for us. You let me walk away without a second thought."

"You're right. That was my position, but that was when I knew that there was no possibility of me being a father. Either way, it was not your job to make that decision for me." This isn't what I needed. At this point, her explanation was unnecessary and didn't matter. I continued to the door, hoping to have a clean getaway before she could say anything else.

"Don't you walk away from me. You come into my home, barely speak, then walk out on me. I need to know how we will co-parent."

"It's going fine, minus this fight you're looking for." I wasn't going to take the bait. She was drinking and trying to start something.

"You can't discuss everything with Nelson. He's not their father."

I cracked up. Is Rain kidding me? He's been their father since the day they were born, hell before that. Since the day he found out she was pregnant. "Yet he's been the most upstanding citizen I know. He hasn't tarnished who I am due to his selfish needs. In fact, he's spoken highly of me and yet finds time to meet me with *my* children when it's convenient for me. I've been able to uncover things that would have taken me centuries to learn through him. He never shuts me out from my children, YOU did. Damn right, he gets more respect and consideration than you. Look Rain, you've been drinking and may not be in your right mind, so I'm gonna leave before either of us say something we regret and wake up the kids. Goodnight." I didn't wait for her response. I got outta there before she could say or do something that had one of us making the paper.

I just had a wonderful time with my kids, and that's the memory I wanted to hold on to.

STEPPING off the elevator onto the 42nd-floor was like being home. Sebastien and Roland were both standing there, displaying wide smiles. Showing off all of their beautiful black man magic, and looking happy as hell to see me. Shooter leaned in towards Sebastien in an attempt at whispering, but I heard every word as if he was speaking to me.

"Santa came early for you, Mr. Bennett." Roland snatched his beanie off his head and headed into Sebastien's office.

"So it seems!" Sebastien said to no one in particular since Shooter has left from his side. I could tell that my presence surprised him, but the smirk on his face let me know that it was a pleasant surprise. I made it to him and offered him a warm, comforting hug transferring all of my positive energy into him. He had me feeling giddy, but I embraced it.

We made it in the office. Some minor changes showed how different his life was over the last year, but I couldn't focus on that for long. He stole my attention. He wanted me. It was all over his face. Sebastien would have devoured me whole if I let him, and in the back of my mind, I considered it. Our sexual tension was buzzing to the point that it was palpable. After a few months of focus, work, exercising, and dating casually, I realized the whole ordeal wasn't his fault, and that I may have overreacted. I still couldn't forget that he never told me the truth of his past with

Rain after having several opportunities to do so. Even with that knowledge, I was unsure if and how to move forward.

"Mani, I thought I needed both of you, but my man Bash took care of it." Shooter squealed, looking like a five-year-old living a carefree life. He danced while rapping his new hit song, except there's a change to the lyrics. He's celebrating his mother's child, I even hear a mention of having so much love for her. Whatever happened before I crept in was the vibe I needed to be on. I didn't have to do much to feel the abundance of love and excitement from both of the men in the room. Whatever the cause for this, I knew it all was handled by the man who always handled his business, Sebastien.

Since I was no longer needed, I stood and planned on exiting the office, but Sebastien asked for a moment of my time. That's the least I could do after almost a year of no communication with him. We said our goodbyes to Shooter, and he left the office just as the face of his beautiful daughter popped up on his phone for a Face-Time call.

"Ms. Barasa, thank you for staying. I know your time is precious, so I won't waste it." Sebastien's confidence is through the roof.

After a few quiet minutes of him seeming to contemplate what he would say next, I sensed a tinge of uncertainty returning.

I decided to put him at ease. "Sebastien, you're worth my time." I didn't need to say anything more.

"This is a nice way to start off after eleven months." And with that the ice was completely broken. He leaned off the bookshelf and made his way into my personal space. "Which is why you need to give me another chance, Imani." He rolls out a marked up calendar. January 1, 2019, has a red indicator with *lost my other half* taking up the entire square of that date.

I can't help laughing in his face. Just as I was about to tell him what I thought, he beat me to the punch.

"Yeah yeah, it's corny, but it's true." He smirked. I'm glad he knew that shit was corny, but it was sweet as hell. That's one of the things I loved about him, he didn't have trouble telling me about his heart and true feelings. "Don't even start with any of your jokes, Imani."

"But-But I can't help it." I laughed louder.

He walked further into my space and shut my laughter down in a split second. Our heads collided into each other, then he took it upon himself to settle his soft, moist lips over my mouth. He gripped my bottom lip into the confines of his mouth, taking the kiss to another level. This felt good. So good that I'm lost in a parade of lust. His woodsy scent only intensified what I've been longing for.

"I miss this," he purred into my mouth. "I miss you. All of you."

Our tongues clashed, slithering down each other's throat. A slight moan escaped my mouth. One hand gripped the bottom of my ass cheek, going for his favorite body part, making himself at home. He casually slipped the other hand inside my pants, bypassing my panties. He remembered all the ways to get me riled up. But I needed to keep my bearings for just a few more seconds. "Sebastien," I sobbed more than announced. "We should talk first."

"We are talking. In the most intimate way. I hear you singing." And damn it if I hadn't moaned my ass off with his fondling.

"How many people have you been with since me?" I slapped myself in the head, embarrassed asking such a stupid question. He wasn't short on women wanting him. I just had to ruin the moment coming off as a crazy woman. I haven't seen the man in damn near a year for god's sake, and now I was asking him where his dick has been.

"The answer is zero. I haven't been in the headspace to be intimate with anyone. I mean bustin' a nut is cool, but all the love-making and intimacy is better with the one you love. I never realized this until we became a thing."

Wide-eyed, I twisted my mouth, not knowing how to react. I can't believe a man of his status, well-traveled, knowing many women in high and low places never experienced that level of love and intimacy, until me! I mean he's thirty-two, sheesh. "Okay. I feel the same way" I nodded. "But still, you had a hell of a year, Bash. You had to have found release in some way?"

"What are you asking? Did I jack my meat, Mani?" Bash got a kick out of that.

"No, Mr. Bennett. That's not what I meant." I dropped my eyes slightly, blushing at the fact that we're this close to each other. Breathing the same air. Sharing a kiss. I was wondering what was next.

"Give me some." I was about to ask, some of what? But he leaned in and retook my lips, taking what he wanted.

"It almost feels like we haven't missed a beat. But I know that things are different. Very different." I responded once he let me up for air.

He inhaled a deep breath, resting his hands on his neat fade. "First, let me put you on. I am very involved with Summer and Savion." I'm glad to hear the news of him being a great father, but the slight pain of knowing Rain will always share a part of him doesn't sit too well with me.

"Wow, I never knew their names. Those are beautiful names."

He gives an awkward glance but takes the compliment. "I mostly deal with Nelson when it comes to the kids. Rain and I barely communicate. There are no plans for this arrangement to change. It works for us, and it works for the kids, so we want to keep it that way."

"You're telling me you haven't sat down and made peace with

her for the sake of the kids?" This shocked me. I always imagined parents needing to be civil to create a healthy foundation for the kids.

"All I'm saying is I acknowledge the situation. I go above and beyond for the twins, not because I'm expecting a pat on the back, but because I can't imagine doing anything else. They are the most important things to me. However, I don't feel compelled to build a friendship with their mother. I respect her because she's their mother. Nothing more, nothing less." Mr. Cocky, self-assertive Bennett, has entered the building and brought me up to speed.

"Duly noted."

"Can we try again, Imani? You told me to take time out to figure things out, and we're one week away from the new year. I would say I met the definition of *some time*."

"Under one condition." I posted against his desk, leaning into his profile.

His posture straightened as he slapped my ass, "Shoot."

"No more secrets. I need you to be transparent with me when I ask you something. That's the only way we'll grow in love and trust. No. More. Secrets. Mr. Bennett." For once, I felt in power, and I sorta liked it.

"No more secrets."

"You only have one shot at this. No lies, no bullshit. The minute that trust is broken, I'm out. No questions asked."

"That's all you had to say." He switched us around so that he was leaning on the desk and I was in front of him. "Speaking of one-shot, let me see how good my aim is. I'm a bit rusty from the long wait."

Sebastien proceeded to use his strength to lift me from the spot I was standing in and moved me to a table in his office, placing me down gently. My back arched backward when he pulled my jeans downward, leaving me in nothing but my hot pink cheekster underwear. I cupped his face between my hands. "You have a condom?"

He drags his mouth from mine. "I don't care to use them on you."

"What if I get pregnant?" I asked, despite knowing I'm on birth control. I wanted to see what he honestly thought about adding to his growing family.

He bucked his hips, prying my entrance open. I'm clueless to when he removed his pants, but I'm no less disappointed. His eyes narrowed half-mast, he whispered, "I'm going to give you babies, plenty of them if it's in God's will."

I can't help the juices that flooded his fullness. We rocked into each other. We've been connected before, but never like this. This is a connection, unlike before. Not that makeup sex, but I need you sex.

The next forty-five minutes were filled with a long, slow ride of absolute delight. Sebastien pleased me, teased me, and devoured me. Sebastien made me feel a sense of belonging. While cuddling like a cocoon on his humongous loveseat, I took it upon myself to pray for guidance. I was ready to forgive him and move onto the next chapter of our lives. Together.

I WONDER if Rain is aware of my presence in her children's life. I guess my reasoning for this thought was because of the pressure on my chest from the little body holding on to me for dear life and making me sweat like I was in a sauna. The new year started with us settling in well with the kids. Having been around a lot of my younger cousins, I'm fully aware of kid's openness to new people. I can appreciate them being so young because let's face it if they were adolescents, things might have not gone as smoothly as they did.

Never in a million years did I think two kids that were no bigger than a minute, could intimidate me. Both welcomed me into their fold and new normal with Sebastien as if they've known me their whole life. No one would have imagined that the hours leading to the meetup, I was a wreck. Our ride to the infamous restaurant, Dorothy Jay's, consisted of questions about how I met their father, and how I managed to grow so tall. I took no offense to this since my height has always been my gift and curse growing up. Savion complimented me a lot, Sebastien thought he was crushing on me. Meanwhile, I just politely blushed at his attempts.

"Summer, it's hot, baby."

"Sorry, Mani, but Savion isn't giving me much space."

Carefully I unwrap her legs from around me, then made my way into the restroom to empty my raging bladder. Summer can be heard puffing at her brother for consuming the majority of the California King bed. It's clear since I stepped foot into what was once a bachelor pad, that a lot of new fixtures were added. Starting with the bedroom. Even though they both now had their own separate bedrooms in his home, when they were here, it was a party of four in Sebastien's bed instead of two. Then there's the playroom that was once an office. His backyard was now kid-friendly. The pool had an added slide and lots of inflatables to keep them busy in the summer months.

During one of their weekend visits, Sebastien convinced me to join them for their man-made campfire in the backyard. An hour later, we were all inside sleeping bags counting stars. Bash didn't give me a transitional period. He trusted me fully with his kids from the moment we decided to restart our relationship. And I made sure that I didn't disappoint them. Being around the kids changed me. I found myself being able to stay calm in situations where I should have jumped off a cliff. Having them around was helping in both my personal and professional life.

When she barged in on me, summer's wild mane covered the majority of her face, just as I finished and was flushing the toilet. She liked the fact that we both had a lot of hair and would often ask me to put hers in a sloppy bun like I would sometimes wear mine. One of the things that we needed to work on was that Summer has no regard for crowding my personal space. If she wasn't such an adorable little human being that I cared for, it would probably irritate me. But it didn't. Summer needed attention, and I was there to give it to her. From observation and hearing her talk about her day, it's clear that she lacks quality time with her mother. We all know Rain works long hours and can be limited in her time with the kids. But they handle it differently. Savion is more of a loner, and the only person he seems to be bothered by is his sister not spending time with him. But Summer, she yearns for that maternal connection. Although it's technically not my job to fill that role, it comes naturally to me to nurture her as best as I can when she is in my presence.

Before we make it back to bed, instead of asking me to read her a book, she asks me to tell her a story to help her get back to sleep. Most of her highly creative story is centered around Nelson, her very own superhero. I couldn't blame her. Recently, I've gotten to know him better and deeply admired him. In no time at all, we were back to sleep.

Just a few short hours later, it was time to get up for another crazy day. Sebastien normally handled Savion in the mornings, and Summer and I made it work. After washing my face, brushing my teeth, and helping Summer through her morning routine, we entered the kitchen, joining Savion and Sebastien. The twins' favorite breakfast of maple bacon oatmeal was already set up and ready to be devoured. Yuck!

I was quiet throughout breakfast as the kids and Sebastien tried to incorporate me into their morning chatter. Sebastien finally took me to the side after he loaded them up in the truck, preparing to take them to school. I told him all was well, I was just a little stressed about an important meeting I had scheduled for the day. He told me I would knock it out of the park as I always did. What he didn't know was that the important meeting was with his baby mama, Rain.

I made my way to meet Rain after she sent me several DM's requesting my time. Riana advised me to decline, but, of course, I did the opposite. Sebastien knew that she'd messaged me, but I never confirmed if I would take the meeting or not. I felt a little guilty about it since I got on him about being truthful and transparent. But I needed to see where this would go before looping him in.

My chest rises with every step hitting the cemented track. I was already a mile into my three-mile run, and there was still no evidence of Rain showing up for a meeting she requested. I agreed to the recreation center because I didn't want to interrupt my morning routine for something that very well may have been a complete waste of time. I needed to continue sculpting my abs, so I worked harder in the winter to relax in the summer. Even the bubble butt that people raved about needed slight work, even though it's mostly genetics from my father's side. The running, hill climb, abdominal work, and lack of sweets does the rest of the work to keep me intact.

Eventually, quick steps creep up behind me, announcing Rain's arrival. She's in great shape, never slowing down to talk to me until she's two laps in. It makes sense why she's curvy in all the right places. "Perfect weather for running, huh?" Rain is unphased at my faceless reaction.

"Uh, I guess." I gripped my wrist over my head to walk off the cramp, making its way up my chest.

Her scarf is halfway off, she seemed to take extra time fixing it to avoid eye contact while talking to me. "I'm not here to be a bitch. I owe you an apology."

I'm flabbergasted by her announcement. "Apology, for what?" I need to understand her, so I moved over to the gray bleachers and took a seat in an area where we could talk privately.

"Sebastien doesn't talk to me besides the occasional simple text message of him picking or dropping Summer and Savion off. Let alone tell me any of his personal business." This is refreshing to know he's been open and honest in the communication he shares with her. I definitely would be coming clean with him about my time with her. I don't quite trust this pretty face in front of me. Still, I'm woman enough to know the importance of proper communication between all parties who will play a role in rearing Summer and Savion.

Rain slips her windbreaker off using the sleeve to wipe perspiration from her forehead. "Ms. Litmam mentioned to me several times, there is a woman playing mommy to my kids. I knew it was you even though I had no idea you and Sebastien had gotten back together." I don't know if she was expecting a response, but I decided I would mostly listen unless she asked a specific question. She continued. "Before stumbling in on you and Sebastien together, I knew of you from following you on Instagram. I'm big on seeing and supporting successful black women take over platforms in positive ways. Your stories are always engaging, which is why I'm a fan. The way you interviewed our favorite celebrities and got them to speak on things others can't bring out was nothing short of amazing. Then to take that expertise and turn it into what you have in the PR world. I have nothing but respect for you. And my daughter has yet another strong, successful black woman to look up to."

I'm in awe. I knew Rain followed me on social media, but to know her real thoughts about me as a businesswoman was touching. I was slowly thawing out to her and making myself more open to receiving what she intended to tell me.

"As hard as this is to admit to you Imani, I do have a fear that Summer will become closer to you because she talks about you nonstop. And that fear is rooted in my own estranged relationship with my mother. I know everyone thinks I work too much, and that I don't spend a lot of time with the kids. But there are certain things I do with them that are specifically *mine*. It bothered me that Sebastien didn't let me know that you were back in his life and would be with my kids because I didn't want you stepping in for things that were *mine*."

Initially, asking God to lead me felt stupid. As if I didn't believe Him enough to show me who He is. Then just as clear as day, I heard Yeay in my brain, "It's a shame you block the blessings God has sent your way. Don't forget your past isn't easy, go lucky, either darling." Then... God answered my prayers. I've been praying for clarity. Was I in over my head with a man with two kids who may never truly accept me? Can I trust the man who acts as if Rain meant nothing to him? I received all of my answers.

Smelling the rain in the air reactivated my senses and motivated me to finish this talk and get out of here. "Thanks for the transparency, Lauren Rain. I know this wasn't easy, but your kids are in good hands. Sebastien would never let anyone around that could hurt them." I couldn't stress that enough to her. "But I do have one question, the names? I love them. How'd you decide?"

"Actually, that's my husbands doing." The look on my face told it all. She proceeded to tell me the long drawn out story about how she and Nelson met, why she didn't tell Sebastien about the kids, and how she's now working on her marriage. She even told me the heart-wrenching story of them losing their eldest son. Again, I was thankful for more insight. Although I may not have agreed with her actions, hearing the story in full from her perspective provided context. "Yeah, girl, we've been doing counseling every other weekend when the kids are gone. I'm learning to work out my personal issues, how to be a better mother, wife, and individual to those I love. My counselor constantly mentions the importance of accepting my reality and dealing with it. I'm a work in progress!" Big droplets expel from her eyes and the sky. This is our cue to go and a perfect end to the confusion and perfect start to clarity. Sebastien had Nelson to communicate with about the kids, but maybe Rain and I could also be allies. I wasn't trying to welcome her into my sister circle, but she was someone who wasn't going anywhere soon.

Ironically, we were parked next to each other, so I noticed the constant ringing of her phone as I'm strapping on the seatbelt in my Volkswagen Passat. She yelled out, "I know you probably thought this was gonna end with you kicking my ass. But I love my face and don't have any plans of scrapping with you. Hell, have you seen you?" I laughed it off, waving my hand at her. Before we pulled off, Rain received a call from Nelson. He said something about Sebastien agreeing to take the kids for an extra night so that they could have a date night. One thing I learned since I've been in the picture is that no one cock blocks more than children, so I'm sure that without those two, Rain and Nelson will have a delightful evening. I just needed to find a way for me and my man to have just as much fun with our additional party of two.

SEBASTIEN
EPILOGUE

I WAS SIPPING on handcrafted cocktails, admiring the view in front of me. I said a quiet prayer thanking God for growth, family, health, and the recent addition to my wealth. It's about eighty people celebrating my recent accomplishment on the rooftop terrace. Downtown Atlanta is serving as the scenic background with breathtaking panoramic views of the lights beaming through and around the skyscrapers and city attractions.

Imani did her magic and had planned this party inviting the people closest to us. She and her team worked countless hours in addition to handling their clients to pull this off. My girl was amazing and I couldn't have been luckier to have her.

"Nah, this isn't your set up, I can tell someone with style put this together." Josh shuffled around the chic outdoor lounge, confirming my thoughts about the awesomeness of Imani B. Relations and team.

"Stop hatin' on my impeccable creative genes. But I can't take credit, this is all my lady." I emphasized.

"You leveled up big time, man. Both of us under forty shattering records. You as a partner at the top firm in Atlanta, and me a judge. Who would've thought it? I'm proud of you, bro." Josh was one of the few that I shared my personal failures with. He's seen me through all the significant milestones of my life, and I reciprocated in every way. Our friendship mattered, his opinion counted.

"Man, it took long enough. I've worked my butt off for this moment. My dad knew I wanted no handouts, but damn he threw every obstacle my way to see how I'd handle it. Last month he stuck me with two of his major clients expecting me to pick up where he left off while he decided to take a month long cruise with my mom. He did it when he knew I would have more responsibilities with the kids and with officially moving Imani into my home. Somehow I made it work without losing my mind and keeping things together with my immediate family." I let him in on another tidbit I discovered. "I learned all the other partners voted me in a year ago."

"Yeah, I heard."

I dang near broke my neck looking at him in surprise. "So we holding out on each other now?"

"Nah. Never that. It just wasn't my place. I overheard my dad talking to ma dukes about it. He tried convincing Mr. Bennett that he's a bit too hard on you, but your dad thought otherwise. Come on, man, you know your pops."

Speaking of the man of the minute, my dad mysteriously joined us away from the rest of the party.

"Mr. Bennett, I'm over here, giving my partner in crime some wisdom about life."

"Is that right, Judge Mitchell?" No matter the tight connection between our families, my father prided himself in uplifting Josh in his career and anything he puts his mind to. As a gift after graduating from college, my dad gave him several stocks. Josh mentioned it being one of the best and most thoughtful gifts he'd ever received. He still talks about the note that was attached to this day, *Be patient, the value will increase.*

"That's right! He needs to take my advice. If he listened to me sooner, he wouldn't have had to wait a year to get his girl back."

They shake hands before dad agreed and they both left to join the other guests.

Deserting my chair, I took a few steps away. "Tonight is perfect." I said it to myself, but I had to acknowledge everything was as it should be. Well, almost everything. The timing is perfect, and I can't miss my chance while my adrenaline cycles through. Instead of waiting any longer, I go to the mic, thanking all the guests in attendance.

Yeay makes a surprising shout out to me. "I told my grand-daughter, don't be stupid." The crowd can't help to laugh at her accent and worse, her pronunciation of my name. "Bastien is a great man for you, Imani." Her mother and father also took time to congratulate me. It's amazing how they feel about me after the whole ordeal, but what was more overwhelming was seeing their support for me, our relationship, and our kids. Imani's father never neglected the relationship that we built during the weekend of Imani's surf competition. We talked weekly for the year Imani went MIA. He's smart though, he never mentioned his daughter's whereabouts and what lifestyle she lived while I wasn't present. I respected him more for that.

After my mother's emotional outcry, that didn't leave one dry eye remaining, Sean and Benji stole the show with their silly antics until I demanded control over the microphone. The first person I thanked after God was Imani. I admitted to the crowd that we had a rough past, and how God revealed so much in my darkest hours. "Despite the turmoil, she came back to me. After I pleaded, of course!" They're entertained by my attempt at a comedy, even though it wasn't a joke. The women especially enjoy the candid, honest moment coming from me and I'm sure most of them have never seen this side of me.

Imani removed her heels earlier, so she's barely below my nose once she joined me at my side. That's my cue. It's now or never. "Ms. Imani Barasa, my chocolate dime piece. The only accessory I need to complete me." Another outburst broke out in the crowd. Those who know me understood the importance in that statement. I'm always sharp in gear, and there's still a small adornment somewhere to polish it up. Today, the woman at my side was that adornment. I kissed her passionately in front of everyone, establishing just how much she meant to me.

Josh interrupted me, trying to covertly place something in my hand. But the way the crowd oohed and ahhed, I think they were on to me. His grin said it all. "You got it playboy?" Josh knew I spent hours shopping for this, he was the only one I trusted with this tradeoff.

On bended knee, I practically begged Imani with my eyes to not embarrass me. "Baby. We've only been back together for a few months. But we can't erase our history. We've come back stronger than ever, and haven't missed a beat. Summer and Savion count on your presence as much as I do. My mother adores you, and my dad acts as if I can't make any decisions without you. And my brothers... Let's just say you were family the moment they discovered your friendship with their wives. You're another sister for them to harass. You've earned a seat at the table. But most importantly, you've earned my heart."

Imani's mother is in tears, and my mother joins her in a hug. Everyone is waiting with bated breath as I ask the question they're anticipating. Riana wobbled in our direction, with Benji close behind, showing uncertainty on his face. As usual, he can't control her, and when he tried to grab her wrist in warning, she raised her hand. "Uh uh, I'm scoping the scene. Let me see the piece he's delivering to my girl." The entire crowd hollered at her antics. No offense is taken. She's that one individual that can get away with such a show. She's used to stealing the show, and today, I appreciate the humor she's bringing to my proposal.

I didn't let her distract me. I continued as if she never said a word. "Imani, do me the pleasure of becoming my plus one. Will you marry me?" Unabashedly, her full lips softened. Gentle kisses have me bucking into her until our passion turns wild and fierce. No one stops us despite the applause from our family and friends.

"Mmm, I love you, Sebastien Bennett."

Riana reels us in. "Sooo, you gon leave us hanging? What's your answer, homegirl? Yes, no, maybe so?"

"Yes, Riana, I'm marrying my Bastien." She then returned to the warm confines of my embrace. I didn't yet have time to place the ring on her finger, as I was doing that, Riana kindly retrieved it for her own assessment.

"Girl, Sebastien sure ain't cheap like his little brother! I appraise this ring at $9500, at least, on the low end." I can now add appraiser to her resume. She's only five hundred short on her quote. Benji had his work cut out for him with this one.

"May I get back to my proposal, Riana?" I needed to stay on track.

I fell into another shared moment with Imani, finally putting the ring on her finger and admiring how it was a perfect fit. I did good, and she wasted no time telling me so. Before we could get a moment to ourselves, we had to endure congratulations from the crowd. My promotion party, now turned into an engagement party. It was perfect.

I gathered Imani and moved us away from the party walking her to the other side of the roof. We stared at our surrounding; miniature cars zoom by below, planes are coasting from above and couples stroll along the sidewalks hand in hand. This reminds me of one of the first times we held hands after our meeting with Roland turned into a lunch date.

"This is perfect timing." She seemed dazed, unable to remove the plastered smile.

"Agreed."

"Hopefully, we can enjoy a few dates before the baby gets here." She shrugged.

Sensory overload. All types of images floated in my brain. Looking down at her feet, it dawned on me that for the last few weeks she hasn't been able to keep her shoes on, saying her feet were swelling. Now I know why! I could almost imagine the beautiful children we would produce. I saw another set of twins, or a miniature Imani. I can't speak but understand the weight in her confession. "How far are we?"

She spun around to face me. "I don't know, silly. I took a test before coming here because I could no longer wait to find out. I'm a few weeks late on my period, though."

"You think you're ready?" I tried to erase the concern from my voice.

"As ready as this wet pussy is for you, daddy. Let's make our exit." My future wife was definitely going to be a good look for me.

We relocated to the hotel across from us, not wanting to waste another minute to devour each other. What I prayed for materialized. Becoming a partner. Growing a relationship with my children who were now Summer Rain Davidson-Bennett and Savion Birk Davidson-Bennett. I was so thankful to Rain and Nelson for allowing me that concession. And now, my future has agreed to be my forever. Imani was going to be my wife. The icing on the cake was that we'd be adding another child to the mix. It wasn't our immediate plan, but I was so happy with the news. Either way Imani was mine and I was hers. From this day forward, I'd give her everything she's been wanting, and we're gonna start with that big ass family she craved.

"Bastien?" She moans seductively.

"Hmmm?"

"I'm definitely ready."

THE END

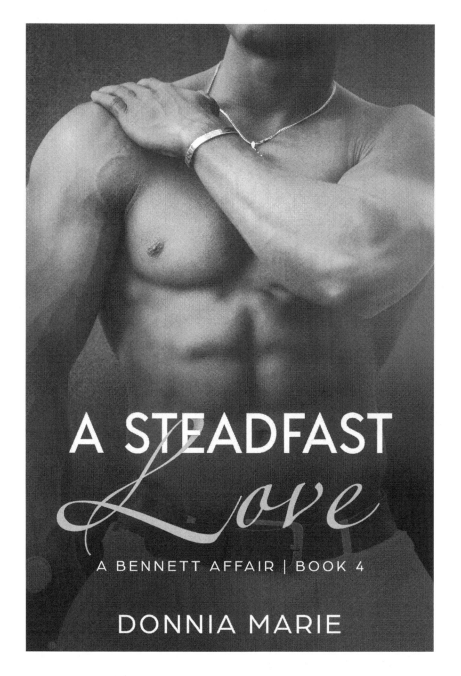

A STEADFAST
Love

A BENNETT AFFAIR | BOOK 4

DONNIA MARIE

Trekking across the vibrating platform at my own pace helped ease the nerves I'd been experiencing for weeks. I listened to Dr. Santori, the President of Pristine Stanford University, call out my name, *"Tavious Miguel Bennett."* Unlike the basic introduction for other students, he set the stage for a King, and I graced everyone's presence as such.

The mob to the left stole my attention; I noticed it was filled with my family and close friends putting the other commencement attendees to shame with their hoots and praise. The massive arena didn't seem to have a vacant seat anywhere. My clan didn't disappoint with the oversized signs, whistles, and blowers.

Once I was out the spotlight, Professor Rigsby caught my attention as her hips swayed seductively in front of me. Those piercing hazel eyes reeled me down a nearby secluded hallway. Her cocoa fingers settled firmly around my wrist when she sank against the wall, drawing me into close proximity to her canvas. An eloquently shaped canvas, to be exact. "Congratulations, Tav." A whiff of peppermint brushed my nostrils when her lips barely teased my mouth. Professor Rigsby's panties were practically in my hands as she continued reinforcing her elated happiness for my success. To be honest, I couldn't believe how fluidic her body flowed, considering the event and large population of people. Lucky for us, no one took notice of my absence.

Perusing the space, I gripped her tighter, wrapping my arm around her backside. I leaned forward, scraping her ear with the tip of my bottom lip. "Professor, I thank you for all the help you provided me over the last year and a half. But I want to keep this professional between us, unless, you know." I retracted, omitting just a bit of space before lowering my lids to my dick, then trailing them uphill to meet her curious eyes. "Unless you want the business. And to be straight with you, I ain't trying to overstep any boundaries."

Rigsby licked her lips, processing the information. In the past, I took three classes that she taught, and her flirtatious ways were persistent from the jump. But she became audacious during my last course, two semesters prior. Chantel Rigsby kept all the fellas in line with her sass and attire, which only furthered our interest in her class, Women Studies. I enrolled, planning to drop it within a few days but decided against it when I took a liking to the class. Most assume the program centers around male-bashing, but no, it evaluated gender, race, and anything else that could be relatable to the general population. What I did discover were her viewpoints on men, and I could tell she has been through a lot with the male species. The ladies loved most of my essays and presentations. Still, they couldn't accept the hardcore truths of their behaviors and the things I found unnecessary with the female community. In the same semester, I found myself working with the only four guys in the room, on a play called *The Vagina Monologues*. After interviewing the ladies on campus, including Professor Rigsby, I became fascinated with the psychosocial development of women.

Another truth presented itself; Rigsby was one of the youngest professors on campus, which explains why she kept a babyface with swag for days. Not one day did she come half stepping and believe me, her hip-hugging pencil skirts, rompers, and long thin

254 BOOK 4: A STEADFAST LOVE

dresses had me turning in my seat from time to time. She could definitely get it.

I lost my balance, falling forward as Professor Rigsby yanked the collar of my half buttoned up shirt towards her. Hastily, I placed my palms against the frigid walls to keep afloat from crashing my mouth onto hers. Unmeasured breathing persisted while her fingers skated up and down my chest. "So, I have to beg for it, Tavi?"

I growled into her ears, "There's no going back, Professor Rigsby." I drove my erection into her direction, flicking my tongue against her neck. "Are you sure you wanna cross that path? I'm no amateur."

She giggled, clutching me by the balls. Oh yeah, she a beast and don't mind risking it all. Her hands massaged the bulge growing steadily in size, and that's when I knew I needed to escape the hallway. I'd been in the arena a few times before but wasn't sure where we could go, but I showed no confusion. We maneuvered the building until discovering an unoccupied room that had a lock. Rigsby didn't allow me to do a thing before she squatted, exposing rosy underwear. She was on her knees in no time and in no time did my jaw sink to the ground.

Text **DONNIA** to **(678) 735-3400** to SUBSCRIBE to the newsletter and stay on top of what's happening, events, book releases and more!

CAN'T GET ENOUGH?

Join our text list for the latest updates, giveaways, and book
releases ⇨ https://eztxt.net/QTl1vd
Or
Text **DONNIA** to **(678) 735-3400**
Prefer email instead, sign up at
⇨ www.donniamarie.com

Want more insight on the characters? Their looks, family, private
text messages, or even things not mentioned in the book. Check
out promotional videos/photos of your faves
⇨ www.DonniaMarie.com/books

EMAIL: Info@DonniaMarie.com

facebook.com/askdonnia
twitter.com/askdonnia
instagram.com/authordonniamarie
snapchat.com/add/donnia07
amazon.com/author/donniamarie
tiktok.com/@authordonniamarie

Dear Readers,

I want to thank you for taking the time to read about Sebastien and Imani's journey through their ups and downs. Writing these two has been a process mentally and emotionally. Allowing the characters to move the way they want, removing my opinions and feelings from the situation, is a bummer. Add on to it, I had a lot going on in my personal life, so yeah, this was a project. A project that I am glad to finally deliver to you.

I thank you for your time and patience in the release of this book, and I hope this book was what you were expecting plus more.

Donnia Marie

This is book 3 of the series, A Bennett Affair. For those who haven't read book 1 FEARLESS LOVE or book 2 UNJUST LOVE, do so now.

If you enjoyed the story, please leave a review on Amazon and all other platforms to spread the word.

ACKNOWLEDGMENTS

I can't acknowledge anyone or anything before **God**!

Tamara I know you're sick of me but I don't care. I can't even tell you how much I appreciate your patience and the dedication you put into this project with me. Forget this project, all the suffering you have to deal with when it comes to my many ideas. I can't help it but thanks for hanging on.

Dorothy & Kelly I can write several pages but for now, I'll just say thank you!

But the ones that feel and deal with me the most, my immediate family **(Chaz & J)**. I thank each and every one of you for the continued support and I love you!

I couldn't close this out without thanking the **readers** and **supporters**. Your emails, messages and feedback have been invaluable to me on this journey. I can't thank you enough and thanks for rocking with me.

ALSO BY DONNIA MARIE

A Bennett Affair Series

Fearless Love

Unjust Love

Unexpected Love

A Steadfast Love

True Love: A Bennett Brothers Novella

The Champion Sisters Series

The Heart of a Champion

The Rise of a Champ by Twyla B. Stone

A True Champion

The Champ is Here by Twyla B. Stone

Spin-off Series

Inaudible Shots

Shooter's Free Verse

SIGNED PAPERBACKS AVAILABLE

www.donniamarie.com

LISTEN TO A BENNETT AFFAIR PODCAST

https://anchor.fm/donniamarie

ABOUT THE AUTHOR

 Donnia Marie is the author of the popular set of books in the Bennett Affair Series! She's quickly gaining momentum with her impeccable skills in weaving the complexity yet real love experienced by couples.

"I write to fill the heart not with just joy of love but the beautifully imperfect love that we're capable of experiencing."

Donnia also emphasizes the need to have each reader form their own perspective and experience of a story.

"What good is a book if you can't picture yourself in it or feel the emotions? Every read should take you somewhere, whether it's to feel or learn."

With several books under her belt and most on audiobook, it's hard to miss her work. If you don't run across her through books or audio, you may catch her performing. Donnia is very involved in the film industry as she's an actress and a serial entrepreneur. Go figure why she's such a travel fanatic. When taking a break, you can count on catching her with family and friends, enjoying the simplicity of life.

facebook.com/askdonnia
twitter.com/askdonnia
instagram.com/authordonniamarie
snapchat.com/add/donnia07
amazon.com/author/donniamarie
tiktok.com/@authordonniamarie

Made in the USA
Columbia, SC
02 September 2023

22355140R00162